DOG DAYS

DEAN KASTLE

ACKNOWLEDGEMENTS

Long is the list of friends and family who helped bring these stories to life, but I have to mention a few. Many thanks go to Mike Pontarelli, authors Steve Karas, Michael DeAngelo, and Lou Anders, and Dean B.—my number-one story consultant. Finally, my wife and motivator in chief, Marilyn, deserves a shout out. You have my love, appreciation, and deepest gratitude.

This one is for Dean Sr. who would have been like, "what is this?"

CONTENTS

CHAPTER ONE

In war, Geth mused, there were winners and losers. Kings rose and fell. Titles changed hands. Fortunes were made.

But for all the wars he'd waged, Geth had never got the hang of all that.

He wouldn't have figured Phelan for one of the big winners either.

"What'll it be?" The little man grinned at him from behind the bar at the Bottom of the Cup, white apron across his chest and everything.

"Ale," Geth said. "On the house."

Phelan snorted but slid a tankard under a tap and poured.

The clank of the door swinging open sounded behind him and Geth turned out of habit. A pair of green-cloaks saluted as they came in, stamping slush off their boots before winding past rickety tables to find a seat. A hearty fire threw its glow over townsfolk and soldiers alike, the acrid scent of wood smoke, alcohol, and sweat mingling under the low ceiling. It stuck to Geth's mustache after he left each night, exactly as it had before the war.

Geth knew it wasn't over, but there in the north of Umbel, it felt like the war had ended. The dead had been buried, and the Ilars were gone. Repairs had begun on Towerrock's bridge, her walls, the ruined portions of the town. Finer establishments, closer to the water, hadn't survived. But the Bottom of the Cup, in all her sordid glory, stood tall. Phelan hadn't waited for the dust to settle before wrangling the dead-man dozen across the rubble to stake his claim.

"So, you decide what you're gonna call the place?"

The little man set that tankard down carefully in front of Geth. The head of foam was perfect. "You just drink your free ale and leave the business decisions to me. And toss anyone who starts trouble, would ya?"

Geth knuckled his brow. "Will do, boss."

The common room filled up as soldiers finished their labors, hauling stone or setting timbers. It was a miracle Phelan had enough ale to go around. But the Ilars, it seemed, appreciated Umbel's brews about as much as Umbelmen appreciated their tart wines. They'd found the cellar stacked full of barrels. Even so, Phelan had already sent Dodger downriver in search of his uncle, a brew-master, to begin restocking the inventory.

A barmaid arrived with a bowl of oxtail stew and a smile. Geth returned the gesture. Gods but it had been a while since he'd had a tumble. His thoughts wandered to Vriana, of course, far to the north and done with him. He looked down at the steaming bowl with a sigh. What a woman. And what a night to remember.

But another arrival at the door stopped Geth's hand, meaty bone halfway to his mouth. A wiry lad of no more than ten searched the crowd until his eyes met Geth's. He knew the boy. He worked for Melagus.

"The gods hate me." Geth swore, dropped the bone back into the stew. He hadn't even gotten a taste.

Phelan leaned over the bar, picked up the spoon, and shoveled a mouthful in his own maw. "Don't worry. I'll tell Blink you said it was delicious."

Geth marched past the boy without letting him speak, across town and over the rough planks of Towerrock's makeshift bridge. The boy trotted to keep up with the big warrior's longer stride but once they'd reached the inner ward, Geth made a turn rather than heading straight for Hadean's war room.

"Hey!"

"Pipe down, son." Geth waved the lad to follow. "Melagus can wait."

Inside the Tooth's dark corridors, he didn't stop until he'd reached Neary's chamber. From the bedside, the witch Amalia looked up at Geth's entrance. She lifted a finger to her lips.

"He's sleeping."

Geth nodded. "He looks better."

"It takes time. But he wants to live. That's what's important."

"Will he..." Geth didn't know what he wanted to ask exactly.

Amalia had the answer anyway.

"My hope is that he makes a full recovery. Or close to it."

"Good." But another thought made Geth frown.

"You're thinking of Iyngaer," said the witch.

Geth muttered a curse. *Bloody magicks.*

Amalia trilled a small laugh, that beehive of hair on her head shaking. "He, too, will survive. And yet even my magicks, as you call them, have limits. The best surgeons in Paellia couldn't repair that knee. He won't escape, if that's your concern. I can promise you that. They're holding him just downstairs; you can go and see for yourself."

Geth pulled a chair from against the wall as quietly as he could. He sat beside her. Neary snored faintly. There was color in his cheeks, below the bandage wrapped around his head. Amalia held him by the hand, her thumb stroking the back of it.

"Sometimes I wonder if we should have let him die," Geth said. "Iyngaer, I mean."

"Of course." The witch smiled. "But the Seer is wise. Trust him. You have plenty of other enemies to worry about, don't you?"

Geth snorted a laugh. "No shortage there." He thought of Towdric down south on the throne, of Palladine, somewhere back east, and of the many Ilars that must still hate him in the north. He breathed a sigh and rose.

"Take good care of him," he told Amalia. "I've got plenty of enemies, just like you said, but a fair few friends."

She nodded, still rubbing absently at the back of Neary's hand. With a silent prayer, Geth left her to it. He let Melagus's boy lead the way to King Hadean's war room.

"Here he is," Melagus said, all smiles. He motioned and his lad shut the door behind them. "We can begin."

Lord Brant, his man, Captain Worran, and a dour old fighter with a bull-neck and a grey beard stood with the counselor and the king at the room's single, long table. Hadean nodded at Geth's arrival, but he looked somber. Geth thought of the boy-king he'd first met back in Umbel

City. In the space of months, it was as if the lad had aged a decade.

And he looked skinny.

"Hey, boy," Geth caught Melagus's messenger before he could leave. "Be a good fellow and go down to the kitchens, tell them your king is hungry. And his council too."

Hadean smiled, a bit of that youth lighting his face. The lad ran off. If Melagus had something to say, he saved his comments this once. Worran poured wine for everyone as Brant spread a map across the table.

Melagus remained standing but motioned everyone else to take their seat. "I have called you here," he said, "as King Hadean's trusted advisors, to discuss the path forward. We all know the usurper Towdric sits the throne in Umbel City and our emissary has returned to confirm his stance."

"Minus one hand," Bull-neck growled.

Melagus's lip twitched but he managed to continue without scolding anyone. "I can't say I expected Towdric to rethink the matter, so here we are. He must be dealt with."

Noises of agreement sounded. Geth couldn't imagine any of them were ready to march off to war so soon after the Battle of Towerrock, but he himself had more than one idea on how to 'deal with' the scratch.

"Sneak me through his gates inside a bale of hay or something. I'll introduce Towdric to the pointy end of my sword and have done."

"Come now," Melagus scoffed. "We could certainly sneak you into the city. But what are the odds you might succeed? The odds that you'd die, now those are odds any betting man would jump at."

Geth glowered at the counselor but held his tongue.

Captain Worran sat forward. "With your permission, my lords, we have armies. How else might we unseat the usurper without a war? His men are loyal, they won't desert him. Not after what he's been telling them."

Melagus picked up where the captain trailed off. "Yes, Towdric has done quite a job of smearing our king's name. He is experienced, wily. It's clear now that he had begun planting the seeds of division as soon as he heard of his cousin, King Aeldan's death. By Towdric's telling, and the telling of the rumormongers in his employ, our young king's ineptitude invited war with the tribes. And nearly lost it as well."

It took some effort for Geth to hold in a choice curse. His hand squeezed the hilt of his sword, the weapon he'd taken off Cald back in the Aldwood. It was almost too long to be sheathed at the hip, but if he hadn't started wearing it there, he'd have had no way to keep himself from swearing every time someone mentioned that sonofabitch Towdric.

"The men won't thank us if we march," Brant was saying, "but we outnumber our enemies this time."

"Three to one," Worran put in.

"Four." Bull-neck had a voice to match that rough beard. "Allowing some time to knock sense into a few holdouts."

Hadean shook his head though. "Towdric must be dealt with, true. But who among you really wants to bring war against our own people? Have the folk of Umbel not suffered enough these past few years?"

The king's eyes flicked from one man to the next. Geth felt his cheeks go hot. Even Bull-neck grimaced under that grey beard. Melagus, however, raised a thin finger.

"My king, we must keep all options on the table. Remember, Towdric is not the first traitor to lead armies against a king of Umbel. And should it come to the blade, we wouldn't be the first to use it. When the viper bites, the good flesh around the wound must be cut away before the poison can spread."

Hadean sighed. "There must be another way. We have three times Towdric's numbers." He nodded toward Bull-neck. "At least. The usurper holds the City of Umbel though. If we march south, he will undoubtedly retreat within the walls, leaving me no choice but to besiege my own fortress, starve my own people, and make true all the accusations that have been leveled against me. No, there has to be another way. And we must find it."

He didn't raise his voice or bang the table, but the look on Hadean's face ended the discussion. Those months under siege, his maturity, his confidence, had steeped like tea. He was good and strong now, Geth reckoned. The big warrior sat a little straighter, proud as ever to serve him.

"But what other options are there?" Melagus asked finally. "Diplomacy? I must say, the sellsword was right to kill your uncle. And Towdric is far worse. Can we really allow him to live?"

"For now, yes." Hadean nodded. "We have *other* business besides Towdric, however, do we not?" He shared a significant look with the counselor.

"The chieftain, Iyngaer." Melagus dipped his head. "The Lady Amalia assures me that he will, indeed, survive his wounds."

Geth frowned. "Well, that was the idea, wasn't it? I could have killed him. Or we could have left him to trudge home and die on the road."

"Master Melagus is not faulting you, Captain Geth," Hadean said. He smiled. "Rather the opposite. He...well, I'll let him tell it."

Melagus smoothed the wispy hairs on his head and cleared his throat. "Iyngaer, a scourge these many months, is now our captive. I must commend our Paellian ally his restraint on the battlefield in sparing his life."

"Of course," Geth lied. "It was the obvious thing to do."

"Of course. By holding the chieftain hostage, we ensure his armies retreat in good order. But there's more."

"And what is that?" Brant raised an eyebrow.

"Let Master Melagus explain." Hadean watched the counselor expectantly.

"For centuries," Melagus continued, "we have warred with the tribes. More so of late. But this latest victory, and the fact that we find ourselves in possession of their chieftain, invites a solution. Rather than executing Iyngaer as punishment for his overreach, we reinstall him as chieftain in Dues, this time as an ally."

Geth's eyes narrowed. "A what?"

"A sort of vassal state." Brant nodded. "Like Adamar." He looked to the counselor. "Clever, Master Melagus. But Iyngaer doesn't need us like Adamar needs Pellon. Will it work?"

Geth found all eyes turned his way. "Are you asking *me*?"

Melagus smiled. Insofar as a he *could* smile. "You have been to Ilia, have you not? Two times actually. I am told you were invited to their sacred places and joined in their rituals. You are counted friend by the Seer, Agrem, a man respected across their forests. You have broken bread at the seats of three of the four greater tribes. And I am informed that you have a...special relationship with the Chieftess Vriana."

Geth squeezed his hilt, *hard*. What else did the bony bastard know?

"Do you think it will work?" Hadean asked, shaking Geth from his thoughts. "By your hand, the Thiring tribe stands leaderless. Melagus's idea was to gift Iyngaer with the rule of that tribe as well, incurring a debt that ensures his loyalty. Between them, Dues and Thiringia span the entire northern border of the realm. With one chieftain controlling all those lands—"

Melagus raised that finger again. "Allied to Umbel—"

"Yes, allied to us, all the way across our northern border, Iyngaer could act as a buffer between Umbel and any hostile tribes. We would have to support our new friend, but this could be the start of something we've never dreamed of. Can you imagine a peace between our two lands, a peace that might last for generations?"

Geth blew a breath out from under his mustache. It was a lot. There were so many ways it could go wrong. But letting Iyngaer live...it was also genius.

"I've gotta hand it to you, 'Grem," he muttered under his breath.

"Agrem?" Melagus's eyes narrowed. "That was *my* idea!"

"Well?" Hadean watched Geth, ignored the back and forth. "Do you think it will work? What do you say? You know Iyngaer better than anyone."

The big warrior frowned, exhaled a sigh. "I guess it's time I paid him a visit."

———†———

The hour was late, but as Geth remembered it, Iyngaer didn't sleep much. He started off in the direction of the chieftain's rooms, pausing to gather Agrem first. The Seer nodded calmly when Geth explained Melagus's idea, like he had expected this all along.

They left Agrem's chamber only to pause in front of the very next door. That didn't leave the big warrior much time to compose his thoughts. A single torch lit the hall, reminding Geth of the night he'd snuck inside the Tooth to murder Hadean's uncle and betrayer. A bloody night by all accounts and hardly a good omen to his mind. He sucked in a deep breath but hesitated. "This is going to be awkward."

"Mmmm."

"What do I say? I'm the one that stabbed him."

"You are also the one who spared his life."

"I only did that 'cause you said so."

"He doesn't know that, mmmm?"

Agrem reached out and knocked before Geth could say anything else. The Seer didn't wait for a reply but pushed the door open and stepped inside.

Geth followed. The chamber was similar to Neary's, furnished with a bed and a few simple chairs positioned around the hearth. A window looked down on the inner ward, but Iyngaer sat with his back to it, near the fire, a great woolen blanket wrapped over his wide frame. His knee was bandaged and a crutch rested against the wall. He turned to watch their entrance with a dour face.

Thinking of Neary, Geth didn't feel so bad about the injuries he'd inflicted on the chieftain. His friend wasn't doing half as well. Neary's wounds, and all the other casualties of this war, could be laid at this man's feet.

Iyngaer must have read the hostility in his eyes. "You come to stand over your defeated enemy, mmmm?"

"If I wanted to do that," Geth said, "I wouldn't have waited so long."

The chieftain's eyes went back to his fire, like he'd already heard all he needed to. Geth paused, but Agrem said something in the Ilar tongue, prompting a sniff from the big tribesman.

"Well, speak then," Iyngaer said. "Will it be the rope? You sunlanders like the rope. Or is it a basement of stone, a tomb for the living. They give me knives with my meals. I will not die underground."

"Whatever you think of me," Geth said, "you should know I'd kill you myself before letting you rot in a dungeon."

"Mmmm?"

Geth nodded. "A mercy. But the truth is, it was 'Grem's idea to spare your life out there, not mine. I'm a warrior, just like you." Iyengaer looked at him and Geth met his stare. "Even so, it wasn't hard to hold back."

Iyngaer just watched him, said nothing. Geth remembered the Truslas, the chieftain's secret capture of Hadean, his leniency at the Misa.

"You've always been my enemy, Iyngaer. That's just the way of it. But I've had worse. At least you were fair. And we both know things could have gone the other way at the Battle for Towerrock. It could have been me sitting there and you sitting here."

Iyngaer shook his head. "The Eagle, the Wolf, and the Snake. It was never meant to be. I should have seen it."

Agrem nodded, hummed.

Geth had no idea what that meant but he pushed on. "If it had been me, surrounded and beaten, would you have killed me? No, after all we've been through, I reckon you would have offered me another path. Because you know how to be a good chieftain."

Iyngaer stood a little straighter. *Treat a man like a god*, old Mather used to quote from the Omnibus, *and you'll see the divine in him.*

Whatever deities the Ilars worshipped, Iyngaer looked about as proud as one now. "What are you saying?"

"The gods were against you on the field that day," Geth told him. "Today, they're back on your side."

"Speak."

"You spared King Hadean once and he hasn't forgotten. He's offering you a deal."

Iyngaer's eyes narrowed. "Sunlanders deals are like snail shells. Easily broken."

"In a bear's maw, yes. But if he handles it gently..."

Iyngaer said nothing. He was still listening though.

"Umbel needs a friendly neighbor along its northern border."

"Yes. The traitor has claimed the throne. You need me."

"You need Umbel even more. Your army is crushed. Your allies are in disarray. The tribes won't be coming back anytime soon."

The chieftain snorted.

"I didn't come to trade insults. I came to put that all behind us. You've earned my respect, Govendi. King Hadean's too. I came here to make friends."

Iyngaer searched Geth's eyes. But the big warrior spoke the truth, there would be no tells. The chieftain's gaze went to his fire and back finally.

"Can the tribes and the men of the south ever be friends?" he asked. "Do you think the wars that have been waged by the longfathers can just suddenly end?"

Geth opened his mouth, but it was Agrem who spoke. "Yes! We cannot go back to the days of the longfathers, mmmm? And we cannot speak now for our sons. But for us, for Iyngaer Lonega, Govendi, and King Hadean, we can say we are friends."

The wheels were turning behind the chieftain's eyes. Did he believe such a friendship could really be? Was he weighing his options? Geth couldn't see that he had any better choice, but the big warrior had saved the best bit for last just in case.

"Ceter is dead." Geth spit on the floor. "And good riddance. The Thirings need a chief. Hadean will support you in ruling *both* tribes, in exchange for your friendship."

Iyngaer's eyes widened, just a hair. He worked that out in his mind, snorted a laugh. "So, protect his flank, his entire border with the forests."

"Still a generous offer if you ask me."

"When a gift is given, something is expected in return."

"Of course," Geth said. "You just said it, protect his flank. But this could be an alliance between the north and the south, the likes of which never has been."

"I have no choice but to accept this, mmmm?" The tall chieftain nodded. "But now I understand. This is not about the deal, as you called it. They've sent you to decide if Iyngaer will abide by this friendship. Or betray your sunland king."

"You won't betray him." Geth said. "You dealt with Hadean fair when he was your captive. And me as well."

"More than fair."

"Agreed. So why not take the path we've laid for you? Accept Hadean's friendship. Go home in peace, Iyngaer. And put that shit-stinking bearskin back across your shoulders."

CHAPTER TWO

It was late by the time Geth left the chieftain—too late to endure the inevitable, smug look on Melagus's face when he received the good news. Geth headed for his bed and left the counselor to stew overnight. He returned to the lord's hall in Towerrock the next morning.

Melagus met him at the table below the dais. "Well, what did he say?"

"Breakfast first," Geth said. "Where's the king anyway?"

Melagus rolled his eyes but sent his boy for the kitchens. A soldier hurried in the other direction in search of the king.

A cook arrived with a platter and a pitcher of watered, morning wine. Geth ate slowly, slurping down eggs, popping links of sausage in his mouth. Melagus muttered under his breath the whole while. Gods forbid he should actually eat something himself. But Hadean arrived and tucked into the meal alongside the big warrior.

"That's better," the king said when he was done, patting his stomach. "Shall we proceed?"

"Right," Geth said. "Here it is: I sat with the chief last night. He's our man."

Melagus only nodded. "What other choice did he have? But did we truly win an ally, or have we just released the bear in our backyard?"

"Iyngaer will hold to his end of the bargain. He's got Agrem to keep him on a straight path as well."

Melagus frowned, unconvinced.

"Iyngaer's injured," Geth said. "And against all odds, we beat him at Towerrock. I think he believes it was the gods' will. Or the longfathers maybe. He said something about the Eagle, the Wolf, and the Snake, but I haven't figured all that out yet."

Melagus flicked a glance at Hadean and back, eyes narrowed. "The three greatest spirits: the heavens, earth, and hell. Yes, our king is the Eagle, it's his sigil after all. You are clearly the Wolf. But the snake...?"

Geth hurried to pop another link of sausage in his mouth to hide a smile. Did the Asp really not see it?

"The next question," Hadean said, "is who will escort Iyngaer home."

"Who indeed?" said Melagus.

Geth found both king and counselor watching him. "You want me to do it, don't you?" He swore.

"Haven't we established the excellence of your two expeditions into Ilia?" Melagus said.

"I don't remember you saying "excellent.""

"*I'll* say it," Hadean offered. "You saved my life."

"As you saved mine, my king." Geth replied. He turned back to Melagus. "Fine. I'll do it. But I'm not going alone."

"Did you think I'd trust you to handle such a task by yourself?"

Geth frowned. "I thought we were past all that mistrust?"

"I trust you well enough." Melagus folded his arms. "You've proven your loyalty. And you have your uses."

"Then why the sour grapes?"

"Just because I trust you to serve the king, doesn't mean I trust your judgment. And it most certainly doesn't mean I like you. I think I'll die if I have to watch you eat one more time."

"That right?" said Geth. He scooped up a greasy handful of eggs and slid them into his mouth just to watch the counselor's face.

But Melagus only smiled in return. "I guess I'll just have to get used to your uncouth ways. It's going to be a long trip to Ilia and back."

Geth paused, mouth still half full. "Huh?"

"That's right. You may have been thinking of your footman and some soldiers, but I'll be joining you as well."

They began making arrangements immediately. Supplies would be needed, men and wagons, horses and tents. Messengers ran back and forth. Melagus scribbled orders on parchments and Hadean scribbled down his signature.

Geth's stomach was full, but all that talking made him thirsty. He was belly up at Phelan's bar again by midday. Young Kerrel joined him, second man of the file now with Neary on the mend. Blink came out from the back to help dole out bowls of stew. Geth watched ale and food flow to the green-cloaks and townsfolk that trickled in, copper rounds flowing in the opposite direction.

"We've had some good news," Blink said, cheerful as ever. "Sergeant Drayic's sent a pigeon from Stoney. He's found those folks that Crookbow had a hold of. They've returned home to rebuild."

He left the inn for Towerrock, heading up to the heights of the parapets to think. He eyeballed every man, woman, and child he passed until he reached the ramparts. A few green-cloaks stood watch, looking bored, but no one paid him any mind.

The wind was cold up there, the river murky and dark down below. "Gods all be damned, how is that man not dead?" Geth muttered out loud. He squeezed the edge of the crenels like it was somebody's throat. The answer didn't matter though. The question was, how to stay alive?

One obvious solution was to tell King Hadean about Ratcher and beg his protection. But that would endanger the king as well. And who would watch Hadean's back while Geth was in Ilia?

Geth's frown turned to a smile. That errand, he realized, might prove a blessing. This once, the forest was his friend. No way an assassin from the Sworn Realms could blend in among the tribes, Geth reckoned. Not even Ratcher.

But one thing was clear: bringing anyone else in would only put that person in danger. Geth grimaced. He had to deal with the bastard alone.

So, what to do?

Ratcher was certain to strike before he left for the north. Why else announce his return? He'd know the file would tell, and he'd know that Geth would soon be out of reach. But that begged the question: why announce himself at all?

"To taunt me, skulking sonofabitch."

Geth mouthed a string of curses. Maybe the whole point was to show Geth he was fine, that he hadn't been hurt in their fight at all. Maybe it was meant to warn Geth to keep the dozen out of it, that his quarrel wasn't with them. That was it, Geth decided. Either way, Ratcher wouldn't have dared show his face if he didn't believe he was about to end things once and for all.

Geth considered how it might go down. No man, not even an assassin, was likely to come at him head on. Even with his blinding dust, Ratcher had been lucky to survive their last clash. And no amount of shine would buy a crew of bone-breakers here, where Geth's sword-arm was known and feared. No, Ratcher would need to get creative.

So, it would be stealth, Geth figured, or poison, or a strike from far. He nodded to himself. It seemed unlikely Ratcher was any kind of a bowman. Otherwise Geth would have been struck dead on some open stretch of road long ago. And neither did the assassin seem the type to favor poisons, given his disgust with the 'amateurs' who'd made attempts on Hadean's life that fall.

down off his horse, pretended to empty his bladder, still casting furtive glances to either side.

No one was there. The grass was tall in places, but there wasn't anywhere else to hide. Still, he'd learned to trust his instincts. He'd heard something perhaps, or felt eyes on his back, he knew it.

When no threat materialized, Geth climbed into the saddle again and rode back the way he'd come, sword drawn. He peered into the ditch beside the road, listened hard, sniffed at the wind. And still nothing.

"Thram's balls."

Town's end lay within sight barely a mile ahead. Geth kicked his mount toward it. He wondered what to do now that his plan to draw Ratcher out had failed. He couldn't tell the dozen, and he didn't want to tell Hadean. But his gut told him Ratcher wouldn't underestimate him a second time.

He would have to tell Phelan.

The first ruined buildings of Greenfell loomed ahead as Geth rehearsed how to explain it all to his friend. The little runt would have plenty to say about how he'd allowed the man to slip in among the file in the first place. Geth's eyes still searched for danger, but saw none, the same hunchback he'd seen earlier coming back the other way, cart empty now, white beard wagging as he steered wide of Geth's path. On the other side of the road, a gaggle of village women stood gossiping, the same lot that had been carrying baskets of laundry into town earlier.

But for some reason, Geth didn't like it. He reined his mount in despite the smiles and batted lashes ahead, scanning the group for weapons, hidden hands. He flicked a glance up at the wrecked homes on the edge of town, searching for a bowman. That feeling of being watched sprang back to mind and he turned his horse just in time to see a lone figure throw something from down the road.

Geth's head went down, braced to get hit, but a thump and a curse from over his shoulder turned him back around. The hunchback was down in the dirt a few yards off, that knot of women looking confused. One of them screamed as Geth kicked his steed in the other direction, sword scraping out of its sheath.

"It's me! It's me!"

He was halfway to the figure down the road when he recognized Phelan.

"Thram's crooked—"

"The hunchback!" Phelan pointed. "The hunchback!"

Geth's eyes went wide. He yanked his mount around, the whirr of Phelan's arm sounding in his ear as his friend whipped his sling overhead a second time. Ahead of Geth,

Geth eyed that beard, thinking of Ratcher's disguise, but managed a salute of fist to heart. No assassin was going to follow him into Ilia, he reminded himself. It was the tribesmen he had to worry about.

Hadean had loaned Geth a magnificent piebald and he shadowed Iyngaer's wagon most of the way. The chieftain kept that long, injured leg stretched out, splinted, and wrapped tight. He winced sometimes when the cart jostled and spoke only to Agrem. But the Seer turned at whiles to chat with Geth. He was full of odd jokes, the sort that made little sense in the Aturian tongue. The way he grinned at his own stories was enough to make Geth smile.

Even so, the big warrior could see through the ruse. Agrem was nervous.

Or sad, maybe. Last time they'd come this way, Eko had trotted alongside. Geth blew out a sigh. Now *there* was a friend that knew exactly when to lean on a leg, lick a hand, or plop down in a man's lap. *Like some overgrown puppy.*

Geth eyed Phelan as they rode, frowning at the thought of losing his own best friend. The little man had no choice except to ride in the same wagon as Melagus, slouching on the bench and looking dejected despite an agreeable turn of weather. That warmer weather was worth a grin. Geth knew full well there could be another bout of cold before winter was done, and yet with the sunshine warm on his face, it was hard for the big warrior to believe the Battle for Towerrock was only a few weeks past.

"Feel that light?" Geth asked Phelan, reining in alongside. "Now that we're out here, you can't tell me you're not glad you came along."

Phelan muttered something coarse under his breath.

Melagus leaned forward to speak past the little man. "Don't worry. I'm sure he'll liven up once we reach Point-fort."

"Why is that?" Geth asked.

"He'll be back among his own sort: Crookbow and his thieves."

Melagus smirked, leaned back.

But Phelan straightened in his seat. "I'm no thief. I'm a lot of things, but that I am not."

Geth came to his friend's aid despite all he knew to the contrary. "I thought we cleared that up? It was me that stole those things back before the siege. And I did return them, didn't I?"

Melagus just sniffed. But it wasn't like him to keep his thoughts to himself for long. He huffed a sigh. "I suppose we'll see how this experiment has worked when we get there. Crookbow, I mean. For all we know, the good captain could be gone already."

"He'll be there," Geth said. "And by my reckoning, the king's plan was a good one: grant the pardons we promised, put Crookbow's lot in green, and put them to work. Point-fort needed a garrison after all."

"Well—"

"You think you know better than the king?"

He clearly did think so, but not even Melagus would say it aloud. "We could certainly use the extra hands," he said instead. "The siege may be over, but for some, belts will remain tight. Much of the seedstock was eaten by the tribes. Cattle and sheep were slaughtered or have wandered off to fall prey to the wolves. We *need* this alliance with Iyngaer. More than he knows."

Geth didn't follow. His expression must have said as much.

"Trade." Melagus explained. "I guess I shouldn't expect a sellsword to understand such things. There's much to be gained from trade with the tribes."

"You intend to trade for grain? I can't believe that. Back in Pellon they say that Umbel is the breadbasket of all the Sworn Realms."

"Well, that's true. One thing Towdric didn't lie about was protecting the south. We still have lands untouched by this war, lands ready to produce wheat and barley as they always have. But the tribes have fish, berries, and cattle of their own. Not to mention animal pelts, wool, and tin."

"I think I see now." Geth nodded. "That explains the 'gifts' back there. You mean to return with a few gifts of your own."

"Now you're getting it."

Point-fort came into view just as the sun slipped below the horizon. Geth recalled his first visit there, finding the place gutted, the garrison massacred. But Umbel's banner flew from the square stone spire and green-cloaks could be seen through the open front gate, hurrying between the sheds and barns. A familiar woman with a fur cap like Crookbow's hailed them as they arrived.

"I can't say I relish the idea of sleeping under the roof of a thief," Melagus said.

"They're servants of the king now. Don't forget that. We couldn't have won the war without them."

The self-proclaimed captain of this band appeared just as the company began sliding out of the saddle, or stretching where they stood. Crookbow doffed his cap to offer an exaggerated bow. His eyes stuck on Geth.

"Well, well, well. Hadean's sharpest sword. To what do I owe the honor?"

"Just come to check on my horse, Palladine. I better not find out he's been mistreated."

"Well, he has," Crookbow lifted his chin, "by whatever bastard named him Palladine."

"I agree. Insufferable, pretentious name."

They clasped hands, shared a smile.

Crookbow waved everyone inside the compound but lingered in order to fall in stride with the big warrior. One glance around the place made Geth whistle, shocked by what the man had managed in just a couple short weeks at the fort. Not a shutter hung uneven, nor did any hint remain of the battle that had been waged there. The thieves themselves looked nothing like the big warrior remembered, clean and proper, rushing to form up an honor guard to either side as everyone filed in.

"You've done a job on this lot, haven't you?" Geth said.

Crookbow held his voice low so as not to be overheard. "The trick is to keep 'em busy. For now, we've got plenty to do. When that runs out, I'll have to think of something."

Geth nodded.

"But I've got no worries. The worst of the worst have already slipped away."

"Cald's lot?"

"Mostly." Crookbow spit. "Good riddance. They may go straight back to thieving in the wood, but that's not my problem now."

Night fell. Geth felt his eyelids going heavy until Crookbow's people lit a bonfire and began roasting little chunks
of venison on skewers over the coals. Iyngaer sat back in the
shadows with only Agrem for company. Melagus, however, spoke with the new captain of Point-fort so long that
Geth became curious. He left Phelan to join them.

"...trade post of sorts. Do you have anyone who can
speak the Ilar tongue?"

"Well..." Crookbow scratched at his head.

"Don't worry. A man shall be found." Even by firelight,
Geth could make out the satisfied twist of Melagus's lips.
"This is a big responsibility. If things do not go smoothly,
I would have no choice but to send a man of my choosing
to oversee."

The counselor exited at Geth's approach, leaving
Crookbow muttering curses.

"What did I miss?" the big warrior asked.

"Master Melagus just dropped something on my foot, as
they say."

"I'll bet he did."

"Good news is I won't have any problem keeping the
band busy now."

Geth reached under his cloak, produced a flask of fiery Ilar liquor. He passed it over without a word. Crookbow took a hearty swig.

"Strong stuff."

"From Ilia. Phelan and I call it 'forest fire.'"

"Thanks."

Geth accepted the flask back and swallowed a few gulps himself, watching Melagus settle in across the bonfire. "I've found that a healthy dose of alcohol is really the only way to tolerate him."

Crookbow grunted, reached for another swig.

———†———

He didn't have to tolerate the man for long though. In the morning, they were on their way. Two days of travel brought them under the eaves of the forest and eventually to the wide river valley of Dues.

A damp spring cloaked the hills in mist, drawing fearful mutters from green-cloaks that had been raised on stories of Ilar magick and treachery. With a year of war behind them now, they'd learned plenty about the tribes first-hand, but few, if any, had ever been there, Geth supposed. Agrem's odd ways and Iyngaer's fearsome bearing did little to allay their concerns.

"Don't worry," Geth told the soldiers. "As long as we march with Iyngaer, we're safe."

But Phelan made a face when Geth said as much to him. "And what if he decides to double-cross us? That's the same scratch that practically threw your hairy ass into a frozen lake. *You* may have forgotten, but *I* haven't."

"You're just irked you saw my pole frozen to a nub and it was still bigger than yours."

"Donkeys have big poles. If that's what mattered, every woman would have a donkey."

Geth chuckled. But Phelan's expression went sober.

"It's not Dues that worries me, truth be told. It's where we're headed after."

"Thiringia." Geth wasn't looking forward to a revisit of Ceter's hall either, but a voice cut in from behind before he could say more.

"And well it should worry you." Melagus spurred his mount up alongside the big warrior, wearing his usual frown.

"You expect there might be trouble?" Geth asked.

Melagus flicked a meaningful glance toward Phelan and back. "You'll both have a part to play in seeing there isn't. I've heard of your talents, Master Phelan. You will listen everywhere you can. And report to me all that you hear."

Phelan muttered something foul under his breath but didn't argue.

"And me?" Geth asked.

"Your very presence is a boon to our cause. They fear you. You killed Ceter after all. Not all of them hate you for it."

"Are you saying you want me to crack a few skulls while we're there? Give a warning?"

"You don't want to encourage him," Phelan said.

Melagus rolled his eyes. "Let me do the thinking, please. I want nothing of the sort. Quite the opposite. I hope you can be civil. You've already shown the whip, now offer the carrot."

"I can be civil."

"See that you are."

"Um...how?"

"Shake hands. Eat. Share a drink. Do whatever it is your sort does."

"He cracks skulls," Phelan said.

Melagus glared at the little man before turning back to Geth. "Just be civil. For Hadean, if not for me."

The counselor flicked his reins until he was riding up alongside Agrem and Iyngaer. The Seer looked like he'd accidentally got a mouthful of crabgrass despite Melagus's smiles.

"What about *his* part?" Phelan said, eyes on that bony back. "You think he'll be doing anything to ensure the tribes don't turn on us while we're there?"

"I hope so. Because I reckon it's going to take more than eavesdropping and handshaking to get Ceter's folk to accept Iyngaer as chief."

———✝———

Except for green surrounds in place of snow-whitened slopes, the great hillfort of Dues hadn't changed since Geth's last visit. The same hide banners fluttered in the wind, the same woody smoke swirled under its great, steep roof.

This time, however, it was a feast that awaited, not a trial. Geth sank down onto his pelt beside Iyngaer's fire with a contented sigh, sipping the wine they offered directly from the skin.

"If Melagus wants me to eat," he told Phelan, "I'll eat. And drink. See? I can be civil."

"Just doing your part for King Hadean."

"For peace, my friend."

Truth be told, it wasn't hard to be civil among Iyngaer's folk. Hails of 'Truslata' greeted him from familiar faces. A few tribesmen, like Iyngaer's man, Fork-beard, even went so far as to drag Geth up for a dance when the music started.

"Go," Agrem said, grinning. "This is how it is done in the forest, mmmm? The men dance with the men, the women with the women."

It was a brotherly exchange—despite Phelan's raised eyebrow—a war dance of sorts, best Geth could tell. Standing in line side by side, the men locked shoulders, skipping and jumping in similar fashion to the dancing he'd seen in Turia. Except they didn't turn in a circle. The strum of fiddles, the trill of bone flutes, and the warm beat of drums enveloped the room in a hearty music, the sort that moved a man to sing or at least clap along. Copious amount of berry wine and forest fire didn't hurt either.

Geth let go and allowed himself to enjoy it. He'd earned the tribesmen's respect, he supposed. Here, it didn't matter that he was from Pellon, a fatherless whoreson or a masterless sellsword. They only knew that he fought well and kept his word. From what he'd seen, mostly they did the same. For that, they'd earned his respect as well.

But Phelan, Geth noticed, didn't get caught up in the celebrations.

"Something's going on," he said when the big warrior sank onto the pelt beside him for a breather.

Geth sucked down some wine. "What do you mean?"

"Him." The little man flicked his chin toward Melagus, seated by himself, eyes bright and watchful but mirthless as usual. "He's up to something. There's been some comings and goings."

"You think he's plotting against the chieftain for some reason?"

"Not against him. *With* him." Phelan took a measured sip of wine. "Iyngaer's in the know, whatever it is. Something about a woman. That's all I could catch. They went quiet whenever I got close."

Geth rubbed his temples, wondering if perhaps he shouldn't have drank so much. Could it be Vriana they spoke of? That might explain why the counselor wanted to keep it from him. Or something to do with the witch Sythme, perhaps, the woman Iyngaer had employed to plot with Pythelle and Eldric?

"Just keep your eyes and ears open," Geth said finally. "Melagus wants the best for the realm, but that doesn't mean he won't sacrifice you or me to get it."

CHAPTER FOUR

As expected, Iyngaer resumed his rule of Dues without incident. The first part of Hadean's plan fell into place. Melagus made public presentation of gifts to the chieftain, a token of Umbel's good will. Among them were gold rings, a whole smoked pig, and dozens of swords for his liegemen—the Ilars' own confiscated weapons, but it was something, Geth reckoned.

The entire contingent climbed back on horseback or wagon bench two days later, bound for Ceter's vacated seat in Thiringia. Iyngaer had enlisted a company of his own warriors for an escort this time. That white bearskin sat solemn across his shoulders, his sword swinging from his waist.

Ready for trouble, Geth mused.

And well he should be. Just because Ceter was gone didn't mean some Thiring or other didn't have eyes on ruling the place. Heavy grey clouds threatened rain as they forded the river, moving west. Geth grew more wary with every passing mile. He'd had to fight his way out of that chiefdom last time he was there, had been hunted through those hills. Melagus betrayed his own concerns.

"This isn't going to be easy." He flicked a meaningful glance at Geth's waist, riding beside him. "You haven't taken your hand off your hilt all day. I'm glad to see you understand the gravity."

Geth cursed inwardly, moved his hand to rest in his lap. "You think we've brought enough men?"

"We didn't dare bring more. That could be regarded as hostile, leading to the very thing we want to avoid. Should Iyngaer be forced into a war, we would be obligated to send aid."

Geth spit. "Last thing we need is to send men north when they should be heading south, to deal with Towdric."

"Let's hope it doesn't come to that. With Ceter gone, Thiringia will certainly devolve into infighting and civil war, if someone doesn't bring stability first. The place is ripe for Iyngaer to step in. In his current condition, however, that could prove a more difficult task than it should be."

He meant the chieftain's maimed leg. Few people knew better than Geth about the Ilar way of settling things—combat—but Iyngaer could hardly stand, let alone fight. "Let's just hope it doesn't come to that," he said. "If it does, I'll handle it. And I won't have to worry about Ceter and his magicks this time either."

Melagus couldn't know what Geth alluded to, but he nodded just the same. "I heard how you duped the witch on the river. I must admit that was a bold, clever move. It is hard to kill such a creature as him."

"I nearly died. Pulled it off it in the end though, with Vriana's help."

Melagus eyed him sideways but kept his thoughts to himself. Geth might have hit him otherwise.

———✦———

They reached Ceter's old haunt two days later, the reception cold and without ceremony. Agrem led them up the hill, ordering Thirings left and right, paving the way straight to the central fire. The seat directly behind it, Geth had come to realize, was the ruler's place. The Seer ushered Iyngaer onto a sawed tree ring that Fork-beard set there and they splayed his injured leg out toward the flames.

Servants watched proceedings with troubled faces. An aged tribesman who seemed to be a sort of steward of the hall frowned openly but didn't challenge Agrem. Geth could just imagine his people scurrying off to tell the tale.

He sidled up beside Agrem. "What happens now?"

"Mmmm. The Thirings will come. We have already called a Misa."

They did come. The company enjoyed their dinner in peace, but they hadn't spread their bedrolls before the doors to the hall burst open. A silver-haired tribesman, in a cloak trimmed with matching silver fox-fur, led several dozen hard-eyed warriors directly up to the fire. Iyngaer watched calmly even as more hostile Ilars slipped in through the back exit Geth had used on his last visit.

Agrem hurried around the bright blaze to face the man. Words flew back and forth.

"What are they saying?" Geth whispered to Phelan. The little man was already at Geth's side, the pair of them standing just a hand's breath from Iyngaer himself.

"You have no chieftain, 'Grem is saying. Iyngaer led you in the southlands once Ceter was gone. He can do it again. I've...heard the whisperings of the trees and the gods and the fathers and they all tell me that he will continue to lead."

Geth frowned as Silver-cloak shot back a reply. "And?" the big warrior prodded.

"He led us to defeat, he says," Phelan continued. "He came limping back like a lame deer."

Agrem spoke again and Phelan translated.

"Agrem says: Then who would lead? Will you find another...lizard...to warm himself in the place of honor at your fire? It was Ceter's poison that began this war. His lies. Ilars don't need southern lands. We never did."

Iyngaer uttered something.

"It was his weak blood that needed the warmth, Iyngaer just told the scratch. Well, he is gone now, the Thiring says. And good riddance."

Silver-cloak spit. Geth didn't need a translation for that. Neither for what he said next, judging by the hard set of his jaw.

"They want to raise their own chieftain," Geth said. "And this ball-scratch is him."

Silver-cloak wasn't done though. He jabbed a finger down at the floor, uttered curses Geth recognized, spit again. A hush fell over the room as the man fell quiet, eyes locked with Iyngaer's. Phelan translated, but he didn't have to.

"He's accused Iyngaer of bringing swords into this hall, a powerful sorcerer, and enemies from abroad. He says Dues has disrespected the Thirings with all that. And—"

"And he's challenged him to a duel."

Phelan nodded. Agrem was already looking at Geth as the big warrior stepped forward.

"Any man that challenges Iyngaer, challenges me!" Geth didn't wait for an answer but drew his sword.

A ruckus erupted; curses flew.

"It doesn't work like that here, they're saying," Phelan explained.

"Translate for me then." Geth took a step forward, lowered his sword but spoke loud enough to be heard by all.

"Any man who threatens Iyngaer Govendi threatens me! We have fought, you're saying? We're enemies? No, we're friends. We're *brothers*."

Silver-cloak snorted a laugh. He spoke, addressing the entire hall as Geth had.

"He says you're not brothers, you're the farthest thing from it," Phelan said. "Did you not almost kill each other?"

"We did," Geth said. "But brothers fight, don't they? In the end, they're still brothers. The chieftain held me captive in his lands. He could have killed me, but he spared my life. And I could have killed him at the battle in the south, but I didn't. We share this. We owe each other everything. And that's what makes us brothers."

There was a pause as Aturian-speakers translated for their fellows. A heated debate sprang up, tribesmen arguing back and forth, aloud and in pockets throughout the room. Agrem tried to shout over them to no avail.

"Doesn't look like theses bastards are gonna accept that," Phelan said.

"They don't have to." Geth moved to step directly in front of Iyngaer. "But they'll have to go through me to get to him if they don't."

That movement wasn't lost on the tribesmen, whether they understood what Geth had said or not. Hands moved to hilts. Serving folk backed to the edges of the great chamber scurrying over pelts and plates. Geth surveyed the men across the room, warriors who likely hated him already. But among the cold hard stares, his eyes met one honey-brown pair that caught his breath.

"Vriana?"

Geth wondered if this wasn't the woman Melagus and Iyngaer had spoken of, but Agrem moved close to the fire, arms raised at that same moment. He shouted until he had everyone's attention.

Melagus slid up beside Iyngaer and Phelan came close beside Geth to translate as the tall chieftain pushed himself up to speak.

"You lay much blame at my feet. You talk of my defeat in the south and the wounds I carry with me upon my return. But you do not speak of my victories.

"I marched our spears deep into the southlands. I sent half of my enemies into hiding behind water and stone, the other half fleeing to the south. The spirits themselves contrived to steal my glory. Eagle, Wolf, and Snake. But from the belly of destruction, I climbed out to return.

"Where is your Chieftain, mmmm? Swallowed under ice. Where are your best warriors? Beside him under the feet of the Great River."

Silver-cloak shot something back and Phelan translated. "Is that your one victory? That you lived to crawl back?"

"I could not take land in the south, but perhaps I came back with something more valuable instead: an alliance with the young Eagle."

Iyngaer held up a hand to display a glittering gold ring.

"He means Hadean," Phelan whispered.

Geth rolled his eyes and flicked his chin back toward the chieftain as he began speaking again.

"That's right. Even in defeat, I won such respect from the Sunlander chief that he sent me back with his greatest warrior, his most trusted sorcerer, and lavish gifts."

Silver-cloak mouthed an especially colorful curse. "So, the young Eagle has bought your friendship? Or perhaps his friendship is a false one, like all the sunlanders before him. Perhaps he sends you north to buy peace at his border, now when he needs it most."

Iyngaer took a careful step forward, peering past Silver-cloak to address the Thirings behind him. "Who wouldn't want peace on their border when they've already eaten plenty at the table of war?"

A loud crack sounded, turning all eyes toward the great doors to the hall. Geth blinked. Somehow Agrem had gone from beside him to that entryway, pounding the base of a staff into the hard floor. The gathered tribesmen gasped all at the same time, but not at the Seer. Vriana stood at his side.

Silver-cloak didn't need to say a word. His expression made plain what he thought of the chieftess. Geth reckoned the hatred between their two tribes must have survived Ceter after all. A smile touched the big warrior's lips, but Iyngaer started in again before he could laugh or cheer.

"I have a new friend in the south, but I have old friends in the north as well. And as I said, who wouldn't want

peace on their border when they have already had their fill
of blood and dying?"

Behind Vriana, her escort of warriors didn't bother to
hide grim smiles. The chieftess herself held a level stare.
The threat in Iyngaer's words was crystal clear.

But Silver-cloak didn't cow so easily.

"Do you expect me to believe, the She-Cat of Laer will
simply pull back her claws because you say so? Did a
woman ever do what a man told her? Not in these forests,
mmmm?"

"A woman can listen whenever she sees fit," Iyngaer
said. "As wife to husband and husband to wife."

Geth froze. His eyes went from Iyngaer to Vriana and
back. All joy at her arrival drained out of the big warrior
as Agrem raised that staff overhead to gather everyone's
attention.

"That's right!" The Seer lowered the staff and stepped
toward Silver-cloak. "The bad spirits surrounding this
Misa can only be driven off by the most sacred of rituals. A
wedding. Let the joy of a great union drive off the ghosts of
the vengeful dead. Let wine and meat and song fill each of
us so there is no room left for ill-will. I propose a marriage
to join two tribes and heal wounds. Iyngaer Lonega has
already agreed..."

Geth braced himself, looked toward Vriana, but her own head was turned toward the entry to the hall.

"...and so has Gemela."

A second collective gasp sounded from the assembly, Geth among them. Tribesmen crowded at the back parted to admit a tall blond in stunning silver and white furs, blue eyes bright.

Silver-cloak uttered a curse, his stare like daggers on a Thiring who stood behind Gemela, the same yellowy hair bound tight to his temples.

"I think it's that man's daught—"

"I see that, Phelan!"

Phelan glowered back, but Gemela had started speaking, and he had no choice but to translate.

"Let there be peace, cousins. Let there be peace, Lord Vongaer."

She dipped her head toward Silver-cloak—Vongaer—but the older Thiring looked like smoke might come out of his ears.

Noises of appreciation sounded throughout the chamber despite whatever he might have thought. If Geth wasn't mistaken, a few of the Thirings that stood close beside Vongaer earlier had drifted a step or two away.

"If we have learned nothing from this great war in the Southlands," Agrem said, "at least we have learned that the mighty do not always win, mmmm? Let us take this wisdom, the friendships we have made, the stories of bravery we've earned, and be done with war for a time."

Gemela dipped her head. She had a beautiful neck to go with those eyes. "This is my wish," she was saying, according to Phelan. "Let us have peace. A child of Thiring blood shall be chieftain of both Dues and Thiringia. Is that not enough?"

Mutters of accord sounded. Vongaer looked gutted. Geth felt a grin split his face, from ear to ear.

Melagus and Iyngaer had seen this all coming, Geth reckoned. With this move, they undercut Vongaer's play for the rule of Thiringia before it even started.

"That's how it's done," said a smug voice. Geth turned to find the counselor standing beside him, arms folded across his chest. "The whip: Vriana. The carrot: a favorable marriage and peace. They'll always take the carrot if the whip is big enough."

"That's about the biggest whip out there."

"Your sword has come in handy once or twice as well. But you see, there are other ways."

Melagus sauntered off, happy enough to accept a horn of wine from a serving lad and take a generous pull. Geth stole a glance at Vriana, breathed sigh. He thanked Phelan with a pat on the back, intent to find the chieftess, but Agrem crossed toward him first.

"Well done," Geth said. "Melagus wants to take all the credit, but I reckon you played as big a part as he did."

The Seer shrugged. "It is done."

"And the wedding?"

"Tomorrow. Afterward, we feast."

Geth started to smile but a look passed over his friend's face. "What is it, 'Grem?"

"Mmmm." The Seer nodded, almost to himself. "Yes, you should come."

"Come where?"

"There is something that must be done before we can celebrate."

Agrem waved and Geth followed. He meandered through the crowd, back out the hall's great entryway. It was dusk by then, the sky gone purple in the east, pink and orange and blue in the west. He led Geth all the way down the tor and out through the hillfort's palisade before stepping off the muddy path.

Stopping at the side of the road, Agrem produced some kindling which he arranged in a carful pile on the ground, then set a clump of something down on top of it.

It was fur.

A sigh left Geth's lips. "Eko." He thought of the beast's end, of that bastard, Towdric.

Agrem struck his flint and blew until the fire took. Standing, he croaked the same mournful tune he'd sung at Baby's burial, then muttered something like a prayer. When he looked to Geth, the big warrior stepped a little closer to the tiny pyre.

"Wise Lady Vorda, welcome Eko to your Bosom. He was faithful, loyal, and brave. He always knew when someone was sad, and he knew how to cheer you up too. He died fighting for his friends. I'll count myself lucky if I can die the same way."

"Mmmm."

They stood there in silence as the little fire burned fitfully then finally guttered out. Agrem knelt to set a finger in the ash before they left, rubbing a smudge on his cheek.

He loosed a sigh of his own, muttered something in his tongue. His eyes were full of mist. Geth didn't know what he said, nor did it matter. He had only one response.

"Don't worry. By all the gods, I swear it. Towdric will pay."

CHAPTER FIVE

An ox was slaughtered the next day, along with several of Ilia's short, domesticated deer. Eager tribesmen hauled urns of wine uphill to Ceter's vacated hall. Ehken Dolae—the Fox Den—hadn't seen a celebration like this in many a year, Geth was told. Still, in better times, such a union as Iyngaer and Gemela's would have called for weeks of preparation.

But in the interest of peace, the wedding was slated for that very evening. The sooner, the better, it was agreed. Message runners had gone out and Ilars from miles around streamed in. The entire town would celebrate.

"They say the festivities could last seven days," Phelan told the big warrior that afternoon, seated on a log ring, feet up on a bucket outside the hall. "I volunteer to stay the full week if necessary, drinking to the happy couple."

"That right?" Geth asked.

"I always do my part, in the name of peace."

But another thought occurred to Geth. "What about the inn? Not in a rush to get back, check on the place?"

"Not in a rush to get back to that sonofabitch, Ratcher."

Geth had almost forgotten about the assassin. He looked down from the heights of the hall to survey ring upon ring of longhouses descending toward the palisade. "Hopefully that slingstone of yours broke a rib or two," he said.

"It should have killed him. But you saw how quick he scrambled off."

With the celebration to look forward to, Geth decided it was better to put Ratcher out of mind. Delicious smells floated on the air and more than a few Duesmen stepped over to offer a skin of forest fire, a pat on the shoulder, a clasp of hands. Somehow, even in the wake of war, he'd made friends among them. Perhaps it was the words he'd spoken for their chieftain the day before, or the surrender he'd negotiated at the Battle of Towerrock, saving many lives.

If that wasn't the stuff of friendship, what was? The day stretched on. Geth found himself wearing as big a smile as anyone, thinking on that. He took a pull at a horn of berry wine. Soon he was smiling from the liquor as well.

Evening approached, purple skies stretching up from the east to chase off clouds lit orange beneath. Man, woman, and child gathered outside in front of the hall, Agrem and a pair of Thiring witches standing by to officiate. As was custom, the ceremony began as soon as the sun touched the horizon in the west. Geth took in the sight, afforded a good spot right up near the doors. The sunsets really were beautiful in that country. The wedding too, if he was honest—a thing of candles, sweet incense, and finally a drink for the bride and groom from the same horn. As the sun finally disappeared behind the hills, a cheer went up and it was done.

Iyngaer turned gingerly on his crutch to present a broad smile to his people. Watching this, the Lady Gemela snatched the crutch away, to slide an arm around and under him. Perhaps she only meant to be helpful, but judging by the hoots and grins that followed, the tribesmen read something more into it.

Geth looked on as the chieftain's beautiful bride helped him hobble inside. He thought of Vriana, another strong, beautiful woman, to be sure. His eyes wandered until he found hers. Her armor was gone, replaced by a vest of fine grey furs, embroidered leathers, close fitted to her curves. A hint of a smile graced her lips—not more—but that was something, coming from the chieftess.

The doors to the hall came open, admitting the newly-weds and as many celebrants as could squeeze inside. Geth headed toward Vriana. A pass of steaming meat on huge wooden platters distracted him for a while, but he ignored a ceremonial exchange of gifts between bride and groom, swiping a whole skin of Forest Fire for himself and striding across the hall to join the chieftess.

He offered the skin, flicked his chin toward Vongaer. "Look at that scowl. You reckon we should kill him now and get it over with?"

Vriana nodded but waved off the drink. "When the music starts, you should dance."

"I'd love to dance with you. I'm not very good, but you could teach me."

She made a face. "Not with me. The men dance with the men."

Geth frowned.

"It's not hard."

"You carry a sword. That's manly enough for me if you change your mind."

A flute trilled a long, high note, and the beat of drums followed. Something like a fiddle joined in. Women clapped and moved out into the cleared space near the central hearth. Vriana left Geth to join their line in a graceful demonstration of steps, kicks, and twirling hips. He sucked down a long pull of forest fire, watching, unable to take his eyes off her.

The men danced next. Iyngaer could hardly walk, but Fork-beard and some of the others carried a sawed tree ring out into the cleared spaced for him to sit on. They danced around him while he clapped and stamped to the beat with his good foot. Geth stood in the wings, grinning, until a pair of hands shoved him forward and he found himself out among them.

Ilars and Umbelmen alike hooted.

"What the—"

Agrem and Phelan stood chuckling behind him. Off to one side, Melagus met Geth's eye. He didn't smile, but he nodded his approval. With the drums beating and all that liquor coursing through his veins, Geth didn't need as much encouraging as he would have thought.

"All right, all right! I can dance! Who said I couldn't?"

Whether they understood him or not, onlooking Ilars whistled and clapped. Fork-beard pulled Geth beside him, locking shoulders as a second Ilar, threw an arm over his other shoulder to start a line. The ensemble grew to a good dozen dancers, linked up abreast. The musicians quickened their beat. Iyngaer smacked his good knee to the time. Geth did his best to jump and kick. He almost kept up.

That song felt like it lasted an hour. Panting but grinning even broader, Geth stumbled out of line when it finished. The line reformed—Thirings right alongside Duesmen, Geth was glad to see—but he hurried away lest he step on anymore feet than he already had. Ahead of him, Iyngaer sat on that tree ring, Gemela's hand resting on the yellow-white fur of the bear mantle across his shoulders.

Geth snatched up his skin of forest fire and stepped in their direction. "A drink!" He offered it to the chieftain. "To your health."

Iyngaer accepted, downing an impressive swallow. He handed the skin to his wife. Gemela took a pull herself, nodding and smiling in turn.

"You have my thanks," Iyngaer said, speaking above the din. "For your words yesterday. It is something to speak for a man, to stand and fight for him."

"The duel? They weren't going to let me do it anyway, were they?"

"No."

They shared a laugh.

"Well, I'm happy for you," Geth said. "I just want you to know that. I'm glad neither of us killed the other. I reckon that makes us friends, right?"

"Mmmm. Two great rams cannot share the same cliff. One of us should be dead. And yet we are here. The spirits—the gods, as you say—have willed it."

Geth nodded.

The chieftain's eyes went somber. "You are welcome in Dues, Geth et Trusla, should you ever have need to come this way. And in Thiringia. Always."

He flicked a glance to one side and Geth followed that look. *Straight to Vriana.* He shook his head. Was there *anyone* who didn't know?

He sighed, heading in the direction of the chieftess for a second time. "Well, if it's no secret..."

Vriana began clapping as he approached. She grinned, eyes full of genuine mirth.

"What? I told you I could dance."

"I saw some jumping. But if you say that is how you dance in the Southlands..."

"Oh yeah? Dance with me then if you think you can do better."

"I think I will win that contest."

Geth motioned toward the other dancers, raised an eyebrow. "Well then?"

"Men with men."

"I forgot. Share a drink with me instead."

"No."

"Not celebrating?"

A hand drifted toward her midsection and her mouth opened, but she clamped it shut, that hand dropping back to her side to grip tight at the leather of her pant leg.

Geth's eyes went wide. "Thram's balls, are you—"

Vriana's chin went up. "What if I am, mmmm?"

"Uh...congratulations. I mean, good luck."

Her eyes narrowed.

Geth cursed himself. Why the hell had he said that?

But what was he *supposed* to say? What was he supposed to *think?*

"There is no luck," the chieftess said, chin higher than ever. "It will be a strong child." She hesitated. "And beautiful."

Geth took several long swallows of forest fire, started to offer her a drink, then took another for himself. Cursing under his breath, he nodded, turned, and made a graceless exit.

It shouldn't have mattered, but the very idea that Vriana was pregnant weighed on Geth. He pushed past laughing revelers until he was outside, breath rising like smoke in the cold northern air. He sucked at his skin of liquor until it was empty.

His head swam. Swearing out loud, he threw the empty skin down the hill and stalked the length of the hall. He peered down over celebratory bonfires that had been lit here and there. But taking the high ground did nothing for him at that moment.

Someone cleared their throat behind him. Geth whirled to find Phelan looking at him.

"What?"

"Did she tell you?"

Geth swore.

"Melagus asked me to eavesdrop, learn whatever I could. Don't worry, I didn't tell him. But anyone who notices she's not drinking will figure out as much."

Geth shook his head. "You're right. I don't know why I should even care. Just because she's pregnant, it doesn't mean it's mine."

Phelan directed a level stare at him.

"It probably is, isn't it?"

"What's your problem with it? That's the real question. Why do you even give a damn?"

Geth sank to a seat on the steps leading up to the hall. Phelan sat beside him. Tribesmen and the odd green-cloak stumbled by in twos and threes, good and drunk, none paying them any mind.

"I guess it could have happened at any time," Geth said finally, "but I never thought of myself as a father. I mean, I never had one myself. Not much of a mother to speak of either. The thought that I would produce a bastard myself..."

"It's not like that, Geth. C'mon, this child will be born a prince! Such as things go up here anyway. And it will have a strong mother for sure."

"But no father."

"Well—"

"You of all people know I could be dead in a week, Phelan. And even if I wasn't, what kind of father would I be? I mean, does Vriana even want me around?"

"That's a lot of speculation, Geth."

"Anyway you cut it, it's about as good as no father at all."

Phelan produced a wedge of cheese seemingly out of nowhere, bit off a chunk, and spoke around a mouthful. "Better no father than a father like mine."

"Maybe. But for me it wasn't easy growing up without one."

Phelan passed over the cheese. Geth just sat there looking at it. Phelan nudged him until he broke off a piece and shoved it in his mouth.

"Do you love her?"

"Love her?" Geth scoffed. "No."

Phelan said nothing.

"Well, maybe a little bit."

"A little bit."

"What does it matter if I love her, Phelan? I'm not the settling down type. I can barely hold a job. And what woman in her right mind would stick to a man like me?"

"A woman who's just the same."

It was Geth's turn to go quiet.

Phelan took the wedge of cheese back and broke off another piece for himself. "All I'm saying is, you're getting ahead of things. Vriana's having a baby, that's it. If she wants something from you, she'll tell you. If she doesn't, nothing's really changed."

Geth grimaced. "Thram's hairy balls." He exhaled a long sigh. "I just didn't see this coming, Phelan. And I hate it when that happens."

Geth's usual response to an ambush was to fight. This time though, every instinct in his body told him to run.

It required a lot more drink, but he managed to pass out. He awoke half on a fur, half on cold wood planks on the floor in Ehken Dolae's hall. Phelan snored beside him. A few tribesmen had already risen to begin cleaning up. Others huddled around the central fire, sipping horns and sharing bread. Geth rolled on his back, stared up into the beams high above, muttering curses.

Agrem arrived just as he finally sat up. The Seer took one look at him and hummed. "Mmmm."

"Phelan told you?"

"No but..." The Ilar shrugged. "I am 'The Seer.'"

He left it at that, stretching down a hand to help Geth rise. He handed over a flask of watered, morning wine and more of the salty cheese Phelan had shared the night before. That smudge of ash still marked his cheek.

"Where's Melagus?" Geth asked. "We've done what we came to do here. I need to get back south, deal with Towdric."

Agrem nodded. "Amalia has spoken to me."

"How did—?" Geth decided he didn't really want to know. "I mean, what did she say?"

"You are wanted in the Southlands. The Snake as well."

"So we're leaving. Good."

"You are, but I must stay with Iyngaer. He will need me in the days ahead."

Geth eyed that smudge of ash on his friend's cheek. "Don't worry, 'Grem. I'll deal with Towdric."

"Mmmm." The Seer's gaze drifted, eyes far away. "Until he is dead, there can be no peace. I have *seen* it."

CHAPTER SIX

Melagus must have been told of Amalia's message before Geth. Preparations to depart had already begun and goodbyes were being said. They would leave at midday.

Geth's head pounded, but for him, the sooner they left, the better. His gut still told him to run, even if it was toward Ratcher and war. These things he knew.

The spires of Towerrock appeared ahead after a few days of hard travel. A brusque wind whipped Geth's hair across his eyes and his knuckles curled cold on the reins. But the sun was shining. For some reason, the North River ran blue and silver under cool skies, not muddy brown or green. Whatever fate might hold for him regarding Ratcher and Towdric, it felt good to be home.

Hadean received them in his war room as soon as they arrived. He knew Geth well enough and didn't skimp on the food. Geth tore into a loaf of warm bread, a joint of mutton, and the ale that was passed around. Melagus, Amalia, and that old bull-necked green-cloak joined in, standing over the king's maps at his table.

"Where's Brant?" Geth asked, wiping crumbs from his mustache with a sleeve.

Melagus frowned, wiping the same crumbs off the map. "Lord Brant has returned to Waterset with Captain Worran and their men," he said. "We'll meet them soon. He's negotiated a meeting with Towdric."

Geth looked from the counselor to the king. "Do you want me to kill him if I get a chance?"

Hadean smiled. "No, we're going to try to negotiate a peace."

"That's a damn sight better than he deserves."

"Perhaps. But we've already discussed other options. Laying siege to Umbel City is our last resort."

"We can't just leave him on your throne, can we?"

It was Melagus who answered, shaking his head. "Consolidating power? No. Let's march an army downriver and see what the sight does for him, shall we? We might find him more amenable to compromise after that."

"Show him the whip so he chooses the carrot, eh?"

Melagus actually smiled. "Yes. But we'll keep the whip handy just in case."

Phelan stood waiting for Geth in the sword-yard as he left the king's counsel. "We need to stick close," he explained. "Ratcher."

Geth uttered a choice one. "I almost forgot about the scratch. To the inn then?"

They crossed the bridge into town, past half-repaired buildings, eyeing darkened doorways and alley mouths all the way. Geth's hand never left the hilt at his waist, but it was for naught. They reached the front steps of the inn without incident.

Hack hailed them with both hands raised. "You're here! Great news: Dodger and Bird-man brought back the brewer!"

Geth looked to Phelan, but the little man hardly smiled. "Has anyone seen Ratcher?"

Hack frowned. "Did you hear me about Dodger? They've already laid up some barrels. We can stop drinking that shit-water now!"

Phelan opened his mouth, but Geth pushed him through the door. A clap on the back ushered Hack inside as well. Geth looked over both shoulders before closing the door behind them.

The dozen hollered their greetings, crowding around to welcome Geth and Phelan. Green-cloaks at the tables grinned, raised drinks to their health. But Geth marveled at the sight of Neary seated among them at the end of the bar. He pushed through the others to join the lanky fighter, lifting him off the ground in a bear hug.

"Neary!"

"Easy, Captain! I'm still on the mend!"

"Right, right. But gods all be damned, last time I saw you, you could barely open your eyes. Now you're up and about?"

"With this." Neary gestured to a cane hung on the lip of the bar by its handle. "I get tired easy yet. And I get headaches. But 'Lia's been tending to me every day."

"'Lia?" Geth blinked. "*Ama*-lia?"

Neary started to answer but Phelan swooped in, grinning. "Tending to you every day, is she? How about at night?"

"Even if she was," Neary said, "a gentleman wouldn't tell."

Phelan's eyes went round. "I knew it!"

The old Umbelman's face turned red. Geth had a snicker himself. For a moment at least, he forgot about Ratcher, about Towdric down south, Vriana up north. Blink appeared with one of his famous dishes and the big warrior tucked in where he stood in spite of the earlier meal with the king. Phelan clapped his hands, sent everyone else back to work.

Geth settled down with Neary. "You look great, Neary. I mean it. There was a minute there..."

"Yeah, I thought I was a goner myself. But here I am. There's only one problem."

Geth already knew. "Ready to hang up your sword?"

Neary looked down at his hands. "Amalia says I don't have any choice. I took a good crack on the head. One more like that, she says, and my wits will be permanently addled."

"Worse than they already are? Can't abide that."

Neary forced a smile, but Geth could see he was troubled.

"We'll find someone to stand in for you," he told the old green-cloak. "Try to, anyway. But your wits were always your best weapon, truth be told. There will be plenty for you to do still, don't you worry."

"I won't be joining you down south though."

"You know about that?"

The Umbelman shrugged.

"Oh right, 'Lia."

"Yeah."

"Well, it'll be alright, it's just a negotiation. Hadean's looking for an accord. I don't reckon he'll find one."

"I hope he does," Neary said. "Me for one, I've had enough of war."

———✝———

Message runners and pigeons went north and south. As a precaution against Ratcher, Geth and Phelan slept in the same room and kept the doors and windows barred. They hardly left the inn. When they did, they went together.

But Ratcher never made a move.

On the seventh day after their return, the order arrived to march south. They'd leave the next morning—all the notables except Hadean himself. For safety's sake, he'd come later with a larger force.

They dozen would stay behind as well. Geth was able to get them assigned to Towerrock's garrison, out of harm's way. They weren't pleased, but he told them Phelan needed someone to look after the inn. He couldn't tell them about Ratcher.

When the morning finally dawned, Phelan was among the first to rise. "Gods but I'm tired of the inside of this place."

Geth grunted. After staring at the same walls for most of the week, he felt the same way.

"What do you think took so long anyway?" he asked. "I thought we'd have left by now."

"They were waiting on two arrivals. One from the east and one from the north."

"And you didn't tell me sooner?"

"How could I?" Phelan spread his hands. "I just now overheard Melagus talking about it with the king."

"Do we know anything else?"

"It's a miracle I managed to catch that much. I've been stuck guarding your back every day, remember?"

That sent Geth's thoughts back to Ratcher. He eyed the men forming up to march. Several hundred would make the journey. Plenty of ranks for a knifeman to hide among.

"We'll be vulnerable out there on the road," he said. "Reckon he just might come for me then."

"For *us*."

Geth grimaced. "I don't think we have any choice, Phelan."

"About what?"

"About Ratcher. There's strength in numbers. It's time to enlist some help."

Phelan's eyes narrowed. "No way. It's too risky."

"We can't watch each other's back all day and all night, can we? When would we sleep? We need to bring someone into the fold. Someone that will understand the need to keep things hush."

"It would need to be someone Ratcher won't suspect. Someone who can help us fight the bastard."

"Or out-think him."

"Sure, but who? That's a dangerous proposition. Who's clever enough to be any help that we don't mind putting at risk?"

Geth's face screwed up, thinking, but the answer was obvious. There was only one man for the job.

CHAPTER SEVEN

M elagus rode up at the fore as the column started off south along the River Road. Geth watched him, thinking what he'd say. He couldn't help riding up and down the line a couple times as well, squinting at soldiers to no avail. For all the helmets masking faces, Ratcher could have been any of them. Or none.

"Maybe he's a horse," Phelan offered. "Did you check?"

"I wouldn't put it past him."

"Did you tell Melagus?"

"Headed that way now."

But a commotion on the road stopped him halfway. A troop of riders had appeared ahead, mounted on the short sturdy steeds of the north. Between that and all the leathers, they could only be Ilars.

Geth kicked his mount in their direction. Smiles and waves hailed him, and yet his gut tightened as his eyes met a honey-brown stare. *Vriana.*

"Thram's balls."

He didn't stop cursing there. He should have expected as much when Phelan mentioned an arrival from the north. Melagus would want to display the whip—his allies—fearsome warriors any traitor to the realm would have to face. And with Iyngaer's plate full in Thiringia, it could only have been the chieftess.

Geth met them halfway between the two parties. "Uh...welcome, Vriana Govendis."

Why did he sound so formal? This time he cursed himself, for his words, and the unconscious drift of his eyes toward her belly. The chieftess watched him, just a slight pinch between the eyebrows to betray her annoyance.

"We are here, as promised, to support the sunland king," she said. "Take me to the Snake."

Geth waved them to follow.

'The Snake,' he'd come to understand, carried no insult. She referred to Melagus, of course, but in the Ilar tradition, the moniker implied wisdom, associating him with the underworld and all the knowledge of the 'Fathers.'

In Umbel, Melagus had acquired a similar nickname, the Asp. It wasn't a compliment, but a result, rather, of his cold, calculated decision-making. Geth snorted a laugh thinking on that.

But maybe the tribesmen were right. He needed Melagus's wisdom too, after all. He started to wonder what the counselor might know of fatherhood, about women even, before he squashed the thought. The two parties joined, exchanged pleasantries, and the company started south once more.

Vriana fell in beside Melagus's wagon. Geth dropped back behind them. He watched the sway of her shoulders in the saddle, cursing himself all the while. *So she's pregnant. Why the hell do I care? She doesn't want me around anyway. And she doesn't need me either.*

But he *did* care.

Gods all be damned! He watched her chatting with Melagus, the sun lifting the red out of the single long braid gleaming down her back.

She slowed her mount after a while—no one could bear Melagus for long—and the big warrior spurred forward, approaching the counselor from the other side of his wagon. There were bigger things to worry about than a woman and his own silly desires, he reminded himself. Like staying alive.

Geth reined in alongside the counselor. "The whip, eh?" He flicked his chin back toward the Ilars.

"The king insisted. It has no teeth though. Towdric will see through it. He knows Hadean's weakness by now."

Geth wasn't sure he understood but he nodded anyway.

"Still, it can't hurt to reinforce our new alliance with the tribes," Melagus went on.

"What's the plan? We'll have to fight the bastard sooner or later."

"Maybe."

"Maybe?" Geth frowned.

"Be patient. We're working on an offer even Towdric couldn't refuse."

Geth didn't like the sound of that, but he kept his opinion to himself. This once. He needed Melagus. He cleared his throat, choosing his words.

"You seek my counsel," Melagus said before the big warrior could speak. "Say it. I'll need something from you at some point as well, I'm sure. Let's call it a trade."

"It's a dangerous trade."

Melagus snorted. "Everything about you is dangerous. It never stopped me before, did it?"

Geth couldn't help but smile. He took a deep breath and began the tale of Ratcher. It sputtered like a candle at first, then caught hold and took flame until Geth himself burned hot with the telling.

"Damn the wrinkled balls of the Red God," Melagus breathed when he'd finished.

Geth had never heard the man curse like that. "I'm in a bind, aren't I?"

"And now I am too! Why in the name of everything good did you tell me? He'll want to kill me as well if he suspects!"

"I told you it was dangerous. But he has no reason to suspect, does he? I mean, you and I have cause for secret talks like this almost every day."

Melagus still looked like he wanted to shake Geth by the collar. But he had to nod. "That's true."

"So, what do we do?"

The counselor blew out a sigh, looked out over the road ahead, muttering to himself. He nodded, shook his head and cursed, and nodded again before turning back.

"You say he's no archer? And he seems to despise poisons?"

"That's right."

"But he's quite adept at disguising himself, going unseen. Fitting in."

Geth nodded.

"This doesn't imply we can rule out other means, only that he *prefers* stealth, avoids other methods. He may fall back on them if he feels he's exhausted his options."

"I still think he'll come for me with the knife."

"And you want my advice?"

Geth nodded again.

"Sleep with your back against a tree."

"Thram's balls, that all you got for me?"

"Yes. And I'm in danger now too."

"Oh, keep your pants on! How many times have you thrown *me* into danger?"

"That's your strong suit."

Melagus muttered another surprisingly ripe curse, shaking his head and turning his eyes to the distance again. Then he snorted, laughed out loud. He nodded and turned to face the big warrior. "Are you wearing armor under your tunic?"

Geth blinked. He hadn't told anyone, not even Phelan. "Yes."

"And you have the thief watching your back while you sleep?"

"I do."

"Good. But I'm going to recommend something more, something you may not like."

Geth frowned. "What?"

"Lay your blankets down among the tribesmen."

"Vriana's people?"

"What, fallen out of love already?"

Geth opened his mouth, but Melagus kept right on.

"They're only a dozen, retainers included. No one will be able to slip in among them without notice."

Geth wanted to argue but found himself smiling instead. "You really are a genius, you know that?"

Melagus sniffed. Geth could have choked him—if he didn't want to kiss him.

It would be like the trip to Ilia again, only on a tiny scale. Pure genius. Even if Ratcher had already managed to sneak in among Umbel's ranks, he wouldn't have a spare set of Ilar leathers in his pack. And the tribesmen were a suspicious lot. He'd never slip among them unnoticed. He'd certainly never slip out alive.

Vriana would insist on a two-man watch each night as well. That would take some of the pressure off Phelan. It was Geth himself who'd be under pressure now, he reckoned. A completely different kind of pressure.

"One more thing," Melagus said, finger raised. "Be wary of anything unexpected, anything that causes a disruption. A good assassin makes use of a man's routine, his regularity. They know where you'll be, with who, and with what. They'll set things up to distract you, then strike in a way you least expect."

"You can stop laughing now." Geth glared at Phelan.

"I can't." The little man rode with one hand at his side. "It's just too good. And the whole time, I get to hear all the Ilars whisper behind your back."

The sky was darkening, and the order would soon arrive to make camp for the night. Geth had told him of the plan to bed down with Vriana's party. Phelan for one, couldn't wait to see him squirm.

"You can't say it's not a good plan," Geth said.

"Oh, it's good. He's a clever bastard, the Worm. Knowing your history, I almost wonder if he didn't come up with it just to torture you."

Geth had started to wonder the same thing.

But, no, sleeping among Vriana's people would certainly offer protection through the most vulnerable hours. He couldn't argue with that. He'd just have to think up some excuse for it with the chieftess.

When Bull-neck finally ordered the column to a halt though, he had yet to come up with one.

"C'mon," he told Phelan, leading his mount toward the company of tribesmen. The River Road shadowed the course of Vorus southwards, and they'd chosen a flat patch of flood plain to make their camp. Vriana stood, directing her people, warriors unsaddling horses, rolling out blankets, lighting campfires.

"Chieftess," Geth dipped his head in a sort of a bow as he approached. She watched him but said nothing.

"Well, uh, as the king's champion, it's my duty to protect his allies in his absence. So, I'm going to have to stay here tonight and keep watch."

"Mmmm."

"For your protection. That's all."

"You think I need protecting?"

"Well, uh...no."

"I am not worth protecting then?"

"No, no, that's not it. I just...you shouldn't *have* to protect yourself. In your state, I mean."

"In my state." She looked at him evenly. "Mmmm."

Gods all be damned!

There was heat in her eyes, unless it was some trick of the orange campfire flickering beside her. She dragged her bedroll across the Ilar camp and sat atop it with her back to him.

Geth cursed himself. But what else was he supposed to say? She *did* deserve protecting, never mind that she was probably in no actual danger on this journey. And even if she didn't agree she needed it, what kind of person would leave a pregnant woman to fend for herself, whether just a friend or something more?

"That went well," Phelan said, striding up alongside.

Geth turned, gave him such a look he stepped back, out of reach.

"Her people think you're trying to get sideways with her."

"Nosey bastards."

"This is gonna be great. I've decided I like that scratch, Melagus. He's alright by me."

———†———

The pattern was set. Each evening Geth and Phelan bedded down among the Ilars, and each night Vriana chose a spot as far from the pair as possible. Even so, it worked. Aside from a single evening under Brant's roof in Waterset, nothing unexpected or disruptive occurred to arouse Geth's suspicions. They approached the walls of Umbel City with only Towdric to worry about.

Message runners went back and forth as the river neared Longsea and the seat of Umbel's kings. No one lost a hand in the exchange this time. The great hill and the keep atop it came into view. As expected, a host blocked their path outside the city but within sight of the River Gate.

Bull-neck had already arrayed the troops across the road. Their enemy flew the same green and white banners as they did, though other banners, emblazoned with a running boar, waved beside them. Geth put Towdric's numbers at about three hundred, enough to a match their own force, not more.

Phelan came to stand beside Geth's mount. "You sure he won't attack?"

"If he wanted to attack, he would have marched a bigger army out to meet us. He's got a lot more men than that."

"So, he's ready to talk."

Geth nodded. "For now. What you should be worried about is Ratcher."

"Ratcher?"

"Sure. What better time to strike than when we're distracted by Towdric?"

Phelan frowned.

"So, keep your eye on my back, would ya?"

The little man gave a mock salute. Bull-neck cantered over with the usual dour expression stuck on that silver-bearded face. Melagus came with him.

"They're not here for a fight," Bull-neck said, as if the big warrior couldn't figure that out for himself. "We've called a parley."

Geth grunted. Melagus had something up his sleeve again, and it involved a group that had joined them under cover of dark the night before. Staying up watching out for an assassin had alerted Geth to their arrival, but he didn't dare stray from the Ilar fires to learn more. He reckoned this was the company from the east Phelan had overheard the counselor speak of.

If Vriana and Hadean's armies were the whip, Geth reckoned, it only made sense those easterners had brought the carrot. "You ready to tell me what you've got planned?" Geth asked the counselor without turning his gaze from the usurper's troops up ahead.

"Towdric's family."

Geth turned, eyes narrowed. "You mean to ransom them? Or demand his surrender in exchange for their lives?"

"No, nothing like that." The counselor frowned. "Is it not plain? I thought you were paying attention."

"I..."

"If you knew Towdric like I do, you'd know he would never pay a ransom. Not for his wife anyway. Or even his son. But his daughter?"

"Loves her, does he?"

Melagus sniffed. "I'd hardly say that. When she couldn't fetch the sort of husband he wanted, he sent her to live among the servants of Neyna in a shrine up in the mountains."

"If he isn't worried for her safety then I don't get it."

Melagus tapped the side of his head. "Think. She's the carrot, sellsword, not the whip."

Geth frowned, but it didn't come to him. A handful of riders from across the field advanced to a point halfway between the two armies. Towdric's bald head was among them. Geth joined Melagus, Bull-neck, and a standard bearer as they kicked their mounts to meet him.

The sound of more horses turned him in the saddle as he rode. Vriana and a pair of grim tribesmen cantered up from behind to join them. She looked right past him, eyes on the enemy. They came to a halt, all together, a dozen paces from Towdric, his man Bushy-brows, and a few others.

Geth flicked the chieftess another glance. She was girded for war, no sign of the fine furs and leathers from Iyngaer's wedding. But still she looked a rare and beautiful thing. Remembering the night of that union, Geth blinked. Melagus's plan suddenly became obvious.

"What's this?" Towdric asked without preamble. "You think to frighten me with your Ilar allies? Ha! Does the boy plan to bring an army of savages downriver to plunder his own city?"

Melagus opened his mouth, but Geth beat him to it. "It's an option."

Towdric eyed him through thin, hateful slits. "The wolf hasn't had his fill of Ilar blood? Eager to wet your maw on Umbelmen now?"

Melagus cut in before Geth had a chance. "We didn't come here to exchange insults, traitor. But don't tempt me unless you want to be made a fool. And don't tempt me to unleash the Paellian, let him have a taste of blood, as you call it. Hadean wouldn't be pleased, no, but it *would* be in his best interests."

Bushy-brows adjusted his hand on his hilt, snarled a curse. Towdric scowled but held his tongue.

"We have an offer," Melagus said. "Such as you are hardly worthy of, but an offer nonetheless."

"An offer of mercy, I suppose? Of course it is. And yet you expect me to believe Hadean would attack his own city if I refuse?" Towdric smiled, shook his head. "You waste your own time. He has nothing of value he can offer me."

"And yet here you are, listening, are you not?"

Towdric snorted.

"Bring her forward," said the counselor.

He turned, waved toward the lines. A single rider came forth—a woman, Geth saw. As she drew nearer, he recognized the white of Neyna's acolytes. If this was Towdric's daughter, however, she looked nothing like him, except for the sturdy eyebrows.

"You think to use my own kin against me?"

Melagus laughed. "I have your wife and son if I wanted to do that. But what I'm offering is something else entirely. Something better."

"Better than murdering innocents?"

"Better than living as king for a month and being remembered forever as a usurper."

"Unless I live out my days as king."

Melagus's tone was flat. "Step down from the throne, Towdric. Now, before it's too late. What I'm offering you is this: walk away and receive amnesty. And in exchange, your grandson shall be king."

CHAPTER EIGHT

Geth watched the wheels turn behind Towdric's eyes. A marriage between Hadean and his daughter? Had he really not seen this coming? How could he even pretend to not be interested?

But judging by the way those eyes flicked from Melagus to Geth and back, he clearly didn't trust it, whatever he thought. "Camp where you are and wait for my answer," he said at last.

"Mind that you answer swiftly," said the counselor.

"Or else what?"

"Then let us exchange hostages. As an act of good faith. How do I know you won't attack in the night?"

Towdric's eyes narrowed but he didn't argue. At Melagus's insistence, Bushy-brows crossed the space to join Hadean's company while Captain Worran, and the young message runner in Melagus's employ went the other way. The two parties turned to go.

"Why the boy?" Geth asked Melagus out of the corner of his mouth.

"He's like a son to me," said the counselor. "We have Towdric's family. He wanted something of mine."

Geth frowned. "I reckon it's more than that."

Melagus didn't confirm it. But he didn't deny it either.

Vriana was the first to canter away. Geth watched her hair bounce, brown braid gleaming red and gold in the sun. He kicked his own steed to catch her up, but she veered away as he came near.

Hoping to play if off, there in front of the entire company, Geth continued straight forward as if that had been the plan all along.

"Well?" Phelan asked as Geth arrived back behind the lines.

"Melagus offered to marry Hadean to Towdric's daughter."

"Ah. So that's who that was. I guess I should have put it together."

Geth nodded. "But Towdric didn't give us an answer. Not yet."

"Well, that's good. More time for you to patch it up with your chieftess."

"Patch up what?"

"Don't even try. I saw how she showed you her back out there."

"Showed me her back*side.*" Geth tried to grin. "And her front side too."

"Not recently."

"Well—"

"Must not have impressed her, that night you spent together."

"Keep talking if you want to get choked."

———

Truth be told, Geth wasn't sure what he wanted from Vriana exactly. But Phelan was right, he didn't like things how they were. Over the course of the next three days, he did his best to sort things out in his head.

They continued to bed down among the Ilars each night, and each night he swore he'd at least *speak* to her. The way she showed that back, and set her bedroll far across the fire, however, he never got the chance.

A messenger from the city approached on the morning of the fourth day, distracting him from his own troubles. He hurried to position himself beside Melagus as the man arrived, but he had no need to hear the words to know Towdric's mind.

"He's gonna accept," Geth said as message-bearer rode easily toward them. "See the set of his shoulders? He'd be stiff with fear if the answer were different."

"Obviously," Melagus sniffed. He received the man and his news with smiles and courtesies but frowned at his retreating back as he wheeled his mount and returned the way he'd come.

"What is it?" Geth asked.

"I don't like it."

"I have to admit, there's something I don't like about it either. Why send a messenger to deliver good news? Why not do it yourself?"

Melagus waved that off. "Towdric's absence doesn't trouble me. A proud man like him will still see this as a defeat. The fact he didn't want us to hear him utter the words is nothing."

"So?"

"It's the timing of it that troubles me."

Geth didn't get it.

"It's been three days." Melagus explained. "It doesn't take three days to make a decision, not even a decision like this. And he's asked for ten days to prepare the festivities. It might take King Hadean some time to make the journey south, but I'd rather seal the agreement the same day he arrives."

"Towdric wants a feast?"

Melagus sighed wearily. "Of course he does. And he wants a speech as well."

"Much as I hate that voice, I'll be happy to let him run his mouth if that's the cost of Hadean's peace. I'd be just as happy to cut his tongue out after, if the king gives the order."

Melagus watched the messenger far up ahead, disappearing inside the city through the River Gate. "Keep your sword-arm loose. It just might come to that."

It would take almost a week for Hadean and Brant to make the journey south, and in the meantime, tents were erected and a proper camp set up for the three-hundred odd green-cloaks and tribesmen in the company. They could have moved it all nearer the village of Rivertown, but there would only have been rooms for a few dozen of the men anyway.

This was a more defensible position anyway, Geth mused. At his insistence, two offset rows of sharpened stakes ringed the perimeter as well. He turned in the direction of Vriana's tent that evening when the work was done.

She met him in front of her campfire. "Still crawling around my shelter like a wet cat, mmmm?"

"For your safety, chieftess. Melagus agrees."

Vriana snorted. Geth left it at that.

It wasn't really a lie. Melagus *had* been the one to suggest he sleep among the tribesmen. Ratcher had yet to be dealt with after all.

And even if Geth *had* wanted more—like an invitation inside—he wouldn't have accepted. Few warriors, man or woman, could have guarded his back like Vriana, that was true. But he wasn't about to put her at risk, not with a child in her belly. *My child, gods all be damned!* She'd already turned away with the shake of her head anyway, through her tent flap, leaving him outside.

"Don't worry, I'll be here," Geth called. He laid his blankets down to one side of the entrance, the other side occupied by one of the chieftess's warriors. The Ilar clapped him on the shoulder, offered a rueful smile. At least her tribesmen seemed to be on his side.

"Wouldn't be if they knew about Ratcher though," the big warrior muttered under his breath. He sighed. Phelan arrived and slid into his blankets and only rose again when Geth shook him awake for his turn at watch.

This pattern continued until the king, and a sizeable army, marched into view. Geth eyed the usurper's men on the city walls. The whip was out and in plain sight now. But the carrot was firmly in Towdric's mouth already. It was a generous offer Hadean had made. Towdric would be a fool not to take it.

And yet he didn't rush to seal the accord.

"You think he taunts us?" Geth asked at the next council, standing among Melagus, Brant, Bull-neck, and Hadean in the large tent erected for their king.

"Who can say?" Hadean looked even older than he had a few weeks earlier, resigned perhaps, to marry a woman he'd only just met. Melagus didn't look pleased either, never mind this entire affair was his design. He looked like he might release one of those rare but now legendary curses.

"Three more days to prepare?" he paced the little tent chamber. "That will feel like weeks to all the soldiers sleeping under the stars and eating road biscuits." He sighed. "Then again, it was I that insisted we hold the ceremony outside the walls."

"You weren't wrong for that." Geth said. "Bastard can't be trusted."

"He can. But only if we take proper precautions."

"Well, I for one don't mind losing a few days to hold the ceremonies out here. Wouldn't put it past Towdric to slaughter the whole wedding party if we held it inside his walls."

"King Hadean's walls," Melagus corrected.

———†———

Those three days passed anxiously. Tables and tents came out the River Gate as a banquet space was arranged on a flat patch just beyond bow range from the walls. A guard was posted to watch over the barrels and foodstuffs that Towdric stored, but Geth assigned himself to aid the effort, allowing several tastings for himself and Phelan well ahead of the ceremony.

"Not bad, these wines," Phelan said, kneeling with his mouth directly under a freshly tapped barrel. He rose and wiped his chin. "Best try the ales over there as well. You know, make sure nothing's poisoned."

The head-cook wrung his hands over his portly belly at the other end of the tent until a menacing look from Geth shooed him off. Rummaging through casks and crates produced cheese, oil, and some dried figs. Geth popped several of the latter in his mouth.

"Dear gods, I haven't had a fig since we came to Umbel."

Phelan hurried over to get his share. "This is what the inn's missing. And olives. And fresh fish."

"Anything else?" Geth mocked him.

"White Adus Spirits. But I guess I'd need a man in Pellon to get those things, wouldn't I?"

Geth looked down at the fig in his hand and frowned, thinking of Towdric's man in Pellon. *Palladine*. Had the bastard gone back? With so many other concerns, the big warrior had hardly thought of him since that night in Brant's keep.

He supposed it didn't really matter where he'd gone. Palladine had left Ratcher behind to do the dirty work. That was more than enough to keep Geth busy until he had a chance to get his hands on the scratch himself.

Even with a limited number of guests, Geth knew the king's wedding might offer Ratcher the opportunity he'd been waiting for. Music, wine, and flickering torchlight—plenty of distractions. But Geth would be ready. He still wore mail under his tunic, and he'd taken to hiding an extra knife in his boot and at the small of his back. He knew he was a fool for it, and yet the warrior in him welcomed the prospect of a fight.

He didn't know what kind of face he was making, but when Geth looked up, he found Vriana watching at him quizzically from the other end of the provision tent.

"Just guarding over the supplies." He cleared his throat, stood a little straighter. Phelan had already slid off somewhere. "Soldiers apt to plunder the place if someone doesn't watch out."

Vriana nodded. "Mmmm. Keeping watch is your favorite duty."

Geth sucked in a breath. "About that. I don't mean to make you uncomfortable, sleeping outside your tent. It's just..."

He trailed off. There was no way to tell the truth without putting her in harm's way. He clamped his mouth shut before a choice curse could slip out.

"Perhaps it is the child." Vriana's hand went to her belly. "Your child."

"I—"

"You do not know what to think, mmmm? Neither did I at first. But it is good if I have an heir. And so there need be no thinking."

"Uh, sure." Geth blinked. "I mean, I don't know."

She raised one of those perfect eyebrows.

"I grew up without a father, Vriana. And it wasn't easy. That's what I'm saying. And now that it's my turn, I wonder what kind of father I could ever be?"

Vriana frowned. "I did not invite you to live in Ehken Laer, Geth et Trusla."

"No, you didn't. 'Course not."

He'd never expected as much, but for some reason, those words still hurt. Emotions warred in him, his stomach tight, his jaw clenched. *Thram's twisted balls!*

"You are angry?" Vriana asked.

"Does it matter if I am? What am I anyway, but a mating stud to sire a little warrior prince for you?"

"Do you think this was my plan? Do you think I tricked you into my furs for such a thing?"

"Well? Did you?"

"I did not."

She met Geth's stare. There had been no hesitation in her answer and there was nothing false about the affront in her expression now.

He softened his tone.

"It felt like something...real."

"It was."

"Then I'm happy for you. For the child, for both of us, whatever you want of me."

She watched him but said nothing.

Geth didn't know that he wanted her to. He'd risked everything to build a life in Umbel, to belong someplace. He couldn't leave Hadean now, couldn't abandon his dozen, his friends.

"The moment," Vriana said, looking from Geth, to her stomach, then back, "it was right. We fought together, almost died together. The spirits brought us to each other to make this child. This child will be something special. So, you are not wrong to sleep beside my tent, to guard over it."

She smiled.

Geth's mouth opened and closed. He nodded but held his tongue.

"Tonight," she said, "I will show you. I will let you feel the baby kick. He is strong."

That coaxed a smile from the big warrior. Even he knew enough about pregnancies to know a baby didn't kick just a few months in. But he wasn't about to miss the chance to get his hands on the chieftess. He nodded again.

"Tonight."

———†———

When night fell and he arrived in Vriana's tent, she took full advantage. Geth was happy to meet her demands. In the morning, she left him again, but this time she rested a hand on his chest as she sat up.

"Come winter, the baby will be born. I will send for you that you may meet your son."

Geth pulled his eyes away from her naked torso. "How do you know it's a boy?"

She turned her head to look at him with one eye from over her shoulder. "They say a girl child is jealous, makes the mother turn ugly while she bears her. I am still beautiful, mmmm?"

Geth reached for Vriana but she rolled deftly away, stood in one motion. She pulled a fur-trimmed tunic over her head and disappeared through the tent flaps, leaving Geth with just his thoughts. And the stupid grin a man wears after a night with such a woman.

That grin didn't stay with him long. He left the tent to meet Phelan's scowl outside. That expression reminded Geth of Ratcher.

"Left me out here all night by myself," the little man said. "All night! While you were having the time of your life."

"And what a night."

Phelan grumbled a curse. Hadean's approach cut him short before he could say more. Bull-neck trailed in the king's wake. Phelan faded away, off to catch a nap someplace, Geth reckoned. He left him to it and turned to salute the king.

"Is it too early to say we've done it?" Hadean said, smiling. "Have we ended this feud with Towdric?"

"I'd rather we hanged the bastard. But if a wedding will suffice, we can always kill him later."

Hadean must have been in a good mood. He laughed.

And why not? He'd avoided war, saved the lives of countless of his subjects, and would gain a wife in the bargain. The prospect of marriage could be daunting too though, Geth supposed. The complications of romance were never far from his mind these days.

He looked to the king. "Are you nervous?"

"Nervous? No. Laying siege to my own city, to my own people, the thought of such a thing, that's what makes me nervous. Terrified actually. What kind of king would that make me?"

"If it had come to that, it wouldn't have been your fault. For all the damage it might have done, Towdric could manage a lot worse with the crown on his head. Just ask Crookbow."

Hadean pursed his lips.

"But getting married." Geth shook his head. "Can't say I've got experience in the matter. It's no small thing, I reckon."

"She's a good woman, Lady Eynid." Hadean nodded to himself. "We've had some time together these past days. We met once as children as well, a long time ago."

"If she's a good woman, that's what counts."

"And I'm a good man. Try to be anyway. We'll dedicate our lives—this union—to the betterment of the realm, we both agree. And if we can both agree on that, I can't image anything else really matters."

Hadean smiled again. The way it lit his eyes, Geth was reminded of the boy-king that had saved his life, an age ago. The prospect of a civil war was the thing weighing on him, Geth supposed. Once that was gone, he might finally enjoy the just rewards of all he'd sacrificed. Hadean offered another smile and a nod and headed back the way he'd come.

Bull-neck lingered. "This isn't over," he said.

"Not 'til the knot is tied well and tight, I reckon," Geth agreed.

"Then let's make sure it is. Keep an eye out though. Just in case."

"Always."

Bull-neck nodded, face even more dour than usual. He started to go then stopped, turned back.

"I'd be happier with Towdric at the bottom of a six-foot hole."

"All in due time," Geth said.

Bull-neck growled something like a laugh and stalked off after the king. Geth decided he liked the old ball-scratch. He couldn't help but feel guilty withholding the threat of Ratcher from him, but then again that was no concern of his, was it? Either way, Geth knew he'd be watching out, watching everything, with a vigilant eye. That was all Bull-neck had asked for.

CHAPTER NINE

The day of the wedding finally arrived, and everything began without incident. Towdric's daughter
Eynid was led out on a white horse, her flowing gown
flawless, her fingers and earlobes jeweled and glittering.
The usurper flanked her, a half-dozen green-cloaks in crisp
tunics and polished helms joining him to make up an hon-
or guard.

Hadean stood waiting, accompanied by Melagus and his
cousin, Brant. The king wore the crown of the realm of
course, green gems inset on a gold band. Vingil hung at his
waist. His knee-length tunic and fitted trousers were the
finest Lach wool, embroidered with intricate patterns at
the cuffs, collar, and hem.

A sister of Neyna officiated, and with a ritual hand-
washing, an exchange of oaths, and a procession of seven
circles around the white-draped altar, Hadean was mar-

ried. Towdric stood there beaming, looking far happier than Geth had expected. Then again, the man was no fool. He had to understand that he could never have held the throne of Umbel for long—not with his few thousand soldiers.

For his part, Hadean looked stoic. Geth kept moving throughout the entire ceremony, watching, listening, instructing Phelan to watch his back and do the same. When the big warrior did pause to steal a glance at the king, the lad looked far braver than Geth imagined he would have, had they traded places. Thram and Awer, all it had taken was mention of a child to set him running.

Bull-neck looked ill at ease though. He ambled over from across the gathering, eyes scanning from side to side before settling on Geth.

"What is it?" The big warrior asked.

"Just look at the smile on that bastard." Bull-neck flicked his grey-bearded chin in Towdric's direction. "The marriage may be sealed, but I don't like it."

Geth's eyes narrowed. "If you know something, have out with it man."

"I don't trust it."

Bull-neck swirled the cup in his hand, muttered something under his breath, and downed it to the dregs. Geth watched him stalk off in the direction of the cooks' tent.

"Bastard's probably just looking for an excuse to get at the meat first," Phelan said, arriving at Geth's shoulder.

The big warrior shrugged.

"You may be right. Look, he's getting into the food now."

Craning to see over the comings and goings of the guests, Geth watched the old green-cloak sniff at each pot, dipping a spoon into one after another. The portly head-cook mopped sweat off his brow but didn't attempt to intervene.

When the plates came out, Bull-neck went so far as to switch Hadean's for Towdric's. A hush fell over the guests. But Towdric tucked in for several huge bites, releasing a loud belch afterward that set a fair few laughing.

"He wouldn't go for poison anyway, would he?" Geth mused. "He seems like more of a knife-in-the-back kinda bastard."

Phelan flicked a glance over his shoulder, replied out of the side of his mouth. "Which only reminds me of Ratcher."

Geth waved that off. For some reason, he was just more comfortable worrying over the safety of Hadean than himself. Still, he knew Phelan was right. He searched the faces of the few dozen guests one more time. None of them could have been Ratcher. The servants were mostly women or boys; too slim to disguise the Paellian's doughy frame. All save the cooks, and he'd already given each of them a good once-over. Surrounding the banquet and its neutral ground was a ring of green-cloaks. No one else was getting in or out.

Geth watched with a degree of assurance as Hadean and Eynid performed their first dance. They looked happy. And he was happy for them. Guests joined in after, but Geth refrained, even after several pointed looks from Vriana. Instead, he eyed the musicians, studied the servants, walked the perimeter just in case.

"Go on, have a dance," Phelan told him. "The coast is clear. For now, at least. I'll watch out for you."

"What makes you think I want to dance?"

Phelan rolled his eyes. "Just go."

Vriana wore a mischievous look when Geth arrived at her table. "Mmmm?"

"In this country," he said, "the men dance with the women."

He extended a hand. Vriana took it in her own strong grip. They paced through the steps of a familiar Aturian dance. Vriana watched the other ladies. She had the turns and pauses down better than Geth before the music ended.

When it did, Geth pulled her back toward her seat. She raised an eyebrow.

"I need to keep watch," he explained.

"Trouble? From Towdric?"

"Maybe."

That wasn't the whole truth, and she looked skeptical, but he reckoned she would have smelled an outright lie. "Mmmm. Then I will keep a watch as well."

They shared a smile. Geth couldn't tell her about Ratcher, give her a description to look out for, but it made him feel better anyway. He squeezed her hand and stalked off for a vantage point where he could keep one eye on the newlyweds and one on the usurper.

As he looked on, Towdric climbed up on a chair, clanking his knife against a goblet to get everyone's attention. The hairs on the back of Geth's neck went up, but perhaps that was just because he hated the bastard so much.

"Umbelmen! Friends!" He raised his cup high, bellowing like always. "Drink to the king and queen!"

That big, bearded head split in a huge grin. It was an expression Geth had learned to be wary of, but the assemblage cheered, obliging with whatever was handy. More than a few of the guests seemed to be drunk already. Hadean and his bride had retaken their seats at the head table. Melagus sat beside them, never so much as lifting his own cup, watching Towdric through thin slits all the while.

"We've come together today," Towdric bellowed on, "to make things right in this realm. To heal. The folk of Umbel have been through hard times after all, beginning with the Affliction, followed by war.

"But today we move forward at last! We eat together. We drink. We celebrate. From two, we have one, a gods-blessed union!"

More cheers, more drinking.

But something about the gleam in Towdric's eye didn't sit right with Geth. Was the man drunk? He simply looked too happy for a man that was about to cede the throne.

"In honor of this new alliance, I have prepared a special gift for groom and bride!" the bastard boomed.

Geth found himself easing forward, closer to the cooks' tent, and closer to Towdric in the process.

"From our sworn ally in Pellon, I have procured the finest dried and honeyed figs! Enjoy them, son! And from my own vineyards, the last batch of a vintage laid down by my father, decades ago! Drink! Eat and drink, everyone! In honor of the king and queen!"

Two serving men hustled from the wings with a platter and pitcher respectively, but Bull-neck appeared, arms raised, to halt them before they could reach the head table.

"Wait!" He plucked a fig unceremoniously from the platter, sniffed at it, studied it closely, and took a careful bite. He poured a measure of wine into a clear glass, swirled it, held it up to the light, smelled and tasted. Towdric looked on, jaw clenched, but at last Bull-neck gave it a nod, muttered a curse, and stalked off.

"A perfect duo. Don't you agree, Captain Rogon?" Towdric said to the old warrior's departing back. He climbed carefully down from his chair to eat the first fig, washed down with several gulps of wine. Geth flicked a glance to Hadean. The king had frozen, one hand clasping Eynid's, but he now wore a smile.

Towdric laughed. More than a few of the guests followed suit. Geth felt his own stomach begin to unknot. "Well, I guess I was wrong."

A commotion from the cooks' tent echoed from over his shoulder almost before those words were all the way out of his mouth.

He turned, hand on hilt. "What the—"

The unmistakable sound of a struggle reached him through the flap. Someone gasped. Geth crossed the distance, pulled it back, sword already drawn, to find the portly cook bloody and wide-eyed on the floor alongside a second, aproned corpse. Further inside, wrestling among the barrels, was Bull-neck and Ratcher.

"You!" Geth lifted his blade. The assassin looked up to lock eyes with the big warrior. Geth leapt over the dead cook on the floor.

With a grunt, Ratcher shoved Bull-neck into his path. Geth caught him with a curse.

"Treason!" the dour captain yelled.

Untangling himself from the grey-beard, Geth lurched after Ratcher. When he looked up, the bastard was already gone, slipping through a tear in the back of the tent.

Rather than follow through the makeshift exit, and maybe meet the end of a knife, Geth bolted back out the way he'd come. He raced past startled wedding guests to round the tent toward the rear. Mere seconds had passed, but by the time got there, Ratcher was already on horseback, galloping toward the ring of green-cloaks circling the festivities.

"Stop him!" Geth cried.

The soldiers could only dive out of the way as the assassin charged them. Phelan appeared beside the big warrior, sling whirling overhead. He loosed his stone, his aim true, but it clanged off Ratcher's back, evidently protected by armor under his cloak.

"Thram and bloody Awer!"

Shouts erupted back at the banquet. The rasp of swords leaving sheaths reached Geth's ear and he whirled back toward Hadean. A clutch of warriors packed close around the king already, a second group crowding Towdric. The fading light of sunset gleamed red on a dozen blades.

"Who dares lift a hand against my servants!" the lord bellowed.

"Why the cook?" someone else cried.

Melagus fairly shrieked. "Poison!"

Accusations shot back and forth. The party had separated into two distinct groups, both armed and cursing one another. At the periphery, the green-cloaks had all drawn steel as well, growling at one another, unsure who was friend or foe, just as confused as anyone.

"Someone follow that rider!" Geth shouted.

Hadean raised one hand, holding his bride protectively behind him with the other. "Peace! Down arms! Let some sense be made before any more blood is spilled!"

But Towdric was already backing away, toward the walls of the city. *Fleeing the scene of his crime,* Geth reckoned. Hadean didn't try to stop him. His new bride, Towdric's own daughter, watched mouth agape but made no move the leave her new husband.

Geth didn't sheathe his sword until the bastard was under the River Gate and out of sight. His eyes searched the guests until he found Vriana. She gave him a nod and he blew out a relieved sigh. Stamping over fallen platters and spilled cups, he joined Melagus beside the cook's tent.

"No one eat anything else!" the counselor was saying.

Geth looked from the murdered cooks on the ground to Bull-neck, kneeling among them, holding his neck. He seemed to have been injured in the struggle. Geth cursed Ratcher's entire lineage.

But had the bastard come for him, or the king?

Vriana stalked toward Geth, sword drawn, oozing menace. Wedding guests and green-cloaks alike moved out of her path.

"Are you alright?" he asked. "Tell me you didn't eat anything from that bastard?"

"Didn't we all?"

"Thram and bloody Awer..."

Melagus's voice rose above the general din. "Call a healer!"

Geth turned to find the counselor on his knees beside Bull-neck.

"I'm fine," the old warrior was saying. "Just got roughed a bit, that's all."

Melagus wore a grim look. "Better to be sure."

Geth flicked his head to one side, motioned the counselor to follow. He spared one more glance for Hadean and

Vriana. Both seemed safe. He led Melagus off to the side, out of anyone's earshot.

"It was him," he said. "The assassin."

"The Paellian? You saw him?"

Geth nodded. "Doesn't make much sense though, does it? Why kill the cooks?"

"Unless he wasn't after just you." Melagus turned to stare off in the direction Ratcher had fled, expression grim.

"I reckon we'll know soon enough," Geth said, "if we all drop dead."

Chapter Ten

The healer arrived from their camp up the road and a concoction was brewed and drank by all. A foul chorus of retching punctuated the night as it took effect. But it worked. Either that, Geth supposed, or there had never been any poison.

And then he saw Bull-neck. "You alright, Captain?" he asked.

He already knew the answer. The old warrior knelt beside a puddle of his own puke, but even in the dim light, there was no mistaking the glazed eyes, the foam in his grey beard. Geth squatted down beside him. He teetered into the big warrior's arms.

"Thram's balls!" He eased the old soldier on to his back. "Healer! Where's the healer?"

A plain-faced woman hurried over, herbs and other medicines in hand, but in a matter of minutes Bull-neck was gone. Geth swore again, gripped the hilt of his sword until his knuckles went white. "I'll have your heart out, Ratcher!"

At his order, the guests retreated to the main camp. He roused the soldiers, put them on alert, and sent scouts to watch for any movement from the city. Better safe than sorry.

"Forget the city," Melagus said, joining Geth as he gazed south through the darkness. "Towdric has played his hand."

"Poison," Geth turned to face the counselor, shaking his head. "Never thought Ratcher would go that route. Was it the figs? The wine?"

"A combination of the two, I think. Only the captain sampled both."

"But—"

"No," said Melagus. "Towdric ate the figs, true. But he already had a cup of wine in hand. He never drank from his father's supposed vintage."

Geth swore. "The bastard would risk murdering his own daughter? At her wedding?"

"Do you put it past him?"

Geth shook his head bitterly. "No."

"All the more reason he must never, *never*, be king."

"He has to die."

Melagus met Geth's eye. He somehow matched the ferocity despite his size. "In this we agree."

The counselor thrust out a bony hand. Geth clasped it. With a nod, it was sealed.

But Geth couldn't stop thinking.

"Ratcher was working for Palladine," he mused aloud. "He's the one who sent Racher after me in the first place."

"They must be in league." Melagus's lip curled. "How far into the east then does the betrayal stretch?"

Geth shook his head. "I can't make sense of it. How would Towdric look if he really had poisoned his own daughter? Who would follow him after that?"

Melagus waved it off. "Perhaps he took the antidote ahead of the ceremony? And tricked his daughter into taking it as well."

"Or are we getting it all wrong? I had some of those figs a few days ago, and plenty of wine. Shouldn't I be dead?"

Melagus thought that through. "Probably the assassin had just added the poison right before Towdric's little speech."

"And that's how Bull-neck found him, lingering still in the cooks' tent."

They fell silent. Geth thought it all through one more time but there was no other way to make sense of it. The timing of it, Towdric's little speech... This was his doing.

If not for Bull-neck—*Rogon,* Geth told himself—Hadean and the lot of them would likely be dead.

Thinking of the old captain, Geth couldn't help but feel a wave of guilt. It was he himself that had drawn Ratcher to the king in the first place.

"Gods all damn you, Ratcher," he muttered. "I'll feed you your own eyeballs when I get my hands on you."

"This Ratcher fellow," Melagus was saying. "Are you certain you saw him?"

"I saw him."

"And are you certain it was Palladine that first hired him?"

"He told me with his own lips."

The counselor's frown deepened, but the sound of footfalls turned them both. Geth blinked. Ship-captain Rondah stood there, red hair catching the torchlight as she lowered her riding hood.

"Captain. Counselor." She dipped her head, saluted fist to heart. "I have news."

"It can't be good," Melagus said. "Tell me."

"Your scouts will see with their own eyes soon enough, but I just intercepted word from within the city. Towdric awaits reinforcements. They'll arrive within hours."

"Reinforcements?" Geth looked from the counselor to the ship-captain and back.

"Uro's shriveled sack!" Melagus swore. "I knew he was stalling!"

"From his cousin in the mountain holds?" Geth asked. "Some other traitors to the south?"

"From the east," Rondah said, voice grim.

"Pellon." Melagus finished for her.

Geth's eyes went wide. "Thram and *bloody* Awer." Palladine, Ratcher, the botched assassination...all the pieces fell into place. "He's sent for aid from King Elius, hasn't he?"

"Who could have known?" said Rondah.

"How many?" Geth growled.

"A fleet. Twenty ships at least. And enough men and supplies to hold this city for months."

Melagus looked like he wanted to curse again, but he just scowled, shaking his head. "It's worse in Paellia than I thought. Far worse."

"What's worse?" Geth looked from the counselor to the ship-captain. "Has Palladine sold King Elius on Towdric's right to the throne? Told him Hadean was dead or something of the like?"

"No. It's worse than that. I sent word of the traitor to Elius myself. He knows the truth of things. And he's chosen to back Towdric anyway."

The implications of what Geth was hearing tumbled through his head. He was no statesman, but he had stood in Umbel City himself not long ago, gazed on the Oathstone where four kings of the Sworn Realms pledged their allegiance centuries ago. From an age of petty kingdoms and petty wars, centuries of relative prosperity and peace were born. It was beneath the Oathstone that Geth had first met King Hadean. To hear how a fellow king now betrayed him made Geth's fists clench at his side, around an imaginary neck.

"We barricade the harbor," he said. "Lock the lily fleet out and choke Towdric off."

"It's already too late," said Rondah. "We'd never get enough ships together in time."

Melagus shook his head. "The king would not have us tighten the noose on the city anyway. After all, it's not Towdric that would choke, it's the citizens. And to what end? Towdric would never surrender, he proved that tonight. We'd have to storm the walls eventually anyway. And wrest the crown from his cold fingers."

———————†———————

In the morning, Geth was summoned to a war counsel in the king's tent. Vriana joined him. The seasons were turning, a humid summer air hung thick and stifling under the canvas. They found Melagus and the king waiting beside a map table at the center of the space.

"Are you sure it's too late to blockade the harbor?" Geth asked Melagus.

"We'd need a week to gather the ships. And judging by Captain Rondah's report, the Paellians will have arrived by now."

Geth snatched a road biscuit out of a basket on the table, shoved it in his mouth, grumbled curses around it. Vriana scowled down at the map. Hadean leaned over it as well, the smile Geth had seen on him at the wedding replaced by a workman-like frown.

"We have been deceived," he said with a sigh, straightening from the table. "And so, our troubles continue."

"Our *war*," Melagus said, stressing the word. "Make no mistake of it, my king. This is war. And war is an ugly business. But we cannot fail at it, no matter the cost. No matter the cruel decisions—"

"We are not laying siege to the city." Hadean turned a hard eye on his counselor. "As long as we hold the ground north of the city, we can ensure control over the harvest, but we won't stop Paellian supplies from reaching the city."

Melagus spread his hands. "I merely suggest we consider all options." He turned to face Geth, waiting.

The big warrior cleared his throat. "Well, er, I guess I don't have a reputation for mercy, my lord. Or patience. Or diplomacy in general for that matter. Or—"

"What I think our Paellian ally is trying to say," Melagus cut in, "is that Towdric has proved a more cunning adversary than expected. Drastic measures may be called for."

"He is the father of my bride," Hadean said. "And for all his duplicity, a great number of red-blooded Umbelmen believe him a good man. What happens if we employ these 'drastic measures?' What becomes of those men? Have we not sown the seeds of future rebellions? Future betrayals?"

"My king—"

"You are not the only man here that has opened a book or two in his years, Master Melagus. You know that as a king's second son, I was groomed to be my brother's right hand. How could I do that when Luhan was bigger than me, stronger? He didn't need me to fight for him. But he didn't care much for books, did he? I could give him *knowledge*."

Melagus smiled, an expression matched by Captain Rondah. Geth and Vriana just listened.

"I studied the histories. I know these things have played out many times before. And always it leaves a scar."

Hadean frowned. "Well, after the Affliction, I think the folk of Umbel have scars enough. This time, we'll do better. And the Kingdom of Umbel will be better off for it."

Melagus nodded, but his lips wore that sour twist. "You speak the truth, my king. But how will we do it?"

"Through mercy. As much as we can spare, at all costs. If we wrestle over the realm like jealous children over a toy, in the process, we'll only break it."

"But Towdric—" said the counselor.

"Has to die," Geth finished for him. A silence fell but Geth didn't let it hang. "There's no way around it."

Hadean exhaled a sigh, but Vriana nodded, slapped her pommel. "Then we will kill him, mmmm?"

Hadean smiled.

Geth found himself resting a hand on her shoulder though. "As much as I like the sound of that, you can't be the one to do it." He turned to address the men. "She's pregnant."

Vriana glared at him. Hadean's mouth opened and closed, but Melagus only snorted.

"Of course she is. She's not the only fighter in the Sworn Realms, however, if that's what we decide."

"Speak plain," Hadean said. "Are you suggesting we send an assassin?"

"Both Towdric and Eldric have attempted such means. Perhaps it is time we tried as well."

"Can we sneak a man into the city?" Geth asked.

"Getting into the city isn't a problem. Getting close to Towdric will be difficult, however. Unless we take chances, employ poisons, or perhaps fire—"

"We won't be doing any of that," Hadean said. "It would be suicide. I won't ask anyone to take that risk, not yet."

Melagus sighed, dipped his head. "The king commands, we obey."

"What about our allies?" Geth said. "Not Pellon, but our *other* allies. We have an alliance with Iyngaer now. Can we not call on the tribes? Bolster our armies, even if it's just for show. Brandish that whip, right out in front where Towdric can get a good look at it."

Melagus answered. "I fear Towdric was right when he dismissed the Chieftess Vriana at our first meeting. What would the king look like if he were to use foreign warriors to attack his own people?"

"The time may come to call upon the chieftain," Hadean said, "but not outside the walls of my own city."

"What about Turia then? Or even Rath?" Geth looked from the counselor to the king. "Pellon and Dues aren't our only allies."

"And drag another Sworn Realm into this affair?" Hadean shook his head. "That could lead to a much wider war. No, that's a last resort."

Melagus raised a finger. "We do have another option, however."

The counselor nodded to himself as if the idea had just come to him, but Geth had the feeling he'd been angling toward whatever he was about to say the whole while. His next words did nothing to change the big warrior's opinion.

"It requires patience, diplomacy, and a fair bit of luck. But it could ensure a bloodless resolution." The counselor flicked Geth a glance.

"Thram's hairy ass, didn't we just talk about this? Patience, diplomacy, mercy and whatever else?"

"We did, didn't we."

He locked eyes with Geth. Geth glowered back. What the hell did *that* mean?

"Out with it, man."

"We didn't talk about our allies in Pellon," the counselor said.

Geth's eyes narrowed. Vriana frowned. Hadean pursed his lips.

But Melagus addressed the big warrior like he was the only person in the room. "We can change Elius's mind," he said. "*I* can change it. But, I can't do it alone."

CHAPTER ELEVEN

Geth spit a curse. "Are you saying you want me to take you to the Golden City?"

Melagus nodded, somber as the grave.

"To King Elius, the man who sided with that bastard Towdric? You want me to take you to *him?*"

Melagus snorted. "I want Rondah to take me. I'll need you in other capacities."

Vriana muttered under her breath. Hadean cleared his throat as if to argue. Geth actually laughed,

But Melagus spoke over them all. "Pellon is fractured. That's our opportunity! They may not be at open war, but there's a power struggle going on behind it all."

"How does that help us?" Hadean asked.

"Elius needs allies. Palladine must have convinced him that Towdric would make the better friend than the true king of Umbel. Perhaps he's already made promises to

Elius. Trade concessions and the like. I'll make it clear the true king is the only friend he needs, a man he might call upon, a valuable ally."

"You think you can change his mind?"

"I have to try. Failing that, we turn our swords on our own city. And the gods only know how many will die."

Hadean went silent, thinking it through. A fly buzzed through the room, landing on the map damn near the markings for the Golden City. The king looked to Geth for the briefest moment then back to his counselor.

"What do you need?"

Melagus actually smiled. "Very little, my king. But we must move swiftly. And in secret. Elius has already sided against us, remember? We are his enemies.

"But I have contacts in the Golden City. His mind can be changed. I'll need some coin for expenses, perhaps a gift of some sort, a symbol, for Elius. Rondah will take me there, that's not a problem. The only other thing I need is *him*." He flicked his chin at Geth.

The big warrior scowled. "You say you've got contacts, and you'll have all the coin you need. So, what do you want with me?"

"Something only you can manage." The counselor looked from Geth to Hadean and back. "I want you to keep me alive long enough to get in front of the king."

Towdric called a parley that afternoon, before anything could be decided. A lad of no more than twelve arrived outside their tent, rolled parchment in his grasp. His fingers shook as he passed it over, but King Hadean only fed the boy and sent him to have a rest in one of the tents.

He watched the lad go with the shake of his head. "He thinks I might be like Towdric, kill a messenger."

"A testament to the lies his master has already spread." Melagus's lips curled. "But it's you who should be anxious, my king. Towdric has already shown just how merciless he can be."

"You can't go to that parley," Geth agreed. "Not as things stand. With those lilies added to the score, he's got the numbers to come after us if we let down our guard."

Hadean looked to the counselor. "Brant arrives tomorrow to reinforce our own army, does he not? Perhaps we should stall Towdric as he stalled us."

"Indeed," said Melagus. "Perhaps another look at the whip would do him some good. I doubt it will change his mind, but his soldiers will see."

"It would be a show of unity as well," Hadean said. "I imagine I already know what he has to say."

Geth had a few things he'd like to say to Towdric himself. They waited a day, however, for Lord Brant and his force to arrive, and another just to let the usurper stew on the sight of ten thousand soldiers massing outside his walls. The sun hinted of summer as they marched to the River Gate and lined up in ranks, glinting off steady rows of spears and tall, waving grass. Red cheeks and sweaty brows peaked out beneath conical helms, between face guards. The traitor Towdric watched from a position on the wall above the gates, flanked by bannermen and scores of soldiers, content to address them from there.

Geth, Brant, and Melagus joined Hadean, each on horseback, cantering within shouting distance. But Towdric spoke before any of them.

"Gathered a few fools, have you?" he sneered down at them. "Come to beg at my gates?"

"Those aren't your gates," Hadean shot back. "When was the last time you even passed inside this city, except to slink in and steal what you could?"

"The throne? The gods know it suits my arse better than yours, skinny pup. How many men died at Towerrock because you couldn't win the first time, at Copper Ridge—And end things with the savages once and for all? You'd have even more fools under your banner if you'd looked out for them."

"Your treason—"

"I have the support of Paellia, boy! You're beaten! It's only a matter of time. Spare the lives of your soldiers and bend the knee. I promise to spare your life in return."

Hadean opened his mouth, but Melagus beat him to it. "And trust *you*?" the counselor scoffed. "Do you think the grunting noises you make pass for speech? Even if we could make sense of it, we could not make reason. It is *you* who are beaten, *you* who will bend the knee. If you would save lives."

"Ha!" That laugh dripped with scorn. "The Asp speaks around his forked tongue to lecture about trust? Wags his jaw as if he were the king himself? No matter. Your betters have something for you, snake. Fat juicy mice. Have a listen, hear how they squeak."

He looked over his shoulder and a pair of plain-clothed servants were ushered forward to the edge of the wall. Geth squinted, stomach tightening as they were prodded at sword point up onto the embrasure between two merlons over the gate.

Hadean must have picked out the nooses around their necks at the same time as Geth. He spurred his mount a step closer. "What is this?"

"Ask your dear counselor."

"I remind you," Hadean growled. "We have your hostages still! Think well before you make a grave mistake."

"Hostages? We'll get to that later. But these aren't hostages, are they, Asp? No, they're spies."

The two servants, an old groundskeeper and a laundress Geth recognized from Erehan Keep, watched Towdric step in their direction with eyes like saucers. Tears wet the woman's face already, and a whimper escaped her lips. Towdric drew his sword, raised his arm to plant it against the small of her back and her chin went up, quivering lips and all. With a shove, he sent her over the edge, her scream cut short as she jerked, bobbed, and twisted on the length of rope. And then went still.

"Bastard!" Melagus yelled. A storm of curses echoed him, but Towdric had already moved on to the groundskeeper.

"Gods bless the true ki—"

Towdric's blade, erupting red through the man's belly, cut his words short, as the usurper ran him through from behind. The groundskeeper doubled over, fell, and jerked to a halt, turning slowly beside the dead laundress.

"Gods all damn you!" Hadean's horse stamped and neighed, echoing his rider's rage. Vingil was in his grasp, gleaming blue and cold.

But Geth kicked his mount close enough to grab his reins. "Not here!" he hissed. "There's nothing you can do!"

Towdric watched them. He didn't smile. "This is how we deal with traitors in the Kingdom of Umbel."

Hadean shook in the saddle. Geth hadn't really known those two and this once he was the voice of reason. He flicked a glance to Melagus. The counselor's eyes had gone wide. Geth turned back toward the wall, and he understood why.

"You spoke of hostages, did you not?" A boy had been lifted up to sit on the edge of the embrasure—Melagus's boy. There was no noose around his neck, thank gods, but Towdric rested that red-stained sword on his shoulder. The lad trembled, sobbed where he stood.

"Careful," Hadean said, his voice at the same time quieter but more menacing. "I have your wife and son. And if you regard them as little as you do your own daughter, I remind you that I have your nephew, the captain, as well."

"You expect me to believe you would harm your mother-in-law, an innocent woman? Ha! But don't think I would kill a child either. No, you can have your hostages back, and I'll take mine. But I'm keeping this—"

With a sudden motion, Towdric reached for the boy's ear, slicing it clear off with his bloodied sword. A soldier beside him gripped the lad by the arm lest he fall to his death. And he would have. The poor child screamed and collapsed to his knees, hands at the side of his head.

"I'm keeping this," the usurper went on, "to remind this lad that a good boy doesn't go listening at cracked doors or looking through keyholes."

Hadean had gone deathly still, but it was Melagus who sat quivering in his saddle now. The River Gate cracked halfway open a moment later and the boy came running out toward them, sobbing louder than ever. Melagus climbed down from the saddle to gather him up in his thin arms. Captain Worran followed out the gates after the child, moving stiffly, and Hadean waved for Towdric's wife and nephew to be brought forth. Geth didn't hesitate to swing a boot at Towdric's bushy-browed nephew as he passed, sending him stumbling to one knee.

"Dirty, foreign bastard!"

This once, neither Melagus nor Hadean said a word. Geth wondered if he shouldn't have had off an ear, maybe one of those bushy eyebrows. He looked to the ramparts ahead. Towdric was gone. As the soldiers and bannermen dispersed in his wake, one shaved head lingered behind, clad all in white.

"Palladine."

The Hand of Justice met Geth's eyes across the distance. Nothing needed be said between them. Their hatred was mutual.

CHAPTER TWELVE

Towdric's parley hardened resolve all around.

"Let it be done," Hadean told Melagus, riding back to the ranks. "Pellon, I mean. Make the arrangements."

"Of course, my king. We can be ready tomorrow."

"Good. My hand aches for swift retribution, but patience will serve us better, don't you think? Paellia's support may have lifted him for now but imagine how much harder he'll fall once we pull it out from under him."

Hadean flicked a glance at Geth, and the big warrior nodded grimly. If he'd harbored any reluctance to make the journey before, the feeling had passed. Something had to be done. The sooner the better.

"The tribes will not honor a peace with this man," Vriana told Geth that evening.

Of course they wouldn't. Everyone but Towdric himself could see how his leadership would only lead the realm into more bloodshed. And probably into ruin itself. Geth kissed Vriana deeply, held her close that whole night. In the morning, he packed his things.

She watched him in silence, followed him out the tent.

He turned, took her hands in his. "What will you do now?"

"I return to Ehken Laer." She glanced down to her midriff. "Too much warm air is not good. Your king will have need of you when you return, mmmm? But in some months, I will send for you to meet your child."

Geth kissed her once more and turned abruptly for the king's tent. He wasn't good with these kinds of emotions. Lucky for him, Vriana wasn't sentimental. He flicked a glance over one shoulder, but she'd already disappeared back through the flap.

Hadean stood with his counselor, waiting to see them off. "Be careful," he said. "With Pellon's fleet behind him, Towdric controls the Bay of Umbel now. Rondah's ship is waiting at the port of Sirona, to the south. Make the journey with haste. You go with my deepest thanks."

Melagus saluted, fist to heart. Geth copied the gesture. Phelan moved a bit slower, but he hadn't complained when Geth asked him to come along and he didn't start now.

"You have no need to thank us," Melagus was saying. "It is only fair that the kingdom should rest in your hands—just, righteous hands, not cruel, hungry claws like Towdric's."

"We'll get it done," Geth said simply. "For you, my lord, and for Umbel. If there's one place I know well, it's the Golden City."

They climbed into their saddles, Phelan, Melagus, and Geth, unaccompanied except for the horses they rode. Five days later, they were on Rondah's ship, the Windskimmer, headed for easterly Pellon.

—†—

Sun on the waves each day, twinkling stars each night—there was a regularity to the sea Geth could appreciate. A salt-tinged breeze filled their sails, and the decks tilted and creaked, the song of their progress. Spring was as good a season as any to be on Longsea, the big warrior reckoned, and he filled his lungs with fresh air, watched gulls wheel overhead as the days passed.

Melagus spent many an hour in the cabin with the captain, but Phelan, at least, rowed when needed and whistled in between. Geth didn't know what to make of it. He crossed the deck to join him, leaning on a rail at the bow, as the first glimmer of yellowy walls and orange-gold rooftops appeared across the waves.

"Golden-*bloody*-City," Geth said, grinning.

Phelan snorted a laugh from over his shoulder.

"I appreciate that you came. You know that right? With the inn and everything else, I wasn't sure you'd want to leave."

"It's a lot of work, turns out. The inn I mean."

Geth nodded, paused to choose his words. "We've come a long way, you know? Being on this boat again brings it all home. But I said we'd prosper, back when we first put on green and went north. And we did."

"Well..."

"Well, what?"

"You were a sellsword, Geth. A fugitive on top of that. But you've made captain now. And I'm happy for you. But what am I, even with this inn I've stolen? Did it ever occur to you that I wanted to be something more than a thief?"

Geth's mouth opened and closed. "So, you don't want an inn?"

Phelan shook his head, muttered something Geth couldn't make out.

"I owe you a lot, Phelan. I'd have been dead without you a long while back."

"And a few times over."

"A few times." Geth agreed. "I'm just glad you're with me now. And the inn can be damned. If you're happy to be back in Pellon, then I'm happy for that as well."

That earned a smile from the little man. "Don't worry," he added, "I won't run off on you."

"Like you did with Brega?"

"There's a long story goes with that. Only Prince Gahalus knows the whole of it. But you can count on me this time. I'll see this King Elius thing through. After that, I can't make any promises."

Geth held up his hands. "Can't ask for anything more. I was really hoping an inn would keep you out west with me, but..."

"I haven't cooled on the idea of my own place. Maybe we could even go partners. I realize now it's a two-man job. But there's a reason I never renamed the inn up in Greenfell. The real owner, or the heirs, will come back someday. And then what? That place was never really mine."

Phelan turned his eyes back to the city, to the white froth and deep blue sea separating him from it. He started whistling again. Seemed he was content, ready for what lay ahead.

Geth reckoned he was content too. He'd never felt so rested now that Ratcher was out of the picture. He didn't whistle, but he found himself humming along to Phelan's tune.

Only when they sailed right past the harbor did Geth's tune falter. "Where the hell are we going?" he wondered aloud. He looked toward the door to the captain's cabin. Rondah had taken the helm, directing the ship, but Melagus was still inside.

Geth didn't bother knocking. The counselor looked up at his arrival, muttered something, and straightened from the map he'd been standing over. "Wondering why we've passed the port?"

"Well, why have we?"

"We're headed to Old Sorn. It's too dangerous to make land directly in the Golden City."

Geth frowned.

"Now you're asking yourself what exactly we're walking into, of course. A lion's den, that's what. In more than just name."

The big warrior pulled at his mustache. "Want to share anything specific?"

"You know this kingdom as well as anyone in the king's circle."

"I know a few things, a few places. Been to the citadel once or twice. But I can't say I know my way around the palace. And I reckon that's where we're headed."

"The long and short of it is that Elius has plenty of detractors in addition to you and me. He needs friends too though. If he's sided with Towdric, it can only mean he thinks he stands to benefit from an alliance with the usurper."

"Detractors? You must mean Lord Ryrus and his lot. They've been scheming after the throne since before I was born. Perhaps we set the one against the other."

Melagus's mouth did that sour twist. "The thought occurred to me. But that might complicate matters in such a way as comes back to haunt us later. Our king would not thank us for inciting civil war in the kingdom of our sworn ally."

"Even if Elius has done the same thing back in Umbel?"

"To be fair, the contest between Towdric and Hadean was already underway. And though Elius chose the usurper over the rightful king, he did not *incite* the war."

Geth snorted. "I'm one to mince flesh, not words."

"Then let me get to the point. Elius has enemies. He also has allies. The levers we may safely pull, are the latter.

Each hold some measure of influence with the king. I think it wise to approach Elius through one of these men or women. To entreat the king directly would be suicide."

"You think he'd kill us, the emissaries of a Sworn Realm?"

"He might. Wouldn't it be easier to stick with the decision he's already made after all, to do a favor for his new ally, Towdric?"

"Thram's balls." Geth tugged at his mustache again. "What about the queen? It's said she's a real firestorm. A woman like that can turn a man in whatever direction she wants."

"Elius is no tender-heart, true. But Queen Lyanne is...just a bitch."

Geth started to laugh, but the counselor didn't join him.

"The woman is so heartless," he went on, "she's all but disowned her own blood, Prince Gahalus. She may be our lever, but I pray she's not. If ever there was a creature that would betray us on a whim, it is her."

"I see."

"I do have one contact that may serve our needs however." Melagus nodded to himself. "Amagoras, the king's 'cupbearer,' his closest advisor."

"I've heard of him."

"Amagoras, I assure you, wants nothing less than what's best for the realm. He's loyal to Elius, make no mistake, but he may be the one man with enough vision to see through the cloud of lies Palladine's kicked up. Amagoras can be reasoned with."

"So, we meet this Amagoras—"

"In secret—"

"In secret. And convince him that Towdric's the one who is unfit to rule, not Hadean. Elius listens to him, sends word to Palladine, and the lilies imprison the traitor within his own walls." Geth dusted off his hands. "All's well that ends well."

"*If* we can get to Amagoras." Melagsu made that sour face. "We cannot let it be known that an emissary from Umbel has arrived. Elius would send soldiers to detain us. Or more likely assassins. He'd sweep the whole thing under the rug, send Towdric our heads, and continue on with one less worry."

"That's cold."

But Melagus was smiling, a rare thing. "Now you understand why I needed the king's sharpest sword to guard my back."

Geth mumbled a curse under his breath. "What's first then?"

"We sail upriver, put in at Sorn. You have some experience there with the place I'm told?"

"Too much."

"We'll stay there for a few nights while I reach out to our friends. If anything new has unfolded, they'll know. After that, we'll head toward the city. I'm counting on you to hide us in some gods-forsaken place where we'll be safely out of sight."

"Gods-forsaken, that's my specialty."

Melagus chuckled. "After that, we'll try to arrange a meeting with Amagoras."

Geth nodded, though he found his hand had strayed to his hilt all by itself. Backstabbing highborns of the sort Melagus described had done in his master back in Turia some years past. He forced that hand away from his waist just as Melagus thrust a small bundle toward him.

"Here," he said. "Keep this. It's a gift for the king. You might as well wear it as we make land in Pellon. I know how your people can judge a man with a glance. Let them see something of your worth."

Geth took the bundle, a piece of leather wrapped around a gold ring, inset with three square green gems. He held it up to catch the light streaming through the window.

"Put it on. Elius is a big man as well. It should fit."

Geth slid the ring onto his left hand. He looked up at the counselor. "Where's your ring then? No, I reckon that's how you want it. No matter, I know your worth."

Melagus dipped his head. He opened his mouth but closed it with a frown.

"What?" Geth asked. "Speak, man, whatever it is."

"Well," the counselor stood a little straighter, composed his hands together, "it's clear you misjudged me for quite some time. You thought me cruel, selfish, a traitor even."

"There's nothing worse."

"Indeed. But I misjudged you as well. You're no mere sellsword, no lawless fugitive. Rough at every edge, true, but loyal and brave beyond a doubt. And skilled."

"And smart. Smarter than you thought anyway. Go ahead and say it."

Melagus scowled. "Smarter than most, that is certain. But what I really want to say is that I mis-*judged* you. I sentenced you to hang. You can see how I could, killing a man under the very Oathstone. Still, I wasn't so different than Towdric at that moment, was I?"

"You're nothing like Towdric."

Melagus frowned.

"I mean it."

The counselor looked up. The barest hint of smile appeared. Geth hadn't thought the man could actually turn the corners of his mouth in that direction.

Melagus extended a bony hand. "So long as you serve Hadean, I shall count you a friend, Geth of Pellon."

Geth spit into his palm, watched Melagus's eyes go wide, then grabbed his outstretched hand before he could draw it back.

"Brothers," Geth said.

Melagus shook, but loosed a sigh at the same time. "I knew you'd make me regret this."

CHAPTER THIRTEEN

Rondah steered the Windskimmer into the mouth of the Arm River, inland, toward Sorn. Geth worked the oars and hardly paid the city any mind as it slid by. The sun beat down hot on his face and back, even in mid-spring. That was something he didn't miss about these southerly climes. The sight of white-garbed soldiers on the walls had his neck hunched a little, like a blow could fall at any time—another thing he didn't miss.

Nobody chasing me, he had to remind himself. Palladine was far to the west, in Umbel. It was Melagus who needed someone to watch his back.

The Windskimmer glided smoothly into Sorn's marina a few hours later and Geth uttered a quick prayer of thanks to Uro for the safe journey. He grabbed his things, hopped over the gunwale beside Phelan. Melagus followed gingerly after.

"News of travelers from Umbel might attract the kind of attention we don't want," the counselor said as they gathered on the dock. "Tell no one where you've been, who I am, or who we serve."

Geth stroked his mustache. "Phelan hates it, but one look at this upper lip and most folk think I'm from Turia. If anyone recognizes me, that's where I'll say I've been."

"I do hate it," Phelan piped up. "But so do the ladies, so I won't complain. Leave more of them for me."

Melagus ignored that. "Rondah will travel ahead, down to Paellia. She'll send word once it's safe to join her."

Rondah arrived, pulling her captain's hat from her red hair to mop sweat from her brow. "I'll leave the ship here, travel by horse down to the city. It could take me a day or two to find out if it's safe to follow after, but I'll send a pigeon to save time. Where do you plan to put up?"

All eyes turned toward Geth. The Velvet Mantle was the obvious choice, he supposed, the finest inn Sorn had to offer, but the arrival of wealthy foreigners could make notice among the local highborn. Melagus would probably faint at the mere sight of Mother's brothel, so that wasn't an option. But there were plenty of others.

"The Juniper. It's just this way, near the marina."

Phelan gave an approving nod, but Melagus scowled. "We'll be smelling river water the entire stay."

"No one will look twice at a couple of travelers there."

Rondah knuckled her brow. With a wave, her crew unloaded the remainder of their belongings. They hadn't brought much. Within the hour, they'd secured a room. Melagus and Phelan each claimed one of the two beds, leaving Geth standing by the door.

"Fine, you can have the beds. I wanted to take a walk anyway."

Phelan frowned. "Take a walk?"

"That's right."

The little man closed his eyes and leaned back. "Give her my regards, would ya?"

Geth didn't deny it. Wending past pedestrians and street vendors, he crossed town toward the Acorn and Branch where Mother would be at work. He found her seated at the bar, back to him, dressed for the occasion, but only chatting idly with a younger woman.

"Miss Largess?"

Her back went straight, eyes wide as she turned. Her mouth opened but she didn't speak.

"Just here to say hello," Geth said.

She looked him up and down. The younger woman melted away, but mother breathed a sigh, hand on her huge bosom. Her lips screwed up and an actual tear slid down her cheek.

"You're alive."

"Uh, last I checked."

"They can't touch you, can they?" She stepped in, hugged him. "They tried their worst," she said into his shoulder. "But look at you now."

Perhaps it was all the years of chastening, or of just being ignored, but those words, the pride in mother's voice, it pulled him up short, speechless. All he could do was lean awkwardly into that embrace, pat her feebly on the back.

"Listen," he managed, "the truth is, I'm here to apologize. For the way I came and left last time. I wanted to make sure it hadn't come back to bite you. I was in a bad way, ya know?"

"A real bad way," Mother said. She leaned back to take in the sight of him. "But look at you now. That ring's new, I reckon. Is that really yours? I don't see those friends, the ones with all the shine."

"Are you about to ask me for a loan?"

"What? No! You don't know what all that coin did for me, last time you were here though. You could say I was in a bad way too. Been in it for many a year, truth be told. But don't I look better now?"

She turned a circle, arms up, smiling.

She did look better. A damn sight better. She'd lost a few pounds, and her face seemed fresh under all that make up. Her chin was up. She moved easily, like the cares she'd borne before belonged to someone else, another lifetime maybe.

"I've given up the drink," she said. "With the shine you left, I didn't have to work so hard, you see? Turns out, I didn't need the wine as much after that."

"That right?" Geth didn't remind her how she'd extorted that coin out of him. "So, you've given up the bottle. But not the trade?"

"The trade? Gods no. I like my job. And I'm good at it too. I like it even better now that I don't need the silver so bad. I can say no to a scratch whenever I feel like it."

"Well, I'm glad to hear it. I just wanted to stop and check on you." He paused, then added, "And let you know I was alright as well."

Mother looked from his face down to her own hands. "I didn't do much for you all those years, did I? Except drag you down, ask for favors. It was easier having a child when you were just a babe, young, tender. But when it got harder, well..."

"Mother—"

"No, let me speak!" She set her chin. "The holy man said it would help."

Geth's mouth worked silently. *Holy man?*

"That's right, I've been at prayer, made a few devotions too. Because I was a drunk, a bad one. You know better than anyone. I never wanted to be a mother, sure, and this isn't the easiest trade. But that doesn't change what I've done or didn't do."

"If you're looking for forgiveness, you already have it. I forgave you a long time ago."

She nodded, patted his arm. "I know. It was that cleric, Mather, wasn't it—that made you the man you are? You didn't learn any good virtues from me, that's for sure."

Geth snorted a laugh. His mother nodded, almost to herself. She patted his arm again.

"I'm not saying I'm perfect now, but I'm better. I feel like your coming here, and looking so prospered, well, maybe that's Mother Neyna's reward for me."

"Maybe."

"I hope that if I do need a favor sometime, I hope I can still ask it?"

Geth's suspicion started to rise, but her eyes were wide, not calculating. "I suppose so."

"Good." She rested her hands on her hips. "Because I hope you know you can ask a favor of me now too."

"At no charge?"

She laughed. "No charge. Except maybe for those rich friends of yours."

Geth didn't remember the air of Sorn smelling so sweet last he'd passed through, but he enjoyed it this time, whatever Melagus said about the proximity of the river. Perhaps that holy man had been on to something. It felt good just to talk to his mother. Damn good.

They didn't stay long though. Rondah's pigeon arrived the next day, bidding them hasten to the city. They found a farmer to ferry them in his wagon, threw their belongings in back, and started out.

"The captain has confirmed that Amagoras Cupbearer is in Paellia," Melagus said after a furtive glance at the driver next to him. The man looked half-asleep anyway. "We'll arrange a meeting with him as soon as we can."

Phelan had sprawled out in the back amid a pile of root vegetables, but Geth walked at the counselor's side. "And it's safe to meet him?" he asked.

"Safe? No. If Elius learned of it, he might send the Frog, Cloak, or some other knifeman after us. I've already said as much."

"So, we meet him in secret."

The counselor nodded. "After that, gods willing, we meet the king. But only once Amagoras deems it safe."

"What if he double crosses us, this cupbearer? What if Elius doesn't appreciate the whispers in his ear, orders the man to set a trap. It would sure make things easier for the assassin if he could choose the time and place to strike."

"Amagoras won't betray us. He wants what's best for the realm. *All* the Sworn Realms. And if anyone in the palace knows the goings on of Umbel, it will be the cup-bearer."

"Same way you know about Pellon? And about Sorn for that matter?"

"Sorn?"

"How did you know I was familiar with the place? And how do you know so much about Pellon? Who, outside of these parts, has even heard of the Frog?"

"Well," Melagus wore that smug look of his, "I must know things if I would counsel a king, wouldn't you agree? So, I've made it my business."

"You have spies is what you mean, like those two Towdric hung. And the child."

"Not Orie." Melagus frowned. "His eyes and ears are open, but I would never send him into harm's way."

Geth eyed the counselor sideways. Horse hooves clopped steadily onward until Melagus heaved a sigh, sagged in his seat.

"Still, I sent him, didn't I? And so, it is my fault. The lad is loyal. And bright. A part of me knew I should have been more careful, that he would have seen things, heard them. And that he would tell me all. But Towdric is no fool. Perhaps he witnessed the boy passing such things on to poor Cedrith and Minie. Or the other way around."

"Or maybe Towdric just cut the boy's ear to spite you." Melagus looked up.

"He's alive, your boy. And he can still hear well enough without that ear. Don't carry the weight of it. Unless that's what you need to fuel your hatred for Towdric."

The counselor nodded, turned to meet his eye. Geth held that stare. He reached over to clap a bony shoulder.

"You still didn't say how you knew about my connection to Sorn, though."

"I know about your mother, if that's what you're asking. And I know you spent time in Adamar, Turia, and among the Mog in the far east. As I said, it is my business to know."

"I was close to King Hadean," Geth mused. "Makes sense that you would ask questions. But how do you know so much about Paellia? For Thram's sake, you even know the hired knives in these parts."

Melagus raised a finger. "Do you remember when I sent Amalia to find you in the wilds? When you were waging your hit and fly campaign against the tribes?"

Geth nodded.

"She had learned that an assassin had come to Umbel from Pellon."

"Ratcher."

"Just so. Though that is but one alias, I'm sure. At the time, it seemed obvious he'd been contracted to murder young Hadean. Previous attempts had failed after all. And so, I began my research. I needed to learn all I could if I hoped to protect the king. There are plenty of other assassins for hire here in Pellon besides Blacksheep and the Number Three, I soon found out."

"Blacksheep?" Geth frowned. "You reckon that's who Ratcher really is?"

"I can't be sure. At one point I thought he might be the Lordling, but I'm fairly certain now he must be the one called Blacksheep."

Geth shook his head. "You got all that from Rondah?"

"Don't be simple. Rondah is an invaluable asset. And loyal, make no mistake. She has a good many contacts of her own as well. But I've made plenty of friends over the years myself. I ask questions, I read. I send letters and receive them."

"So, you learned this from your pen pal?"

"I communicate with those who share similar interests, similar curiosities, often those who have ties back to Umbel. I help them as I can, in turn. I pay them if necessary. Every king needs such knowledge at his call, a man beside him that is useful, clever, wise."

Geth thought that through. It made perfect sense. "And for Elius, that man is his cupbearer, Amagoras."

"Indeed. That's why we must meet him. He may be the one soul in all Wide Eria that's able to change King Elius's mind."

CHAPTER FOURTEEN

Aside from the flies, they made the distance from Old Sorn to the Golden City unmolested. A bright, southerly sun bathed fields of wheat, olive groves, vineyards, and tile-roofed towns in its glory. On these final miles of the great King's Passage, foot traffic weaved in and among a steady stream of carts, horsemen, and other wagons like their own, flowing in both directions along the wide, paved road.

They reached the Golden City before dark, passing the guards at the gate without incident. Geth eyed those white tabards warily. He pulled his shirt sleeves down over his tattoos, but no one paid him any mind.

He walked beside Phelan, still bouncing in the bed of the wagon. A forest of tenements and shops, and the musty throngs of its denizens closed in and around as Paellia in all her greatness swallowed them.

"Last time I was here," Geth mused, "I was riding alongside that bastard, Clydon."

Phelan nodded. "Brega had sold you out. Anything for a copper or two, old wench."

"Still owe her one, I reckon. But I did put a dent in Clydon's nose."

Phelan grinned. "Ah, the good ol' days."

They booked a room at the Netmender's Daughter, near the wharves, where the same drunks and trawlers Geth remembered from his last visit still occupied the booths, mixed in with an assortment of smugglers and even an honest traveler or two from abroad. Here, he could let his Mog tattoos show. But he hid that ring.

"The smell," Melagus whined. "Again."

"You wanted secrecy, didn't you?" Geth said. "Well, there will be plenty of foreigners in this part of town. No one will look at us twice, long as you don't put on that fancy tunic you've got in your pack."

Melagus snorted. "How would I get the stench out afterwards?"

Geth claimed a few chairs and waved for a round. Rondah caught up with them within the hour, but Phelan insisted they share a meal, sample the fried smelts, before any business. When the plates were cleared, the captain gave her report.

"It's done. Amagoras will meet you."

Her hat rested on the table beside her elbow. She smiled, but Geth didn't miss the dark circles under her eyes, the fine wrinkles around her lips. Somehow the orange light of the hearth only accented the white hairs among the red at her temples.

"It wasn't easy, I gather," Melagus said. "How could it be? We've given the Cupbearer much to think about, a problem he didn't have before we arrived."

Rondah shook her head. "It wasn't that. If I'm honest, it seemed he was expecting us. It was just so damn hard to get to him."

Geth frowned, shared a look with Phelan and Melagus.

"He's being watched," she explained. "They weren't hard to pick out, but someone's got eyes on the man."

"You weren't seen?" Melagus asked. "We do not want news of our arrival to reach Elius by any other means than the Cupbearer."

"I wasn't seen. He knew about the watchers as well. He seems to think they might belong to the queen."

"All the more reason to be careful," Melagus muttered. He went quiet for a moment, bony face wrinkling up in thought, then added, "Set up the meeting outside, on the streets. Let me know where, what time, and I'll be there. If my information is correct, Amagoras loves cherries."

"Cherries?" Geth repeated.

"Just watch. You may learn a thing or two."

In the morning, after listening to alley cats fight over fish bones all night, Geth was roused by the counselor and they set to work. Melagus asked the way to the fruit vendors' row, where he purchased an entire load of cherries and a wheelbarrow to haul them. Geth got the honor of carting it back to the inn. Rondah had already returned with the meeting all set up.

"Midday, right beside the great cistern," she said. "He'll be there."

The sun was already beating down hot on Geth's neck at that hour, but if there was a spot in the city to find some relief from the heat, it would be beside the water. Cistern Plaza sat just beneath Elius's citadel, so it made sense in that regard as well.

The Cupbearer arrived right on time. He wended through the fine-garbed lordlings, merchants, and ladies that crowded the great plaza, a tall, lanky man with an embroidered skullcap over his bald head. Melagus snatched the handles from Geth and wheeled the cart in the man's path, looking nothing like an actual fruit vendor in the big warrior's opinion.

But it worked.

"Ah, cherries!" said Amagoras. He motioned his entourage—a footman with an armful of tomes and three white-clad guards—to a halt. Geth sat with Phelan, watching from a seat on the lip of the cistern itself, but hurried to fall in behind the guardsmen, forming a line to get at Melagus's produce.

"...and she practically tore the smallclothes off me," Geth said, just loud enough for the lilies to hear him. "Her breasts were like ripe melons, I tell you. Her ass as round as one of those Southie wine urns."

"And that was yesterday?" Phelan caught the gist and played along.

Geth flicked a glance at the white-clad backs ahead of him. "The day before," he said a little louder. "Best part is, she only charged a dozen rounds."

A snort sounded from one of the three guardsmen. Geth smiled inwardly.

"And this was down near Neyna's Square?"

"No, man. You know that little moonshine cellar between carpet row and the butcheries? The one on the corner?"

"Yeah?"

One of the lilies had half turned and Geth pushed on. "She works above there. Private like, no handler, no brothel. But you'll see her walking up and down the street."

"Ah, independent." Phelan had his back to the lilies. He rolled his eyes but kept on. "What a catch."

"The best kind. You'll see her walking, unless she's with a client. You can't miss her."

One of the guardsmen grumbled something and Geth followed his eyes to the Cupbearer. He seemed to be haggling with Melagus—pretending to, at least. Geth cleared his throat to get the lilies' attention again.

"Just look for those tits. And...red hair about this long. She's got a nice gap between her front teeth too, so you know she likes her work."

"Oh, I know the sort." Phelan made a face at Geth, back still to the guards. "But twelve rounds, man?"

"You gotta' be clean. She won't even look at you if you're not clean. But for twelve rounds, she'll bounce you off all four walls."

"I could use a bounce like that myself," one of the guardsmen chimed in. The other two chuckled. The footman with the books wore a nervous smile.

Geth silently thanked the gods. "Just don't all go at once, mind. I was hoping to pass by again tomorrow and I don't want her tired out."

More laughter. Geth flicked a glance toward Melagus. The counselor gave him a nod.

"I just might marry this one," the big warrior added. "I swear it."

"Crazy scratch," one of the lilies chuckled.

The three lilies, the footman, and Amagoras himself started off. Melagus exited in the opposite direction, one hand on the small of his back but free of the wheelbarrow. The Cupbearer had bought the entire load.

Geth hurried to catch Melagus. "How'd it go? What did he say?"

"Was that the only story you could come up with? Dear gods!" The counselor flicked a sour look at him. "Red hair and a gap tooth?"

"C'mon, that's not the part that got your attention, is it?"

"It was the tits," Phelan called from over Geth's shoulder.

The big warrior nodded. "Everyone loves to eavesdrop, and what better way to catch a soldier's ear than woman-talk?"

"Was it not a bit overdone though?" Melagus asked. "More than a bit, truth be told."

"Made them listen though, didn't it, just thinking they had a chance?"

Phelan shook his head. "I'm with the Asp on this one. But I guess it worked."

They passed around the edge of the wide cistern, basalt statues on their islands, watching watercarriers and passersby crossing this way and that throughout the plaza. Geth flicked a glance over his shoulder in time to see Amagoras and his entourage disappear under the center of the three huge stone arches leading into King Elius's citadel.

"Regarding Amagoras," Melagus said, pausing to follow Geth's eyes, "he agrees. Towdric cannot be allowed to rule. He doesn't think Elius will want to hear as much, but he will present it and advise if it is safe to press further."

"There could be an easier way."

It was Phelan who'd chimed in. Melagus's eyes narrowed.

"What are you saying?"

"Prince Gahalus—"

"No way." Geth put his hands up. "Last time you saw the lad, it nearly landed you in the Tower of the Moon. He'd probably have you arrested on sight."

"Not if I paid back the money."

Melagus snorted. "He finally admits he's a thief."

"A gambler," Phelan said. "And a damn good one."

"A damn good cheater maybe," Geth muttered. "But that doesn't change anything. It's too dangerous, we can't risk it. From what I hear, he's on the outs with his mother anyway."

"And well he should be," Melagus said, "if half the tales are true."

"Oh, they're true," said Phelan. "And that's just the ones you've heard of."

"All the more reason to steer clear," Geth said.

The counselor nodded curtly. "Then we agree. We have a route to the king, a trusted route. And by this time tomorrow, with any luck, we'll be standing right in front of him."

———†———

"I don't know why I have to wear this if I'm just your footman," Phelan said. He scowled down at himself, arms held out to display the baggy, embroidered sleeves of the green tunic Melagus had brought for him. His trousers hung on him as well. Finely cut garments, but clearly measured for a larger man. The smell of rotting seafood and saltwater wafted in through the one tiny window of their quarters at the Netmender's Daughter.

"Any servant of the realm," Melagus said, "must wear proper colors. This is Paellia, not some Ilar hillfort in the frozen north. You know as much."

"Then how come *he's* not wearing green?" Phelan flicked a petulant glance at Geth.

The big warrior retuned a smirk.

"Because," said Melagus, "he looks more fearsome as he is, a rough-cut sellsword with a short temper and a long sword arm."

"Rough-cut?" Geth turned a dark look on the counselor.

"As all fine gems begin," Melagus amended.

Geth muttered a curse but allowed Phelan to trim his mustache and run a comb through his hair. In truth, he'd insisted on wearing his own tunic, a bulky thing that hid the mail he'd first donned, in secret, as a precaution against Ratcher. Melagus didn't press the issue, so long as Geth wore a green kerchief at his collar.

"That scarf looks ridiculous," Phelan said, pulling the front of Geth's tunic straight and giving him a final nod.

"It's a kerchief."

"Sure it is."

They left for the citadel on foot, only stopping long enough to hire a small coach halfway there. Geth and Phelan walked behind it, but Melagus played the proper dignitary on the seat beside the driver. Rather than enter through the Leonine Gate with its fluted columns, stone lions, and three grand arches, they veered wide around the water in Cistern Plaza to approach Elius's palace from a secondary entry. Geth cast a wary glance over his shoulder. Only the basalt statues on their islands looked back.

"I don't understand how arriving through a side door hides us with this coach and all the finery on our backs," Geth said.

"By Paellian standards, this isn't finery," Melagus replied. "We'd need at least two rings per hand to make notice in the citadel."

"I suppose I won't have even the one after this meeting." Geth looked down at the green gem on his finger. "But the point stands."

"Without a proper retinue, in Elius's halls, we could be anyone. Or no one, as far as most watchers are concerned. Now if we were to be seen passing others to join the king directly in his throne room, that might raise eyebrows. But Lord Amagoras has agreed to usher us through to a private meeting."

In all his years, Geth had only ever been inside the citadel a handful of times, back when he was a lily himself. Once for the Games, and once when his company had been picked to form an honor guard for the king, lining the series of broad stairs that ascended from the Leonine Gate to the palace itself. That was the only way up or down that he'd ever seen.

But the serving lad who admitted them through a second gate into the citadel led them on foot up a series of winding paths until they passed through a wide garden somewhere behind the palace. Down a colonnaded walkway beside the southern wing of the palace, they arrived before an ornate, gilded door.

"Make your prayers now," Melagus said under his breath.

A pair of lily guardsmen eyed them suspiciously until Amagoras himself arrived from down the hall, motioning the soldiers aside with an impatient smile. They pushed the door open and held it for the two counselors. Melagus and the Cupbearer traded bows and pleasantries. Amagoras led the way inside.

"What do we do?" Phelan whispered as the door closed, leaving them outside.

"Wait here."

"Then what was the point of this ridiculous tunic?"

The air was mild up there, in the shade of the gallery, the smell of the fruit trees and the tang of the sea wafting to Geth's nose in intervals as the breeze shifted. He clasped his hands behind his back, trying to look natural while still taking in all the finery of the fabled Lion's Den. Frescos in rich blues and reds adorned the yellowy stone walls. Sunlight filtered past spear-shaped cypresses, through pale-leafed olive trees, to sparkle on little pools and marble birdbaths. He kept one eye on the guardsmen just in case, their whites as pristine as everything else around them.

A stiffening of those lilies turned Geth as a woman and her entourage appeared around a corner from what must have been the central hall. Geth watched her approach out of the side of one eye. Gold gleamed on every finger, even her thumbs. Streaks of silver shot through the dark curls piled and arranged on her head.

"The queen," Geth warned Phelan. The little man turned in time to bow at her arrival. Geth copied the gesture.

Queen Lyanne flicked a glance over the green of Phelan's tunic, the kerchief around Geth's neck, and frowned. She pushed through the door without a word. Her own pair of lilies and a girl with a basket of flowers waited outside, but an elderly man with watery eyes followed her in.

The silver in her hair reminded Geth of nothing so much as bolts of lightning. A good omen or bad? He hadn't yet decided if they'd avoided a strike when the door opened again to release Melagus, Queen Lyanne, and her husband, King Elius.

"...such a pleasure to hear from young Hadean at last," Elius was saying. Geth didn't like the way he omitted the word 'king' but the smile he wore didn't seem overly forced. He had a wide mouth and a strong, dimpled chin beneath it. His wife smiled as well, hers a perfunctory gesture, no more.

"And we," Melagus said in simpering tones, "look forward to a continuation of the lasting allegiance of our two realms. And the mutual support that can only lead to greater stability, peace, and prosperity."

He bowed low. Elius dipped his head before turning back inside, the way he'd come. Lyanne followed after. Melagus waited for the door to close before waving Geth and Phelan down the hall.

"Is it done?" the big warrior asked as they walked.

Melagus pursed his lips. This once, Geth wasn't sure if it was that sour expression or something else.

"He heard what we had to say," the counselor said as they walked, boots clicking on marble tiles. "And I have no doubt Amagoras will sue for a reversal of his previous stance. The Cupbearer knows as well as anyone what it would mean to allow Towdric to take the throne."

"He walked you all the way to the door," Phelan put in. "That's something for a pompous ass like Elius."

Melagus turned to give him a nod. "True. But I had hoped we might avoid the queen altogether."

"Did she say anything?" asked Geth.

"No. And believe me, it would sit easier if she had. She didn't miss a word that was uttered, I can tell you that much."

Geth frowned. He flicked one more glance back the way they'd come, just in time to see Lyanne's watery-eyed manservant speaking close to one of the lilies that had accompanied their queen. The scent of fruit trees couldn't mask the reek of malevolence that woman gave off.

They weren't halfway down the citadel's hill when Amagoras's voice pulled them up short, calling from behind and actually running to catch them up. "Counselor! A moment, please!" He motioned them into an alley between two buildings with an anxious glance over his shoulder.

Geth rested a hand on his hilt. "What is it?"

"The queen," Amagoras said, still huffing from his jog. "I fear she may be up to something...unseemly."

Geth turned toward Melagus.

The counselor wrung his hands. "I feared that she might intercede."

"Whatever you do," said Amagoras, "be wary. Gods forgive me for saying it, but she is a shortsighted woman. She won't give a thought to the consequences if she counsels her lord king to side with Towdric and against King Hadean."

Melagus scowled. "I had heard the Hand of Justice, Palladine, was her pet. I guess it's true. It seems she intends to support his unhealthy attraction to Towdric."

"So it would seem. Therefore, I urge you make haste back to your accommodations. And do not let yourselves be seen on the streets until you've heard from me that it is safe."

Melagus nodded.

But Geth eyed the cupbearer sideways. "And how do we know we can trust you? Lay low? We haven't got time to spare. Our king is at war."

Amagoras spread his hands. "Of course. But the esteemed counselor will know that I only want what is best for my realm and for my king. Do you think I haven't heard of Towdric's doings? Of the innocents he's killed, how he failed to answer the call to war in the north? It's even been said that he cut the ear off a child, in public, for all to see.

"He rules with a closed fist rather than an open hand. Some might say he gave the thieves of Aldwood their just deserts. But even if such methods were effective, my little birds tell me the tribes of Ilia would never honor the truce you fought so hard to win. And so, a return to war in Umbel. More war in Umbel means less wheat in Pellon."

"Just what I told King Elius." Melagus grimaced.

"Indeed. There are some who might look to profit from instability, even in a sworn ally. But I assure you, none of those are faithful servants of the king."

"Lyanne couldn't plot against her own husband, with Ryrus," Geth asked, "could she?"

Amagoras shook his head. "No. Even if she did so despise her lord, she doesn't think like that. She simply wants what she wants. *Now*. And she's not afraid to break things to get it. She'll pick up the pieces afterwards. Or see to it that someone like Palladine sweeps them under the rug."

The Cupbearer escorted them all the way to the side gate where they'd entered, bid them gods-speed. Geth waved away the driver and wagon that waited. Too conspicuous.

Amagoras issued one last warning. "Hurry back to your lodgings and do not venture out again until you've heard from me. I promise I'll do everything in my power to convince King Elius of your cause. And rein in the queen as well."

Melagus thanked the Cupbearer and Geth turned them right, northwards, as they left the citadel, angling away from the open space of cistern plaza. Masses crisscrossed and thronged the cobbles, but it was still too exposed for his liking. His eyes searched for danger ahead. He kept Melagus close behind, Phelan bringing up the rear behind him.

"We've got a hook in our tail," the little man said as they rounded a corner to turn back west, in the direction of the Netmender's Daughter.

"You sure?"

"Yeah. And it's wearing white."

"Thram's crooked cock."

Geth pulled them up under the awning of a carpet seller's stall to dare a glance back the way they'd come. Sure enough, a lily rounded the corner a moment later, stopping to peruse some olives at another stall but casting furtive glances up the street the whole while. The sweat that rolled down Geth's side had nothing to do with the heat.

"Follow me," he said.

Down the street a little further, he sped up and turned right, down a narrow alley. He ushered his friends ahead of him then plastered himself against the wall at the corner. Seeing that, Phelan hurried the counselor away at a clip.

The lily came around the corner at a good pace himself, too fast to dodge the haymaker Geth leveled at him. Spit flew from the soldier's mouth and his whole body spun as the blow connected. A sound like a butcher's mallet tenderizing meat echoed up the alley and he went down in a heap, moaning where he lay. Geth might have uttered a triumphant curse but for the gold armband above each of the lily's elbows.

"Gods all be damned." He hurried to catch up with his friends. "We need to get off the street. If Lyanne's got the city watch doing her dirty work, it's only a matter of time before they find us."

"Or we get sold out," Phelan said. "Any street kid or horse groom would do it for a copper."

"Can we make it across the city to the Netmender's Daughter?" Melagus asked.

Geth shook his head. "I hope you didn't leave anything valuable back there."

Melagus made that sour face but held his tongue. Geth took a breath to calm down and think.

Every instinct told him to get out of the city, but he groped for another way. "We need to stay clear of the sort of place travelers go," he said. "They'll be looking for us there. That means the port, the wharves, and wherever the shined-up merchants take their swill. We need to go deeper into the city."

"We'll stand out," Phelan warned. He hooked a thumb at the counselor. "He will anyway. Maybe we ditch this place and come back to Paellia once things cool off."

"We don't have such time," Melagus said. "Have we come all this way for nothing? And how ever would Amagoras find us if we left Paellia?"

Phelan opened his mouth, but Geth cut him off. "As long as we hole up someplace safe, we can wait it out, here, in town. Somewhere we've got friends."

"And where's that?" the little man asked.

Geth gave him a meaningful look. "There's an inn near Northgate—"

"Oh no. No way, not her."

"She's close, Phelan. And it's our best chance."

"Who?" Melagus piped up. "What?"

"I know a woman," Geth started.

"An *ex*," Phelan said.

"And she's a friend?" Melagus raised an eyebrow.

"She hates my guts," Geth breathed. "But she won't turn us in."

CHAPTER FIFTEEN

"I should turn you in right now."

Eora's hands rested on her hips, a stance that always made Geth nervous. He twisted the ring off his finger—the ring intended for Elius—offered it up. "Take this, as a token of...well, as an apology."

Her hands moved from her hips, but only to cross over her chest. Not an improvement. She hardly looked at the ring.

But her foot started tapping. Geth took that for a good sign. At least she'd think it through before succumbing to the anger in her eyes and making good on the threat.

"You never change, do you, Geth?" Eora said. "I made it clear a long time ago, I never wanted to see you again."

"And that was *a long time ago*." He held up both hands. "I respected your wishes, didn't I? It's been ten years."

"I said I never wanted to see you *ever*."

"Take the ring, Eora. Let us hole up for a few days. You know I wouldn't be here if I wasn't desperate."

"You're always desperate. It's how you live. One disaster to the next."

Geth pulled at the end of his mustache. It was hard to argue with that. Things had changed in the service of King Hadean—a lot more than Eora might believe—but not the disaster part.

He looked to his friends. Melagus and Phelan stood shuffling their feet a few yards back. They'd arrived by way of the alley behind the Oak and Hart inn, Eora standing in the door to the stables, blocking their entrance. Geth had to think up something quick before someone saw the three of them and remembered it when the watch came around asking.

"Look," he said, "I'm a new man. Mostly. Would the old me have been able to offer you a ring like that? How do you think I even got it?"

"Cut it off a dead man's hand, I reckon."

"I got it from him." Geth pointed to Melagus. "He's counselor to a king. I'm not running around with any old mercenaries these days, Eora."

"But you're still running."

"I'm trying to do what's right. I've got a real lord now. A *good* lord. And if it takes one disaster after another to help him, so be it."

She snorted. Geth heard shuffling behind him, but Gods be praised, Phelan had the sense to lay low and leave it to Melagus to intercede.

"Dear lady," the counselor bowed almost as low as he had in the palace. "I fully understand how you might mistrust, Captain Geth. It took many moons for me to trust him myself. And I can't say I like him even at this point."

"You don't like him either?"

"Not really. But I *trust* him."

She looked to Geth, shifted her weight from one foot to the other. Maybe hearing the title 'captain' had helped.

"Go on," she said.

"I trust, dear lady, because I've personally groomed him."

"You expect me to take him in because he's got a fancy ring and scarf around his neck now?"

"It's a kerchief," Geth grumbled.

Eora turned in his direction with a scowl. "I see you still carry a sword. And I see you're still on the run. That tells me all I need to know. Now get out of here before I call the watch. I mean it."

Geth sighed. For his part, he was ready to move on, but Melagus stabbed a finger at Eora. "And that would be on your conscience, that you turned your friend over to his enemies. Whatever you believe about the captain, I know he never betrayed you. He'd sooner die."

Eora flipped that dark hair over her shoulder. Her chin went up, but she couldn't contradict the counselor. Geth held out the ring again, halfheartedly.

She took it. "Fine, you can stay for a night or two. But after that, you leave. I don't need you in my life, Geth. Now or ever."

———⊢————

Eora showed them into a room on the second floor, closing the door behind them without so much as a goodbye. Phelan collapsed flat onto the single bed. Melagus strode to the window to peek through the curtains.

Geth checked the bolt on the door and stood with his back against it. "Now what? Sit here and wait for Amagoras to give the all clear? What if that takes a week?"

"I loathe the thought," Melagus replied. "But I struggle to think of an alternative."

Phelan sat up, cleared his throat pointedly. "There is one other option."

"Gahalus?" Geth asked. He shook his head. "No way. Why are we even talking about him?"

"You don't think he holds any sway?"

"He walks with a sway, but that's because he's drunk most of the time."

Phelan rolled his eyes. "I'm telling you, he can get us in and out of the palace. The young rascal would revel in it, I wager. He can get us in front of his father if anyone can."

Melagus turned from the window to face the little man with a frown. "Get us in front of Elius? We've already been in front of him. And where has it gotten us?"

"In front of Lyanne then. He's her baby. If he speaks for Umbel, she'll listen."

"Lyanne hates Gahalus." Melagus shook his head. "I have contacts throughout this city and all of them agree; the queen and her younger son despise one another."

"You're wrong. Have any of your contacts drank with the prince? Diced with him? Have any of them snuck through the window of a brothel and—"

"We get the point," Geth said. "But I've heard the same thing as Melagus. Lyanne hates the boy."

"She hates the things he's done maybe. And maybe he's done them to spite her. But what mother hates her son? Especially a good-looking lad like Gahalus, a manly, sword-toting scratch."

Melagus sighed. "Love him or no, she'd have us done away just to one-up the boy." He nodded as if to himself. "She's already decided as much it seems."

A knock at the door made Geth whirl. He leaned close to speak through the crack. "Who is it?"

Eora's voice filtered in. "Who else would it be? I'm the only person who knows you're here."

Geth unbarred the door, his nose immediately filled with the savory smell of some sort of soup. Pork and grain, he guessed. A tray with three bowls and a loaf of brown bread appeared, followed by Eora's arms, then the woman herself. She set the meal carefully down on the bed—there was no sideboard—and wiped her hands on her apron.

Geth snatched a bowl and began slurping from the rim. "Oh, thank the gods."

"Some things never change," Eora muttered.

Melagus cleared his throat. "This must be your inn?"

"I work here, but it's not mine. Not yet."

"I see."

"The owner has agreed to sell it to me once I've paid off the debt."

"What she means to say," Geth put in, "is that we aren't staying for free."

Eora scowled at him before turning back to the counselor. "I run the place, yes, but there's a fair way to go before it's actually mine. No one stays for free, not even me."

"And what is it called?" Melagus asked. "Your soon-to-be inn?"

"The Oak and Hart. It used to be a popular stopping point after a hunt in the Kingswood." Eora gave them a pointed look. "These days my inn shelters the hunted, it would seem, rather than the hunters."

"It's not what you think," Geth said. "Not this time."

"No? It's worse, isn't it?"

Geth opened his mouth and closed it. She *knew*.

Beyond an ability to heal like Amalia, Eora had an uncanny talent for nosing out the truth. Geth sighed. There was no use denying it.

"We merely brought King Elius a message. A message from a king to a king. But it seems it was a message he didn't want to hear."

Melagus raised a finger before Eora could reply. "It's not the king we're running from, mind you. In fact, it's the queen."

"Lyanne." There was a bitter familiarity in the way she uttered that name.

"You know her?" Geth asked.

"More than I care to."

"Is she stubborn?" Melagus asked. "Will she tire out or keep up the chase? Or do you think we might change her mind?" He watched Eora. "We are prepared to reward her handsomely."

"The first thing you must know," Eora said, "is that she's a witch."

Geth, Melagus, and Phelan exchanged looks.

"If she wants to find you, sooner than later, you'll be found. As for changing her mind, she may be a witch, but first and foremost, she's a woman."

"That means 'yes'," Melagus said. "Unless I'm mistaken. Her mind can be changed if it suits her. But what of her son, Gahalus? Is it true that they've fallen out?"

"If you intend to get to Lyanne through her son, you've got your work cut out for you."

"But it can work perhaps?"

Eora muttered something like a curse under her breath. "She would do anything for him. That much is true."

"Ha!" Phelan clapped.

"But either way," Eora went on, "you better get to it. If Lyanne is after you, I want you out of my inn by this time tomorrow."

"I'll need coin," Phelan said, almost before the door had closed behind Eora.

"Hold on," Geth frowned. "This sounds like a bad idea already."

"I told you I'd have to pay back my debt."

"No one said we're going after Gahalus. Where would we even find him?"

"What other choice do we have, Geth? She's putting us out."

Geth's frown deepened. "Will it even work? Can Gahalus change her mind? Or are we just exposing ourselves for nothing? Maybe it's better we lay low and wait for Amagoras."

"We either try the prince," Phelan said, "or jump on Rondah's ship and head back. You heard Eora, if Lyanne really is a witch, we can't hide from her. She's got the watch on her side as well."

Melagus had stood silent, watching the exchange, until both Geth and Phelan turned to him at the same time. He exhaled a long sigh.

"I fear the thief speaks wisdom this once. If Lyanne is truly a witch—and I do not doubt it—we must act swiftly. Or admit defeat and flee."

"Thram's hairy, balls."

Geth paced the little room, yanked at the end of his mustache. To return emptyhanded to Umbel would mean it had all been for nothing. Hadean would have no choice but to lay siege on his own city, drawing this whole affair with Towdric into another lengthy war. Not an option.

But did they stand to gain anything from Prince Gahalus?

"We have to try," Melagus said, reading Geth's mind.

"Fine. Do we have the coin?"

"How much do you need?" Melagus reached for his belt pouch.

The amount Phelan uttered made the counselor's eyes bulge. But they had it.

"There's only one or two places he can be," the little man said. He stripped off that green tunic. "But I'm not going anyplace wearing *this*."

"Alright, we'll get you a change." Geth tore off his kerchief as well. "I'm going with you though. The prince might not remember you as fondly as you think."

CHAPTER SIXTEEN

They bought the tunic off the back of Eora'a cook and left straightaway. Melagus didn't argue about staying behind. He'd be a fish out of water in the sort of drinking halls Gahalus frequented and he knew it.

The sun was still high in the sky as their boots hit the cobbles. Even those days, centuries after its peak, the Golden City was immense. But the place Phelan expected to find the prince wasn't too far, gods be praised. From the working man's district of the Oak and Hart, they moved south, hoods up despite the heat, until they'd arrived at a tavern called the Sable Dragon. Smithies, armories, and other craftsmen's shops lined streets crowded with local folk, off-duty soldiers, and more than a few watchmen.

"You sure he won't turn us in?" Geth asked as they ducked inside the common room.

"No way." Phelan nodded to the man behind the bar and slid into a chair off to one side. Geth took another, both seats positioned against a wall with a good view of the door. Two foamy ales arrived but Phelan pulled Geth's back and out of reach before he could get a sip.

"Easy on the drink tonight, you hear me?"

"I know what I can handle."

"Just trust me on this. Sip it slow. We might be here a while, and you'll need your stamina."

Geth eyed him from across the table. He was up to something, but the big warrior played along. Phelan downed half of Geth's ale in one pull before sliding it back over. Fortunately, it wasn't long before the prince arrived.

He was a lanky lad, Gahalus, but broad across the shoulders like his father. A mop of curly hair—dark as the dragon on the tavern's placard—gave him even more height, and he wore an impressive sword. A thick-necked, bald-headed bodyguard trailed him, eying every corner of the room before pulling out a chair for the prince at a four-seater on the opposite side of the room. A few of the regulars dipped their heads or knuckled their brows, nothing more.

"Looks like Prince Gahalus is no stranger to this lot." Geth watched him over the rim of his drink. "But how'd you know he'd be here?"

"I've been asking around since first we arrived."

Geth eyed his friend sideways. "Oh, have you?"

"You think I trusted the Worm to get things done? Ha! There's a reason he brought us along, Geth. This is our town. We know which turds float and which sink in these parts."

Whatever the big warrior thought of that, it seemed Phelan was right. Would they get anything from it though? Before he could ask what the plan was, the little man had kicked back his chair and started across the room. Geth swore, hurried to follow.

"My prince!" Phelan bowed low. "It's been far too long. I see Rudie's moved on, but I like the look of your new company."

The stern-eyed bodyguard glowered back in reply, folding thick arms across a chest as wide as a barn door. Lamplight gleamed almost as bright off his head as it did off the pommel of his sword, but Gahalus himself snorted a laugh.

"Well, if it isn't the Eel himself." He looked to Baldy, hooked a thumb toward Phelan. "Not a man as slippery as this one, not in all the Sworn Realms. Slick as they come."

Phelan bowed even lower. "You may be thinking of a certain dice game and my hasty departure. But rest assured,

I have your share of the winnings. I'm glad we were able to catch up and settle the debt."

Gahalus's eyes narrowed. Phelan reached for the purse at his waist before the lad could speak. He doled out silvers, chatting all the while.

"A tidy job, wasn't it? More fun than I've had in months. We turned a nice bit of coin that night as well."

"Did we? I seem to recall that you fleeced everyone at the table. Including me."

"You, my prince?" Phelan stacked the last coin next to the rest and slid the sum across the table to rest in front of Gahalus. "How could I fleece my own partner?"

"Partner, is it?"

"Did you not want your fair share? That's all of your monies in front of you, plus one half of the winnings we took off the others."

Gahalus scanned the stacked coins for a moment—figuring sums Geth reckoned—then shook his head. "At least you're a generous one, *partner*. But let's trace the strings attached and see where they lead. Then we'll know the sum total of what you've laid on my table."

Baldy snorted. "Well spoken, my prince," he rumbled.

"Sharp as ever," Phelan came back. "One of the things that makes you such good company. And a good partner.

As for Rudie and the rest of those...*friends*, I can't say I miss them."

"The lords and ladies you robbed?"

"*We*, technically." Phelan flicked a meaningful glance down at the silver on the table.

"Well, they weren't true friends anyway, were they?" Gahalus looked to his man again. "Not even Rudie."

"No," the big bodyguard agreed. "Better off without 'em."

Phelan grinned. "And fair game for the fleecing. We can agree on that."

Gahalus chuckled

Just like that, the tension melted away. The prince gestured to the empty chairs. Phelan sat next to him, half-sprawled, casual as you please. Geth took the remaining chair beside Baldy.

"How about another, drink?" the little man asked. "On me." He waved for the barman before Gahalus could reply.

"Well, some things *have* changed," the prince muttered.

"Thank the gods. I had to leave these parts for a while—you may have heard that a certain Hand of Justice was looking for me? I landed in Umbel. Fell into some real serious business out there, but I came away at a profit."

"Umbel? I can believe it."

Geth shot his friend a warning look at mention of the realm, but it was already too late.

What was he thinking? Half the watch was probably looking for them. Could Gahalus be trusted, or was he just as likely to turn them in? The drinks arrived, four red Paellian wines. Whatever Phelan was up to, Geth didn't appreciate the way his foot got stamped under the table when he tried to reach for his cup.

"Ah, Umbel." Phelan let loose an exaggerated sigh. "I can't say I miss it, truth be told. They've been at war out there. I found myself caught right up in it."

Geth kept his mouth shut, listening and trying to figure out Phelan's angle. The little man relayed to Gahalus the goings on in the westerly Sworn Realm, and also neighboring Ilia. Most of what he said was true, though he embellished his own part and left out the whole imprisonment bit. He said nothing of Geth whatsoever. At least his account of Hadean didn't sell the king short.

Gahalus absorbed every word. Geth wasn't fooled by the way he casually swirled his wine. No, this lad wasn't stupid. If his mother and father knew what was going on in Umbel, Geth reckoned he had to know something of Towdric and all the rest as well.

But did he also know the king had thrown his weight behind the traitor? Or that the queen herself sought to bury them, Hadean's rightful envoys?

"Fond memories, I'm sure," Gahalus said when Phelan finished. "Enough heavy talk though." He cast a wistful glance around the room, but the little man was already waving for the barman again.

"White Adus," he called. "Something special for a special patron."

"You really did fall into a shiny patch, didn't you?"

"You doubted me?"

Gahalus was smiling, despite the irreverence. Geth shifted a boot this time before Phelan could step on his toes, but he did spill his liquor while the other three drained their shots. Even Baldy wore a mellow look by the time a third round arrived—wine again. The room livened up as a fiddler began strumming, a mixed crowd shuffling in at day's end. A couple of girls danced and a dice game had sprung up in one of the corners. Lilies, fresh in from work, arm-wrestled, hooting and cursing as bets crossed back and forth with each win or loss.

Geth saw Phelan's eyes flick from the lilies to him and back. Like that, Geth knew his plan. A part of it at least. "Thram's balls..." he muttered into his still-full wine. The little man turned to Gahalus, leaning toward him to whisper conspiratorially.

"Let's have some fun, shall we? I've got time to kill if you're up for it."

Gahalus snorted. "I doubt you do, but I'm always up for some entertainment."

"Aren't we both?"

"But is *he* up for it?" The prince turned to regard Geth, one eyebrow raised.

Phelan laid a hand on the big warrior's shoulder before he could reply. "My footman? He's *always* up for it."

Geth swallowed another curse but played along as Phelan approached the gamblers surrounding the arm-wrestling. They paired him against a white-clad lily of medium stature, but quite strong, Geth reckoned, if his confident smirk was any indication. They sat and squared off. The bets were laid and soon enough, Gahalus and Phelan were collecting coin.

"Didn't I tell you?" The little man clapped the prince on the shoulder. Gahalus grinned, his cheeks more than a little rosy from all the drink. A round of ale on the royal tab went some ways to brightening the mood of the men that had lost.

Geth had been sure to drag the contest out, making it seem hard-won, and a second match-up was picked for him as soldiers, off-duty watchmen, and regular drunks attempted to recoup their losses. It was the oldest hustle in the book. Still, neither Phelan nor the prince had pushed the bets high, and even though they had to suspect, they couldn't resist another bite. Geth defeated the second opponent, a thick-limbed watchman, in the same manner as the first.

More than a few of the losers grumbled as Phelan and Gahalus swept up the coins, but others who'd won in the side-betting laughed and hooted. Once again, the prince stood, bought a round, and frowns melted away. The lad spun one of the dancing girls playfully before settling back down in his chair. A few of the lilies had begun singing. Even Geth could appreciate the atmosphere. They loved the rich bastard.

"You know," Gahalus swirled his wine, looking down at it for a long moment, "fleecing aside, I never set the Hand, Palladine, after you."

"I know." Phelan met his eye. "It was your mother."

Gahalus didn't have to answer. A fleeting grimace told it all.

"Well, I have to come clean," the little man went on. "It's her I wanted to talk about anyway."

"My mother?"

"It was the gods' truth, what I told you about Umbel. The war with Ilia, the insurrection. She had a hand in all that."

"No." But there was no conviction in the denial.

Phelan nodded. "Turns out she set her hound, Palladine, on better folk than me. Or maybe it was his doing. Either way, she's backed the traitor Towdric. *Against* Hadean, the rightful king."

"Our lord," Geth put in, "and friend."

Gahalus's eyes flicked to the big warrior.

Phelan continued, before he could speak. "More heavy talk, I'm sorry to bring it up. But I know you're not the idler they say you are. You know what's right and wrong, what's wise and what isn't."

"Unlike some others," Baldy muttered, downing his drink.

"Would you call it wise to challenge the queen?" Gahalus asked.

"If it's in the service of a king."

Gahalus smiled, shook his head. "So unlike the Phinnie I knew. In the service of a king? I hardly believe it."

Phelan leaned closer, voice low. "Ask around. Your mother's got the city watch looking for three men from Umbel as we speak. You're looking at two of them now."

"A good son would turn you in then, make her happy, wouldn't he?"

Phelan spread his palms. "Our lives are in your hands."

"They couldn't call me idler then," the prince agreed.

"But some might call you traitor. And that, I think you could never abide."

Gahalus's eyes narrowed.

"Hear me out," Phelan said. "That much at least."

"It isn't much fun, this serious business. That's not why I keep you around."

Phelan dipped his head. Geth still didn't know his endgame. Phelan's gaze flicked back toward the arm-wrestlers and a smile touched his lips.

"At least we had some fun with the wagering," he said. "My man here, he's as strong as an ox. Not the first time I've won coin because of him. In fact, I've never lost."

Gahalus snorted.

"It's true. I've never seen him lose. Not once."

Geth lifted his cup to hide a smile. He had to admit, Phelan played it well. Gahalus fell right into his lap.

"What do you say, Tham?" The prince looked to Baldy. "Think you can best Phinnie's footman?"

"Maybe not with my *feet*," he goaded, "but with my arms? I'm sure of it."

It all made perfect sense now. Phelan hadn't been wrong to keep Geth off the drink. Silently, the big warrior thanked him for it as he rolled out his shoulders.

Gahalus rubbed his hands together, waving at the barman for another drink. "What's the wager? Three golds, make it interesting?"

"Three golds?" Phelan's eyes widened. "I haven't fallen *that* deep in the shine. What say we leave the coin out of it. But if my man wins, you hear me out on this 'serious business.' You can still decide yay or nay if you want any part in it."

"Only a fool would wager anything more."

Phelan nodded. "Just hear me out."

"It's a bet." Gahalus whistled to call over some of the lilies and watchmen from the other tables. He turned back to Phelan. "Put one silver on it as well. It's always more fun when there's money on the line."

CHAPTER SEVENTEEN

Geth eyed Tham and his big bald head from across the table. A real beast. Probably slower than Geth himself in a fight, he reckoned, but plenty strong. A half dozen drinks couldn't take that away from him.

But it *would* cut his stamina.

"Best of three," Geth said. "Just to be sure."

Tham laughed.

Gahalus quickly agreed. "A silver each match, Phinnie. Put them on the table where I can see it."

Phelan dipped his head and produced the coin. He squeezed Geth's shoulder and stepped back.

Tham rolled up his sleeve, set his right elbow on the table, flexed his hand. Geth left his shirt sleeve up, but his tattoos peeked out at the cuff anyway. They clasped hands.

Gahalus smacked the tabletop and they started, grunting and heaving, using their left hand to grip the opposite table edge for balance and leverage. Gods the bastard was strong! Geth felt his arm and shoulder burn, tremble, as Tham slowly forced it back. He could have conceded—there was no turning the tide—but he fought to the last.

Geth's arm finally gave out.

"Down!" Gahalus shouted.

Tham raised both arms, hooted. Sweat beaded his forehead, and he sucked in air. "Yeah!" He pumped his fist. But those celebrations only buoyed Geth's hopes. A man didn't celebrate an easy win with that kind of vigor. It had taken something out of him.

Sweat rolled down Geth's side as he twisted in his chair to switch arms. If he didn't win now, with his stronger, left arm, it was over. He set his elbow down and waggled his fingers straightaway, not leaving Tham the chance to catch his breath. The big bodyguard growled and took it. Their eyes met, icy blue and intense dark. Geth growled back.

With another smack of the table, they began. Geth heaved, temples throbbing, and jaw clenched as he strained for every ounce of strength. They sat there, locked in place, neither man budging, until slowly, Tham's arm began to give.

He held on, just as Geth had, to the end. The thought occurred to the big warrior that he should ease up, drag things out even more, but he didn't know how much longer he could hold out himself. The back of Tham's hand touched wood and a roar went up from the onlookers. Geth's arm went limp just a moment after Tham's. He didn't have the energy to celebrate.

"One more!" Phelan shouted. "For pride! All the pride in the world, and one bright silver to boot!"

Gahalus watched the little man through narrowed eyes. But he wore a smile. Tham muttered curses, hurrying to set his right elbow on the table before Geth could try to continue with the left. The big warrior clasped his hand and prayed. *Thram and Awer, give me strength. It's the least you can do. I know you're loving this, you haughty bastards!*

A final slap of the table and they heaved, cords standing out on necks, veins on foreheads. As with the previous contest, their arms shook in stalemate for what seemed an eternity. But as with the left-hand bout, slowly, it was Tham who began to give way.

The entire Sable Dragon had gathered around by then, hollering and clapping, including the innkeep. It was all just noise in Geth's ears, but it was *a lot* of noise. As Tham's arm shook, the clamor increased. A sense of triumph fueled Geth. He pushed for the win until Phelan's foot pressed on the top of his boot.

It could only mean one thing. Geth swore inwardly, spittle dripping from his mouth. But ever so slightly, he eased back. The shouting and banging of tankards grew even louder. Tham's strength grew with it, as newfound confidence surged through him. Geth tried to drag it out, but once his angle was broken, it only took seconds for the big bodyguard to force his arm all the way down.

"Victory!" Gahalus shouted.

Liquor sloshed and spilt as men jumped up and down or threw their drinks in frustration. Backs were slapped, curses grumbled, coins traded.

"That was a close one," Phelan said, leaning down close to Geth. He handed him a fresh ale. Geth glowered at his friend, snatched the tankard and drank the whole thing down.

Gahalus stood behind Tham, a hand on either of his big shoulders. "Still undefeated." The prince's face was good and flushed. He wore a drunken smile. Baldy nodded but thrust a hand toward Geth. Phelan stepped on the big warrior's boot and pressed until Geth reached forward and accepted the handshake.

"Well fought," he mumbled.

In twos and threes, the onlookers retreated toward their seats or in the direction of the bar, leaving Geth and Phelan with the prince and his man. Baldy smiled into his ale like a toddler with a slice of cake. Geth swore he'd wring Phelan's neck if this scheme of his didn't work.

"I haven't had that much fun in a fortnight," Gahalus grinned, settling back in his chair finally. He shook the pair of silvers he'd taken off Phelan in one hand. "I only wish I'd wagered more."

Phelan dipped his head. "Ah but you've taken much more from me than coin tonight, rest assured."

"Have I? It's that 'serious business' you're talking about again. Do you really think I don't already know what you want from me?"

"I reckon you do." Phelan set down the single silver he'd won during Geth's second bout against Tham. "But let's say I don't and wager a bet. It's always more fun when there's something on the line, as you said."

Gahalus looked down at the coin, a smirk on his rosy face. He nodded to himself. Lifting his cup, he pulled down a healthy swallow of wine then looked from Phelan to Geth and back.

"You want me to speak to my mother," he said.

Phelan didn't so much as blink, but the lad smiled just the same.

"Her lapdog Palladine has urged her to back Towdric's claim on the throne and you need me to turn that around. Or at least convince her that Pellon should remain neutral.

King Hadean—your friend—doesn't stand a chance otherwise."

"King Ha—" Geth started, but the prince raised a finger.

"There's more." He faced the big warrior. "You are
no footman, but a wolf. *The* wolf, in fact. What's more,
you're the man Palladine has been hunting for a good long
while—the man that escaped the Tower of the Moon and
set fire to the Hand's estate on the way out."

Geth opened his mouth, but Gahalus cut him short
once more.

"No use denying it. The tattoos are right there. The
mustache, the brooding eyes..."

Phelan shifted in his seat "Well—"

This time it was Geth who did the interrupting. "He
had it coming." He leaned to one side and spit on the floor.
"All of it and more."

Phelan's eyes widened.

Across the table, however, Tham actually giggled.
Galahus matched that gesture with a chortle of his own.
Geth blinked. Somehow the big bodyguard was drunker
than the prince, despite outweighing him by about a hundred pounds.

"I couldn't agree more," Gahalus said, lifting his cup.
"And I salute you, Wolf. To the bottom."

He downed his drink and Geth hurried to follow suit. "So, what now?" the big warrior asked.

"What now?" Gahalus leaned back in his chair. "We hop a ship to Umbel, put Palladine in his place, and all's well that ends well."

Phelan offered a rueful smile. "If only was so easy. Glad as I am to learn that you share our opinion of Palladine, Pellon's soldiers won't answer to him alone. But if you could speak to your father, an order from him would do it."

"You were right when you started with my mother," Gahalus said.

He'd started to slur and Geth worried they were losing him. "Your mother then," he said.

"I'm sure you know we don't see eye to eye."

"We've heard a few things."

"That she's evil?" The prince smiled. "That she's a witch? It's true, you know, on both accounts. I could talk to her. Not sure it would do any good though."

He swirled his cup, took a good long drink. But there was a certain gleam in his dark eyes. He swallowed, looked from Geth to Phelan again, wheels turning in his head. Geth wasn't sure he liked that look.

"Unless..." The prince let that word hang.

Geth stifled a curse. "What do you want? Just say it. Whatever it is, if it means you'll call off Palladine and his troops in Umbel City, we'll do it."

Gahalus grinned, turning toward Phelan. "The thing is, you've settled the debt you had with me, Phinnie, but I, in turn, owe some silver out myself. You know how I like to gamble and such. Well, these debts...let's just say my mother finds them an embarrassment. One of many I've caused her."

"Debts you say?" Phelan frowned. "And this isn't something you could deal with on your own? Or have Master Tham handle?"

"Oh, I suppose I could just ask Mother for the coin and be done. But that would defeat the purpose. And to handle it any other way than to simply pay up, well, that could prove dangerous."

Phelan frowned. Geth thought of Oram back in Sorn, how he himself had settled his mother's debts. "I know how to deal with moneylenders," the big warrior said.

Gahalus's eyes flicked back and forth between Geth and Phelan. "If I were to handle that debt, now that would catch Mother's notice, maybe even win her favor."

"Then consider it done," Phelan said.

Gahalus reached down to slide Phelan's silver coin off the table and into his pocket. He smiled. Geth downed his tankard and pushed his chair back.

"Alright, tell us which moneylender and we'll be done by sunrise."

"I doubt it." Gahalus leaned back in his chair, closed his eyes like he might nod off right where he sat. But he managed to finish. "She's a big fish, this one. A real tramp if you ask me. They call her Lady Brega."

CHAPTER EIGHTEEN

Geth didn't bother swallowing his curses. "Thram's hairy, twisted balls!"

Across the table, Gahalus came awake, shared a laugh with Tham at his expense. But Phelan nodded, eyes narrowed in thought.

"The Wolf's tail seems to have dropped, Phinnie," the prince said. "Are you still up for it?"

Phelan kicked back his chair, stood, and offered a bow. "Rest assured, my prince. Brega won't know what hit her."

Geth grumbled another choice one, knuckled his brow toward the prince, and followed Phelan outside onto the street. They moved at a clip, down shadowed lanes, avoiding darkened doorways as a course of habit.

Geth didn't speak until they'd put a few blocks between themselves and the Sable Dragon. "Well, that was a waste of time."

Phelan shook his head. "Is that all it takes? Mere mention of the name 'Brega' and you're pissing down your leg?"

"Don't be an ass, Phelan. We can't get to Brega. She's too smart, too connected. And did you forget about that personal army of hers?"

"Look, she's dangerous. But anyone with the stones to take a debt from Gahalus was gonna be dangerous. We can do this. You know you *want* to."

Geth snorted. "Of course I want to. But I'm telling you, it can't be done. We don't have the manpower, the time to plan. What did you have in mind? Storm her manse, kill her, plus a few dozen bodyguards, and then burn the place down? Phelan, I'm only one man."

"You're not thinking, brother. What we need isn't more manpower. What we need is the power of a woman. One woman to be exact."

Geth eyed his friend sideways.

"Eora."

"She's a healer Phelan, not some murderous witch."

"She can do things! More than just mending bones I mean. I've seen her. Plus, it's Brega that financed her in buying the inn. She's the one holding the debt Eora still owes."

"What?"

"That's right. And if helping us means wiping clean her own debts, she won't be able to say no."

Geth thought that through as they walked. He didn't know what Phelan had in mind regarding Eora's talents, but if she did in fact owe the lady, she could help them lure Brega out at the very least. The little man was right; with Eora's help, there was a chance.

"No one knows better how Brega operates," Phelan said, reading his mind. "We draw the spider away from her web and squash her. I can sneak back to her manse while she's out, steal her records or burn the place or some such."

"While I kill the old wench."

Phelan didn't answer.

Geth swore. He didn't like the idea of killing a woman, even a real bitch like the lady, but he didn't get a chance to think on it long. The noise of footfalls behind them had been steadily growing until it became obvious they had a tail. He nodded to one side and Phelan followed him around a corner. He managed a furtive glance back the way they'd come as they rounded the bend.

"Watchmen, two of them. And one lily soldier, unless I'm mistaken."

Phelan sighed. "Probably followed us out of the Sable Dragon. No other way to end up with a mismatch like that."

"That wench of a queen must have put a bounty on us," Geth agreed.

"I know a good spot up ahead. Wait 'til they hit that corner, then run."

Geth nodded, and as the three men behind them came into view again, he took off at a run. Phelan took the lead. They turned about a half dozen times until Geth was totally lost. Fortunately, they'd lost their pursuers as well.

Phelan waved Geth to follow down one last turn, the pair of them still panting as the Oak and Hart finally came into view. "Here...we are," the little man said, half doubled, hands on hips.

Even with their tail far behind them, Geth couldn't shake the feeling he was being watched. He looked both ways down the alley, up onto the roofs, saw nothing. They entered through the stables out of an abundance of caution.

Melagus stood pacing the length of their room when they arrived. "Well?"

He looked to Geth, but the big warrior let his friend have the moment.

"We met him. I put on the charm. It's done."

"He'll speak for us with the queen? Excellent!"

"He will." Phelan motioned for calm. "But we need to do a job for him first. Nothing we can't manage."

Geth shook his head, muttered under his breath, but Melagus didn't notice. He exhaled. "Thank the gods. The way you smell, I thought you went swimming in a barrel of ale. I was afraid that meant you'd failed, except in getting drunk."

"I never fail at that." Phelan winked.

He'd certainly drunk his share, but Geth was sober enough to note the counselor fidgeting with the hem on his tunic. "What is it?" Geth asked. "What happened?"

Melagus grimaced. "I received word from Amagoras. The queen has proved difficult to steer. What's more, my contacts tell me things may have worsened for Hadean."

"Worsened?" Geth looked to Phelan and back. "How?"

"Towdric has launched an offensive against Hadean's position north of the city."

Geth snorted. "He hasn't got the numbers."

"No, not for an all-out attack. But enough to send a band in secret across the pickets. They burned much of the army's stores."

Geth blinked, looking from Melagus to his friend and back. "Sonofabitch. That's my move."

"That's right," the counselor finished. "Now our forces will be short on supplies." He blew out a sigh. "It seems Towdric was paying closer attention to the Wolf last winter than we thought."

Dawn met them groggy-eyed, and, in Phelan's case, still half-drunk. Even so, they set to work first thing. Geth sent Melagus to fetch Eora. She seemed to trust him the most. A nail-biting hour later, the counselor returned with the innkeep, a tray of morning tea, cheese, and day-old bread in hand.

"Master Melagus tells me you need something," Eora said. "Again."

Geth opened and closed his mouth, trying to choose his words, but Phelan beat him to it.

"There's a bone in this soup for you too, Eora."

Her eyes narrowed.

"What if I could wipe away your debts and win you full ownership of the inn *today*?"

She laughed. "I don't care how many kings you're working for these days, Phelan. There's no way you could pull that off."

"I can and I will. For a fifty percent stake in the business."

"Ha!"

"All I need is for you to lure the Lady Brega out of her lair."

It was Eora's mouth that opened and shut this time. She straightened her braid down her left shoulder, frowning fiercely. "Even if I did coax her out," she managed finally, "what makes you think you can get her to forgive my debt?"

"Forgive?" Geth laughed. "Brega's never uttered the word. But if you can get her out, I reckon I can convince her. Phelan would sneak into her place and destroy her ledgers just to be sure."

Eora's pretty mouth twisted. She flipped her braid from one shoulder to the other. "I think I know what you mean by 'convince.' And even if I'm wrong, it's an honest debt I owe her. To do anything other than pay up would be stealing."

Phelan rolled his eyes.

Geth barked a laugh. "Ha! You're worried about cheating *Brega*? Paellia's biggest thief? Did you know we worked for her? You certainly don't know how she sold me out, tried to have me locked up in the Tower of the Moon."

"Well—"

"It's true," Phelan put in.

"After all I'd done for her," Geth said. "And let me tell you, I did my share—she turned on me for a handful of golds. If I told you the things—"

"Alright, I get it. But why? What is it that *you* need from Brega?"

"Let's just say, yours isn't the only debt we need to clear."

"Out with it." She folded her arms. "I'm not doing this unless I know exactly what the three of you are about."

It was Melagus who answered. He moved close to the innkeep, expression sincere. "Dear lady," he said. "We must also clear the debts of young Prince Gahalus. A great sum, we're told. But should we succeed in this, the prince has agreed that in return, he shall speak to his mother, the queen, on our behalf."

"And you need this? For the king you serve?"

The counselor gave a solemn nod.

Eora blew out a sigh. She turned to regard Geth for a good long moment. Her hands settled on her hips, but this once, the big warrior reckoned the threat in that pose was for Brega.

"I'll do it," said Eora. "I suppose she deserves as much. But I won't have her killed."

"Eora—" Geth began.

She shushed the big warrior with a look. "Here's how we'll do it. I'll ask to add a sum to my loan, for a renovation or some such."

"To borrow more against the inn?" Geth asked.

Eora nodded. "A hefty amount. She'll want to come see the place, make sure it's still in good order. We'll handle her then. But we won't hurt anybody."

"How we gonna do that?" Geth asked.

"By stealing her memory."

Phelan directed a smile at Geth. "I told you she had other talents."

Eora glared at the little man. "And when this is done, you only get a third."

It was all set up within a few hours. Eora made the trip to Brega's manse to request the loan. She must have sold it well because the lady told her to expect a visit within a few hours. That left just enough time to prepare.

They met back in their little room. "She'll have several guards with her," Geth said. "A couple of them will wait outside. And probably one more behind the inn. We'll need to strike their memories too or they'll squeal. And we'll need to get the lot of them away from here afterwards, to her manse—anyplace else really. She can't remember she was ever at the Oak and Hart."

Phelan nodded. "I'll bust into her place while she's gone. Most of the boys will be out collecting. That will leave just a few servants and maybe two or three of the boys."

"Won't they see you?" Eora asked.

"I doubt it. I know exactly where the lady keeps her valuables. No one is allowed in those quarters. The ledgers will be there."

"But the servants?"

"I've done this sort of thing before."

Eora sniffed.

Geth didn't like the sound of it either. "You don't think it would be easier to just burn the whole place down?" he asked.

Phelan shook his head. "I'll be in and out before anyone can lay a hand on me, don't worry. They may see me, but it won't be until I'm on my way back over the wall."

A look from the little man cut short any further argument from Geth. The big warrior gritted his teeth but held his tongue. Between Phelan's task at the manse and dealing with Brega's entourage, there were plenty of ways things could go wrong. There was no point telling Eora though—Melagus either, for that matter. It had to be done. Time was running out for Hadean.

Phelan smoothed the front of his tunic. "Better be on my way then." He started for the door. Geth stuffed the last of the old bread in his mouth and walked him all the way down to the back alley.

"You don't really expect it to be so easy," Geth said.

"When has anything ever been easy?"

"She'll have six men with her, at least, for this meet-up. Odds are I'll have to bleed at least a couple of them. You know damn well you're wading into a load of shit yourself."

Phelan grimaced. "I may have to set fire to the place after all, huh?"

Geth nodded. "And then there's Yoric."

"The scribe." A silence hung between them for several long seconds. "Little bean-counter knows everything, doesn't he?"

"He'll have to be dealt with somehow."

"With any luck, he'll ride along with the lady, and you can wring out his memory as well."

"If he doesn't?"

"Pray that he does."

Phelan disappeared down the alley and around the corner. Geth turned his thoughts to his own task. For the most part, he just needed to stay out of sight and not blow the whole ruse. He hadn't the faintest idea how Eora's magicks worked, but he'd be ready with his sword if it didn't go to plan.

They waited, Eora in the common room, Geth in an empty second floor chamber with a view of the street out front. His fist clenched and unclenched on the hilt at his waist, recalling how Brega had sold him out, the scorn and jealousy of her other bodyguards, the ridicule of Clydon, her master-at-arms. A slingstone from Phelan had served that bastard his just desserts, but the lady, she had something coming.

He thought of Hadean and the army back home. They'd be tightening their belts by now, if they hadn't turned to plundering the countryside already. That wouldn't endear the king to anyone once he'd won back the throne. No, this once, what Geth wanted and what needed to be done coincided perfectly.

The appearance of a party on horseback down the street signaled Brega's arrival. Geth studied the toughs she'd brought along. Two ahead of her and three behind—one man short of the half-dozen Geth had expected. The lady herself rode side-saddle on a snow-white mare, the same severe expression on her face as always, the same tight bun atop her head. The first of her bodyguards stepped inside the inn, came back out to give a nod, and the rest of the party began to dismount.

Geth hurried downstairs to listen from the landing of the stairway at the back of the common room. Eora had closed the place for the afternoon, clearing out the whole staff just in case. Melagus stood in as her one servant. He wanted to listen in as bad as Geth evidently, and he assured Eora he could deliver a few mugs of tea as efficiently as anyone.

"...so gracious of you to come all this way, my lady," Geth heard Eora saying as he crouched at the bend of the steps, just out of sight. He risked a glance around the corner. Best he could tell, three of the toughs had joined Brega, the other two out front with the horses, keeping watch.

"It's always a good idea to kick a brick or two," the lady said. "You've kept the place running well enough thus far, but I need see the asset itself before I extend the loan."

"Never missed a payment, have I, my lady?"

Brega didn't answer, the old bitch. Geth eased a few steps back up the stairs as he heard a chair scoot back. She'd wander the common room, he expected, eyes drinking in all they could in the dim light provided by a pair of lamps and the two large front windows. She hadn't come here for nothing.

"Where are all the wenches?" Geth heard Brega ask over the noise of chairs scooting back into place. He imagined Eora dipping her head respectfully across the table.

"I've closed for a few hours to properly receive you, my lady. I've sent all my people home except one." She clapped her hands. "Mel!"

Geth heard the sound of the door to the kitchens opening behind the bar, then footsteps, and the jangle of spoons in earthenware mugs. Melagus would be bringing in the tea.

"Chamomile," Eora's voice said. "Just the smell of it does wonders."

The noise of footfalls receded, Melagus turning back the way he'd come. Brega spoke as the door to the kitchens squealed open and shut. "So, to work. We're talking about no small amount of debt, Eora. You want to make improvements to the place?"

"Yes, my lady."

"The facility seems adequate for the unwashed sort in these neighborhoods."

"The guestrooms are quite bare, my lady. And I'd like to lay down my own barrels of wine."

"Enterprising." A spoon clinked as someone stirred a cup. "Risky as well, considering the sum you're asking. But if you would like to put the place up as collateral, I'm sure things will all work out."

Geth felt his lip curl.

He'd spent enough time working for Brega to recognize the trap she'd laid. The hook was set now, or so she thought. Her plan was to give Eora as much line as it took, as much coin, to wear her out with the payments until she could reel the younger woman in without a fight and take the inn for herself.

The cups clinked again, and Eora started to hum. What Brega didn't know, greedy bitch, was that she was the one being hooked. The room fell silent except for Eora's soft, breathy hum. Geth felt his mouth relax. He'd sat down dreamily on the steps before he realized what was happening.

"Bloody magicks."

He shook his head, pinched himself, then risked a few steps down, ducking to get a view of the common room. Through the spindles of the banister, he saw Brega, frozen over her tea, transfixed. Eora's eyes were closed, lips too, as she hummed. Steam wafted up from the teacups, silver and gold in the lamplight.

Brega's three bodyguards stood slack-jawed beside her. Geth descended another few steps, peered down the length of the room and out toward the other two outside. They stood there with the horses, chatting, seemingly unaffected.

"How does it smell, Brega?" Eora said softly.

Brega's mouth barely moved. "It's nice," she mumbled.

It had worked on the four inside, but the pair out front would have to be handled. Eora must have been thinking the same thing. Her eyes opened and reached out to take the lady's hand.

"Why don't you invite your friends inside for some tea? Mel will see to the horses."

Brega rose obediently. Eora walked just behind her, humming softly from over her shoulder. At the door, the lady motioned them in. Eora turned to make way for the pair of them to enter and it was then Geth saw that she was carrying those two mugs of tea.

"Must be in the steam," he muttered.

Sure enough, the two of them moved with a dream-like lethargy until Eora had led them all back around the table. *Gods all be damned, she's done it!* Geth was nearly to the bottom of the stairs when a set of hinges squealed behind him to admit a man with a cudgel through the back door.

A sixth bodyguard. Geth swore. He didn't have time to back up the stairs before the man's eyes fell on him.

"You!" he snarled. "Awer's crooked cock!"

"Clydon?"

CHAPTER NINETEEN

Geth's sword rasped out of its sheath, but the master-at-arms had already fled back out the door. Startled noises sounded behind the big warrior as he dashed after him in pursuit.

Clydon didn't get far. He'd already been past his prime when Geth had fled, but Phelan's slingstone seemed to have given him a limp as well. Still, the old bastard whirled in time to parry Geth's swing with his cudgel, the force of it knocking him down to one knee.

"Wait!"

Clydon raised both hands. He was a sorry piece of shit, old and half-broken, but he was still one of the meanest cunts Geth had ever met. Ignoring that cry for mercy, he drove his blade straight through the bastard's sternum. With a twist, it came free. He didn't have time to savor the moment, much as he wanted to. He turned and sprinted back to the inn.

It was hard to make out details in the dim interior after the bright daylight behind the inn, but there was no mistaking the gleam of bared steel. Eora's voice had risen from a quiet hum to a wordless, almost frantic, keening, her face pinched up as she struggled with her magicks. Geth wasn't taking any chances. In a few strides he was among the five bodyguards clustered around Eora's table, hacking at the first with a vicious swing.

That was the wrong thing to do. Blood sprayed the lot of them as Geth's sword connected, and Brega's mug fell from her hand, shattering with a crack as Eora's spell shattered as well. The other bodyguards shouted almost in unison as the first man went down. Eora screamed, Brega shrieked, and a brawl like few others in Geth's life unfolded.

A straight thrust came at him over the twitching body of the first tough, Geth twisting to avoid it. His momentum took him into the side of the table where Eora and Brega sat, bowling over furniture and women alike. He couldn't spare more than a glance for them, feet catching in the table legs, but he managed to keep upright, backpedaling out of the way before the next blow could land.

The four toughs still standing raised swords and clubs as Brega—all fifty pounds of her—sprang on top of Eora with a nasty curse.

"Ahhh!"

"Turian dog!" one of her toughs spit, recognizing Geth at last. They fanned out, teeth bared. Geth didn't wait, dropping the long, unwieldy blade in his hand to hurl the first chair he found right down the center of them.

More curses followed, but that chair bought Geth time. Some kind of crockery crashing against the wall beside one of the bodyguards offered another distraction, drew yet more expletives. The curses turned to howls when Geth grabbed the edge of a table, turning it sideways to catch as many of the bastards as possible as he pushed it across the floor like a huge broom, sweeping them back, until one leg caught a snag and the whole thing flipped over.

"Geth!"

Brega was on top of Eora, battering at her with those thin hands. But the crash of more crockery hitting the walls and the threat of the four men in front of the big warrior were all he could handle. Three of them had been backed off by that table. The last came at Geth with a long-handled club. A bowl of some kind hit him across the shoulder and Geth sprang in with a straight jab to knock the scratch stright back to the seat of his pants.

The same table Geth had pushed into his enemies came screeching across the floor at *him*. They drove it longways like a battering ram and Geth sidestepped to let it pass. But that wedged him up against the bar, his attackers within arm's length, he himself weaponless. The closest man lifted a short sword. Geth reached behind himself, over the counter, for something, anything.

"Here!" Melagus voice sounded.

A heavy, roundish weight hit the big warrior's palm and he raised it just in time to meet the swing. Glass and spirits showered the pair of them as the bottle of spirits in Geth's hands exploded with a deafening crack.

"Look out!" Melagus cried.

Still wedged between the table and the bar, Geth turned, barely dodged the swing of another tough. The man's sword missed, hit the wood of the bar and stuck, leaving the bastard cursing as he tried to yank it free. Geth threw out his right hand to clutch the man's wrist, holding the bodyguard in place to meet the haymaker he swung with his left. It connected with a meaty thud, sending the bastard spinning, away and down.

The man with the club was up again by then, the swordsman with liquor all over him recovered as well. They came at Geth from both sides, but he dropped like a gopher into his hole, down below the table, scurrying out from underneath toward the side where he'd punched the third tough out. Scrambling over the man's groaning form, he saw his sword on the ground ahead of him. With a lurch, he grabbed it, rolled to one side, and came up to his feet in a crouch.

The brawl was over, the battle just begun. Geth couldn't spare a glance for the women, not with Brega's two bodyguards facing him and a third about to rise. Fortunately, the big warrior's reputation must have preceded him. Or maybe it was the fact that the toughs were down a man already with nothing to show for it. They hesitated, looked from one to another.

It was only a matter of time before one of them ran for it though, alerted the others. If that happened, Geth knew their plan would have failed, it would all have been for nothing. The whole of Brega's little army would descend on them in the space of an hour. There was no winning against those odds.

"C'mon, you cowards!"

Geth went for the man to his right first, slashing wide to steer him toward the bodyguard next to him. Brega's tough parried the blow, but Geth had succeeded in bunching him into his fellow. The timely streak of a bottle through the air distracted the first man and Geth's next thrust caught him under an upraised arm.

"Agghhh!"

With a cry, he collapsed. Geth aimed a downward cut at the bodyguard behind him, knowing full well the third man would try to circle behind him, but at least he'd be moving away from the front door and escape. A raised club caught the blow, cracked in the process, taking the force out of it. Footsteps behind Geth made him whirl before he could finish the man.

A second club was already in motion by the time Geth saw it, but his sword was up, taking the swing in an arm-shuddering parry that split the weapon clean in half. Off-balance, the tough behind the club fell right into Geth's arms. Geth turned a circle, shoved him into his fellow, then freed his sword for an overhand chop.

The low ceiling came to the two bodyguards' rescue, thwarting Geth's attack as the blade struck the beams overhead. The one clubman disentangled himself from the other, but the big warrior managed a slash at the first while he was still scrambling to snatch up the sword of his fallen companion. The swing opened up a red gash in the side of his neck, blood hissing out in a red mist, then spurting as the wound tore itself open.

"Geth!" someone cried.

The other clubman had flanked him. Before he could turn, the noise of another bottle shattering made him flinch, cool liquid and glass shards showering down the back of his shirt. Geth turned. Behind him, the last of Brega's bodyguards raised a hand to his head, teetered over with impossible slowness, liquor and glass in his beard and all down his face.

Geth looked up to find Melagus standing crazy-eyed behind the bar, panting, yet another bottle poised in a raised hand. Seeing the final tough fall, he dropped his arm, slumped unceremoniously against a column.

"Eora..." Geth breathed.

Down on the floor, among the broken shards of crockery and splinters of furniture, the innkeep sat beside Brega, holding her close in her lap like a child. She'd started humming again, but from deep in her chest this time. Geth blinked, shook his head and looked away before her magicks could take hold.

Maybe the steam *was* the key. Brega didn't go down so easily this time. Her jaw clenched as she tried to pull away, but Eora held on tight, hummed even louder. The lady whimpered and mewed like a crying babe. Geth felt *something*—he couldn't say what—and at last Brega went limp. The room fell silent except for the weak scrape of a dying man's boots on the floor and Geth's heavy breathing.

Eora's wide eyes found him. "We weren't supposed to kill anyone. What have you *done?*"

"Outside," Geth mumbled. "Clydon. We were made. I—"

"You killed these men right here in my common room."

"I'm sorry, Eora. I had no choice."

"I don't kill, Geth. I *heal*."

The big warrior heaved a sigh, turned, leaned down to wipe his sword on a dead man's tunic. That way he didn't have to meet her accusing gaze. He stood straight, sheathed the weapon, and chose his words.

"You didn't kill anyone, Eora. I did. But believe me, these men had it coming."

Eora left Brega seated on the ground, stood, found a chair and sank into it. She looked at the lady, sitting there slack-jawed, a dab of blood on one cheek. Eora must have been having a good long think about all the evil the old woman had done over the years, Geth reckoned. When she looked back at him, she only nodded.

"Maybe we've done a good thing. Brega's still alive after all."

Melagus shuffled to the front door, peeked outside, then barred it. He looked down at the sprawled bodies, twisted his lips. "Perhaps I was a fool not to expect as much."

Geth frowned but held his tongue. Melagus looked from Eora to Brega. He stepped closer until he stood over the moneylender, waving a bony hand slowly in front of her face.

Brega may have been alive, but you almost couldn't tell. Whatever Eora had done, it had wiped away far more than the memory of a few debts. Her head turned slowly toward Melagus. She never blinked.

"Is she..." Geth started to ask. "Will she...?"

Eora, closed her eyes, rubbed her temples. "I don't know."

Whatever the future held, for the present, Geth reckoned Brega had been shocked right through, reduced to a simpleton, or something like it. "Better than she deserves," he muttered.

"I lost concentration," said Eora. "Pushed too hard. I think I took away everything, made a child of her again."

Geth frowned. "You're a healer. Is it beyond you to bring her back?"

Eora blinked, matched that frown.

"No." Geth said, answering his own question. "Why would we want to wake the monster?"

Eora raised a finger. "I won't have her harmed. She can stay here, at the inn. Maybe I can mend her enough to be of service. Now that I think of it, it's a mercy really, isn't it? To take away memory of all the evil she's done, let her live out her days in innocence?"

"Truly," Melagus agreed.

Geth stepped closer to rest a hand on the innkeep's shoulder. "You're a good person, Eora." *Too good for the likes of me,* he thought.

Thankfully, Phelan arrived breathless through the back door before an uncomfortable silence could settle in. "There's—" He skidded to a halt, eyes on the bodies, and hooked one thumb in the direction he'd just come from. "I was gonna tell you there's a dead man in the alley."

"It's Clydon," Geth told him. "And you're just in time to help clean up."

Phelan didn't argue. One by one, they hauled each of Brega's bodyguards to the stable. The stalls were crowded with seven new horses and six dead riders, but Eora didn't complain. Phelan relayed how things went at the manse while the four of them scrubbed blood from the floors.

"You were right," he told Geth. "I had to set fire to the place after all. I don't think it really took, but her records didn't survive. Of that, I'm sure."

"So, it's really done?" Eora asked. "Is the Golden City free of the Lady Brega once and for all?"

Melagus raised a finger. "Most importantly, will it be enough to help Gahalus sway his mother?"

"I'll go find him now," Phelan said, straightening from the floor.

He left out the back, the way he'd come. Geth hadn't asked about the lady's steward, Yoric, but the scribe would probably wet himself if he so much as saw the mansion in flames. With no records, no master-at-arms, and no Brega herself, Geth couldn't see how her moneylending empire could do anything but collapse.

Melagus set down his rag and blew out a sigh. "I should check in with a contact as well, get a message to Rondah. We'll need her ship if all goes to plan."

"Be careful," Geth said.

Melagus followed Phelan out the door. Geth realized that left just himself and Eora to deal with six dead bodies and a blood-splattered room. He picked up Melagus's rag, muttering a curse.

"Don't worry," Eora said. "I'll send for my staff. They'll help."

"They have experience dumping bodies?"

"They'll do whatever I ask."

"You don't think they'll go straight to the watch?"

"I heal people, Geth. But I also *help* them. There's more to the Oak and Hart than you know. This is a safe place."

"Are you saying it's some kind of a front?"

Eora frowned. "It's still an inn. You of all people know what a hot meal and cool drink can do for someone in need."

"Of course." Geth met her eye, offered a smile. "So, helping people, just like back in the Lows, eh? I'll never forget that I owe you my life, Eora."

She brushed that off. The cook and stableboy did, indeed, return. Eora even coaxed Brega into sweeping for her. They locked up the stable and the common room was soon tidy enough for the evening's business. After nightfall, they'd use a wagon to haul away the bodies, it was decided. In the meantime, they waited for Melagus and Phelan to return.

Geth sat in the shadows, watching Eora work as her customers floated in one by one. There were plenty of regular customers, come for a bowl of broth and an ale. Or wine and bread and cheese. But there were women with children clutching at their legs, oldsters, a cripple, even a drunk beggar.

That one got a cup of tea and a broom. Others took a meal, or a room for the night. The cripple received a poultice for his foot. But it was the touch of Eora's hands as she wrapped it up that really did the trick, Geth reckoned. His limp wasn't half as bad on the way out.

Melagus returned through the front door. "Rondah will be ready. Now it's up to Gahalus. And Phelan."

The little man arrived soon after. His face was flushed from more than just the Paellian heat.

"What is it?"

"Watchmen. I lost them, but it was a close one."

"Gahalus?"

Phelan nodded. "It's done. Pack up, boys. We meet him in the Lion's Den tonight."

———†———

They left under the cover of dark, hoods pulled over their heads, eyes scanning the streets for watchmen. The prince had told Phelan he would see them directly to the queen. He'd spoken on their behalf already, but he also promised to join them and lend his support when they met her.

"It's risky," Geth said as they walked. "You said it yourself, Melagus; King Elius might be more inclined to murder the three of us than change his position, sweep it all under the rug."

"And the queen is even worse," Phelan put in.

The counselor marched in between them, that sour twist firmly on his lips. "All true. And I've heard nothing from Amagoras Cupbearer. We must assume he's made no headway."

"Are we sticking our heads inside a noose then?" Geth asked.

Melagus answered as he walked. "If the prince has done nothing else, the mere fact that he knows of our mission is a boon. Who else knows? That's what Elius will ask himself. Would he risk killing the envoy of a Sworn Realm if his court might find out? It would certainly make him think twice."

Geth took some consolation from that. They made the distance to the citadel within the hour, untroubled by footpads and thieves, only dodging watchmen once. They arrived at the same side gate they'd used before. The same lad received them, leading them up the same stairs, through the same garden, past the same colonnade, lit grey by a bright moon this time.

But Geth had that feeling of being watched again. The boy left them at a different door just down the hall from the other, knocking once before retreating the way he'd come.

An elderly porter opened it, but the lamp-lit chamber within was empty except for a few cushioned chairs, a couch, and table with a tray of fruit and wine. He motioned them inside. "The queen shall join you."

He bowed. Melagus copied the gesture, followed a breath later by Phelan and Geth. But one look around the place gave the big warrior a bad feeling.

"At least there's a back door," he muttered, noting the exits. He glanced at the fruit but didn't dare touch it. His reflection stared back at him from a wide-brimmed wash bowl set up beside a lamp on a sideboard.

A good half an hour passed. That fruit and wine started looking good.

"Where is the prince?" Melagus asked.

"He'll be here," said Phelan.

"What if he isn't?" Geth plucked a grape, sniffed it, and set it down with a frown.

"He will. He's not a liar."

"Alright, but what if she betrayed him? What if we've—"

The door creaked and the prince came in, all long limbs and wild hair like Geth remembered, Tham right behind him. That roguish smile was nowhere to be seen though. He looked about as tense as Geth felt.

"She'll be here in a moment," he said. "I've softened her up already. And let me assure you, this business with Brega made quite the impression."

"Then why do you look like you've shit your pants?" Geth said.

Melagus glowered at the big warrior.

"...er, my prince," Geth amended.

Gahalus smiled. "She's going to like you. That might be the thing that does it."

Geth exchanged a look with Phelan. Tham stepped closer, flicked a glance at Geth's sword and held out his hand. "I'm gonna need that."

"It will be a private meeting," the prince explained. "But your weapons will be right outside the door."

Tham offered a reassuring nod. No sooner had the big bodyguard stepped outside with Geth's sword and Phelan's dagger, than the queen appeared from the opposite door, in the back, embroidered gown flowing behind her, silver streaked proud through her dark hair.

"Here they are," she said with a predatory smile. "Just the men I've been looking for."

I'll bet you have. Geth kept those thoughts to himself and bowed alongside Phelan and the counselor.

"Yes, mother." That from Gahalus. "These are the men who humbled that overreaching moneylender, Brega. Half the city will thank them for what they've done."

"Yes, but it's a very expensive thing they ask of me now. Do you know the concessions Towdric has made to ensure our support? He's promised rare dyes, tin, and wheat at bargain prices. For years to come."

Melagus cleared his throat. "My queen, if you know anything about Towdric, you will know that he won't keep his word. He's already forsaken his oath to his king, has he not?"

"Perhaps. But what would he do with Umbel's wheat if he doesn't sell it to Pellon?"

"No doubt he'll send some to Ilia, try to secure a peace with the tribes. There are markets far to the west as well, through the ports at Isthmus."

The queen sauntered over to the table, poured herself a cup of wine, settled down lazily among the cushions of a couch. "He'd risk the ire of a sworn ally?"

"He'll send a shipload or two," Melagus made that famous sour face. "Just enough to keep up appearances. Then claim Umbel has run out of surplus. How could anyone contradict him? He might send a special shipment to Lord Ryrus or some other rival of King Elius, just to keep everyone off balance."

They weren't small accusations the counselor made, but Lyanne looked bored. She popped a grape in her mouth and closed her eyes. "Mmm."

"My queen," Geth said. "Forget bargains and promises. The only thing you need to know is that Towdric won't win. It's time to back the right horse, switch allegiances."

She opened her eyes, swung them toward the big warrior. "But he's winning now. And so shall he continue, as long as Pellon stands behind him."

Geth ground his teeth. He'd balked at roughing up Brega, but this once he wouldn't mind choking a woman. Just a little. Then again, he doubted her son would appreciate that. Or that it would work.

Melagus came to Geth's aid. He cleared his throat. "If I may be blunt, my queen," he said, voice dry. "You wouldn't have met with us if there wasn't something you stood to gain. Tell us what it is you want."

She smiled. Beneath that streak of silver hair, her eyes flashed in such a way that Geth had no doubt she was, indeed, a witch. She sat a little forward, not much, but enough to make it plain the counselor had her attention.

"Perhaps I merely wanted to see the men who took down the Lady Brega? That's no small feat for three men, all alone in a foreign land."

Melagus nodded. Lyanne's eyes were on Geth and Phelan, however.

What does she know, Geth wondered.

Gahalus knew plenty about him, that was certain. But had Palladine, or someone else, told her as much? Would the captain have dared repeat how Geth thwarted him, escaped from his prison, and burned his manor? Or did she have a network of spies and informants much like Melagus?

"You want our service," the counselor said finally. He dipped his head. "We are men of Umbel, sworn to King Hadean. But should you support him, we in turn would be indebted to aid you as a true friend and ally."

"*You* are a man of Umbel." She pointed a slender finger at Melagus. "These two, by rights, belong to Pellon. And me."

"What do you want?" Geth growled.

"A smart woman can think of many uses for a strong man." She flicked a glance to Phelan. "Or a clever, resourceful one. Stay. Serve me, and Pellon's ships, and all her soldiers, shall depart from your shores within a fortnight."

Geth felt his jaw tighten. He was reminded of Pythelle, what seemed an age ago, and her attempt to ensnare him. Was she lying? He'd swear anything to this woman, he decided, if it would help King Hadean. And he wouldn't hesitate to break those oaths either.

Phelan had already nodded and bowed. Geth pretended to think it through, playing hard to get, then followed suit a moment later.

The corner of Lyanne's mouth turned up, just a hair, but the expression never came near her eyes. "So be it." Her gaze flicked to the sideboard with the cleansing bowl. She looked back, smiled that dangerous smile, and rose from her seat.

"Then it is done." She sauntered over to pluck a few more grapes and started toward the back door again.

"And the king will abide by your decision?" Melagus asked.

"Of course he will."

She tilted her head, waited for them to bow, and waved her son to join her as she headed back out through the rear door. Gahalus flicked a glance and a nod back at them and Tham clapped Geth on the shoulder as he passed.

The door shut. "I don't like it," Geth said. "That was too easy."

"I agree." Melagus's eyes spoke more than the twist of his lips this once. This once, he looked scared.

But Phelan sucked a wedge of an orange, unconcerned. "You heard Gahalus the other night. If his mother likes to keep a scratch like Palladine for a pet, why not add the pair of us to her stable? Doing the dirty work of the high and mighty is our specialty."

Geth jammed several grapes in his mouth, cursed right through them. "Thram's balls, Phelan. Haven't you had enough of that sort of life?"

"What if we play the part just long enough for Hadean to be rid of Towdric?"

Melagus shook his head. "What if Lyanne is the one playing the part? What if she's playing her son as well? What does she know of you, Geth?"

The big warrior frowned. "Can't say for sure. But Gahalus knew a lot more than I thought he would."

"What if she had no interest in supporting Hadean at all? What if the whole purpose of this meeting was to serve you up to Palladine, her pet? Or take you off the board as a favor to Towdric?"

Geth frowned, tried to think that through, but a small noise from outside the door stole his attention. That feeling of being watched settled over him again. Could there be a peephole between the tiles of a mosaic on the wall? Phelan stood, frowning as well. As Geth's eyes skimmed over that wide bowl of water, a sudden realization hit him.

"Thram and bloody Awer."

Melagus's eyes widened. "What is it?"

"The water." Geth stepped across the room toward the sideboard to peer down at his reflection again. "Pythelle used something like this to communicate with the witch Sythme in Ilia. What if Lyanne's been using the same magicks to communicate with Pythelle all along?"

Melagus's eyes narrowed. "If she is, bending her allegiance to Hadean would require that she betray not only Towdric, and Palladine, but also a sister witch. I doubt—"

He didn't get to finish the thought. The door swung open and a good dozen watchmen crowded into the room, blades already drawn.

CHAPTER TWENTY

Geth recognized the one in the lead from their first meeting with the king and queen. *Lyanne's man.* There was no mistaking the hard set of his jaw. Geth had positioned himself behind the table with the fruit and he slid one hand under the lip, ready to heave. The other moved to the tray with the grapes. *Like this is a bloody food fight.* The gods had to be falling over laughing.

But behind Geth, the door at the rear cracked and a familiar voice filtered through. "Lights out, Wolf!"

Ratcher?

Geth's eyes widened, then shut hard. He flung that table with both hands. The tray of fruit went flying with it as something dusty whooshed past his cheeks. Men swore, cried out. Geth fumbled, one hand out, searching for Phelan, but a strong grip yanked him backward.

"This way!"

Ratcher again. Geth twisted, swung a haymaker, missed, stumbled, and almost fell. No blade struck him though, no fist or boot. Those hands grabbed him again and hauled him toward the rear door. "C'mon, damn it!"

"Wait!" Geth cried. "Phelan! Melagus!"

"No time!"

They were through the door in a breath. Geth heard it click shut. Ratcher pulled him down some sort of hall at a run. Geth's face had begun to burn from what had to be more of the assassin's blinding dust.

A dozen steps down the hall, he risked opening his eyes, pulled Ratcher to a halt. "Give me a sword, I'm going back!"

"They're already gone. Escaped, gods willing."

"Escaped?"

"Gahalus said he would get them out."

"What if he failed?"

"No time to find out, Wolf. This is the palace. There's gonna be lilies all over the place in a matter of seconds."

True to Ratcher's words, a troop in white tabards rounded a bend down the torchlit hallway and started their way. Heavy footfalls echoed off marble floors. "There!" one of the soldiers shouted. Ratcher threw his shoulder into a door to his left, grabbed Geth, and crashed into a room full of young ladies.

A few of them screamed. An older woman hugged a book against her chest like a shield, opened her mouth to protest. But they were already through the opposite door and out into the night before she could breathe. Tall columns ran in a row, supporting a long portico against the side of the building. Geth recognized the gallery to the south of the great hall, the heart of the Lion's Den.

Ratcher led the way from those heights down the great central stairs toward the Leonine Gate and Cistern Plaza beyond. More lilies appeared ahead.

"This way!" Geth cried. A soldier of Pellon himself once, he remembered filing in from narrow lanes on either side. He chose the left side, angling toward the sea wall, the quickest way out. But another troop of lilies appeared ahead of them before they could reach the wall.

Ratcher drew his sword.

"Give me that," Geth said.

The assassin didn't hesitate. "All yours. Just don't kill me afterwards."

The lane was narrow. For all their numbers, the soldiers ahead could only come at him two at a time. Geth raised his blade and screamed. Fear lit the eyes of his enemies as he charged, but with more of their fellows coming up behind them, there was nowhere to run.

A sweeping cut knocked the first lily's blade aside and a boot into the chest drove him back into his fellows. The man to his right had turned to claw his way backward but an overhand chop with Ratcher's sword dropped him like a sickly ox. Someone darted a thrust over the head of the man Geth had kicked. He caught it on the upswing, sending a second kick into the poor bastard in front and crumpling him and the man behind him as they got tangled up. Geth backpedaled and lifted his guard, but the rest of the soldiers had already turned to run.

Ratcher dodged past Geth to finish the two men on the ground with the lightning-quick swipe of a dagger at each man's neck. Blood sprayed Geth across the face but he didn't reckon it would be there long.

"Follow me!" he yelled. "To the sea!"

Ratcher sprinted behind him. "You're crazy!"

"I know!"

The lane ended at a ladder going up. Geth hurried to the top. Ratcher arrived panting behind him a second later. They stood facing a long wall of merlons, the southern parapet of the citadel running to the right and left. Men with torches appeared to either side, shouting. He handed the sword back to Ratcher and climbed up between the stones.

"Gods all be damned," Ratcher muttered.

Geth looked down. Moonlight gleamed on dark waters below. "Can you swim?"

"Jump already you crazy bastard!"

———†———

Sometime after midnight, they arrived dripping and cursing in a decayed building near Neyna's Square. Ratcher waved Geth to follow over collapsed beams and crumbled walls. The whole place stank of shit. The assassin pulled back a canvas curtain to reveal a cave-like hole in the rubble at the rear. A faint orange glow emanated from the tiny room. Once inside, Ratcher fumbled in a corner until he'd drawn back the shutter of a lantern.

"This is Blacksheep's lair?" Geth asked. A bedroll rested to one side, a pack and a few supplies to the other. That was it.

"Long story."

Ratcher dug through the pack until he produced a half-empty skin, and a loaf of bread wrapped in cloth. Geth had already sunk to the seat of his pants against one wall. The assassin tore the bread and offered him a half.

"It's not poisoned." Ratcher took a bite himself, sat against the opposite wall and chewed. "I hate poison."

Geth grunted. The way the man's jaw worked, it may not have been poisoned but it was certainly stale.

"What's in the skin?" he asked.

Ratcher took a swig, smiled. "The last of my Ilar berry wine. Now that's something I'll miss."

Geth grumbled a curse. He bit into the stale bread and accepted the skin to wash it down with some of the Ilar drink. This once, after all they'd been through, it wasn't so bad.

"What an escape, eh?" Ratcher's pudgy face cracked in that smile again. "I'm not gonna lie, I don't usually take chances like that, but hey, we made it out alive."

"Sure," Geth snorted. "You gonna tell me why though? What the hell is going on? Why the hell am I drinking wine all friendly next to you all of a sudden?"

"We'll get to that."

"What about Phelan and Melagus then? We just bloody left them back there. You really trust Gahalus to save them?"

Ratcher blew out a sigh. "Didn't have a choice."

"What if the prince was part of the set up?"

"He wasn't. He didn't know his mother planned to betray you."

"But *you* knew." Geth watched the assassin for tells.

"I did. Because I've been tracking you for weeks. And the queen's been tracking you as well, for almost as long. Once I was sure she'd decided to take you out, I knew she was never gonna change her mind. But that was a good effort, the arm wrestling and all, trying to get Gahalus to convince her."

Geth's eyes narrowed. "How did you know...? Wait, you were there?"

Ratcher nodded. "But I needed to speak with you alone. I couldn't risk you outing me. Or worse, trying to kill me."

Geth rubbed at his temple. It was almost too much to think about all at once. Ratcher, Gahalus, the fate of Phelan and Melagus...

"Don't worry, I'm about to explain," Ratcher said, reading Geth's mind. He took another pull at the skin and offered it back.

The big warrior snatched it with a scowl, drained it to the last. "Well?"

"I need your help."

Geth watched Ratcher's face. He was serious. Geth couldn't help himself. He started laughing.

"I know, who would have thought?" Ratcher shrugged. "It's a long and twisty story."

"Let's hear it."

Ratcher took the wineskin back, frowned at it and set it aside. He wiped his hands on his pants, exhaled a long breath.

"Well, you realize by now that Elius has sided with Towdric, however thin his claim on the throne. And you know that Lyanne wants you dead. What you *don't* know is that the pair of them tried to murder King Hadean as well."

"Their own sworn ally? Taking sides with Towdric wasn't bad enough?"

"Everyone isn't as loyal as you, Wolf. What can I say?"

"How does King Elius and all this circle back to a certain assassin?" Geth asked. "You already told me you were hired to kill me by Palladine and no one else."

Ratcher dipped his head. "Aye. With Lyanne's blessing. Not that she cared much about you either way. It was all about Palladine getting even. But the job on Hadean, that was a careful plot, hatched by Towdric, with the help of Elius and Lyanne."

"I reckon this is where it gets grimy," Geth said.

Ratcher grinned.

"They wanted you to do it," Geth surmised, "but you didn't fancy killing Hadean, did you?"

"You've got some wits in there after all."

Geth ignored that. "It would have been a dangerous job. And that's not what you came to Umbel for. Much harder thing, to kill a king, than to knock off some sword-toting mercenary like me."

"There was more to it all than that." Ratcher leaned forward, eyes intent. "For one thing, they said it had to be at the wedding, take out as many of Hadean's people as possible, innocents be damned. *A wedding!* That's not why I got in this business."

"Wait, I saw you at the wedding. *In* the cook's tent."

"I'll get to that." Ratcher lifted the skin, sucked out a few drops, and sighed. "As I was saying, I wouldn't do it. The mighty king and queen of Pellon didn't appreciate that."

"They wouldn't, would they? Sonsabitches."

"They came after me. I'd taken half the payment up front. And, they couldn't let it be known that the king of a Sworn Realm had signed off on another king's murder, could they?"

"I reckon they couldn't."

"They already had a couple of other assassins in Umbel, but they sent for the Frog as well. He came at me with all he had. Now that pissed me off. I hate the Frog, more than I can tell you.

"But, to make a long story short, the Frog had to leave me be and concentrate all his efforts on Hadean and his wedding. The day loomed closer. And what was I, after all, but an inconvenience? For my part, I decided to hell with Palladine's contract—he's Lyanne's pet anyway—so I was off your tail even if you didn't know it. My plan was to thwart the Frog, stick it to the lot of 'em."

"But the cook—"

"Yeah, I know what it looked like. I got there late. It took me a while to figure it all out, that's all. And that's how they had time to get the poison into the figs and wine. I was looking for the Frog, you see. But it was his apprentice that did the deed, a man I didn't recognize until it was too late."

"That was the dead man in the tent?" Geth surmised.

"Yes. But I was too late. Thank the gods for that old soldier. I did manage to run the Frog out of town though. Hadean's in no danger of him, thanks to me."

Geth did his best to digest all that. Ratcher had killed the poisoner and tried to save King Hadean? And it was Elius and Lyanne behind it all? Just as much as Towdric? How far back did their dealings go? He rubbed his temples. He wished they had more wine. Berry or otherwise.

"Alright, so Elius, Lyanne, Palladine—they all double-crossed you," Geth said. "That still doesn't explain why you're helping me, except that you say you need my help. Why in the name of the gods would I help you?"

Ratcher had the decency to look sheepish. "We've had our moments, Wolf. I can't deny it. But we've had some good times too. Like when I marched with the dozen. And tonight! That was fun. If you're honest, between this night and the wedding, I've actually saved your life twice now."

"Still doesn't explain what you could possibly want from me."

Ratcher forced a nervy smile. "I need your help, Wolf. Because of what I did for Hadean back in Umbel, there's a contract on me now. And every assassin left in Pellon wants a piece."

CHAPTER TWENTY-ONE

Geth just looked at Ratcher.

"Thram's hairy, twisted, stinking..." He shook his head, ground his teeth. But the curses kept coming. "Puss-infected, disease-dripping, twisted-ass bollocks! Gods all be damned man! If the watch is already after me, why would I want you drawing all those assassins to me as well?" He stood to leave.

Ratcher jumped up. "Listen to me, Wolf! You know your way around this town, and maybe there's a small chance you can get out of here even with all the watch and half the lilies after you, true enough. But what about Hadean? Elius and Lyanne tried to kill him. Are you gonna let that stand?"

"I may just take a stab at killing them on my way out."

Ratcher shook his head. "That's not the way to do it. Unless you want to touch off a war."

"Why not?"

"Look at those tattoos." He flicked a glance at Geth's arms. "Everyone knows you're Hadean's man. If you go after the king and queen, the problems Hadean has now will be nothing compared to what's coming."

Ratcher was right. Geth uttered more curses. Pellon had the army, the navy, and the lack of virtue—evidently—to squash Hadean's reign. Especially now, with Towdric's insurrection weakening his hold on the realm.

"Once I find Phelan and Melagus, I'm headed back to Umbel. I'll deal with Elius and Lyanne later, like you said."

"Let me help you."

"You're a marked man, Ratcher. How can *you* help *me?*"

"They'll be coming after you before long too. If they aren't already."

"I'm going my own way."

Ratcher tried to take Geth by the arms, but he shook him off. "Alright, do what you like. But once they kill me, do you think Elius won't send those same assassins back to finish Hadean?"

Geth glared at him.

"Could you live with yourself if you made it all the way back to Umbel only to bring Hadean's murderer on your heels?"

"I can protect him."

Ratcher spread his hands. "What better way to protect him than to deal with those bastards here, in the Golden City, with an assassin of your own up one sleeve?"

"Thram and bloody Awer."

He had a point.

———————

Geth needed sleep. Ratcher could have killed him long ago if he'd wanted to, so he figured there was no risk in it. In fact, the assassin was snoring before Geth had closed his eyes himself. Geth looked at that baker's body, blocky head, chubby cheeks. He should have known the man would be a snorer.

Geth was stirred awake by Ratcher's return through the cave-like entrance sometime later. The big warrior rubbed his eyes. He hadn't even heard him leave, but under the assassin's arm rested a satchel he didn't have before.

"What's that?"

"Breakfast." Ratcher winked. "And some other stuff. We'll need a disguise now that the watch is looking for us. If we want to move out in the open, anyway."

He upended the sack. Geth pulled his attention from the wheel of cheese and loaf of bread that fell out to take stock of everything else. A bundle of clothes, leather arm bracers, a few odd bottles. And a razor.

"We'll have to shave both our heads," Ratcher said. "I have a black robe for myself, a leather apron for you."

"So, you're going to be a cleric of Vorda and I'm a blacksmith?"

He nodded. "Fitting, don't you think?"

"I could have been the cleric. Do you know how many men I've sent to the Dark Lady's halls?"

"Droves, I'm sure." Ratcher snorted a laugh. "But you're a hack, my friend. Myself, I'm an *artist*."

Geth rolled his eyes. It made sense though. A big man like himself would play the part of blacksmith well. He shucked out of his bloodstained tunic and pulled the fresh one on over his chain shirt. The only problem was the elbow-length sleeves.

"Here," Ratcher said, tossing over one of the bottles.

Geth caught it out of the air. "What is it?"

"Face paint, the kind the ladies use. For your arms. Between that and the bracers, those tattoos won't show a bit. And once we shave your head and mustache, no one will look at you twice."

Geth smeared the concoction on and slid the bracers onto his wrists. Ratcher knew what he was about. The description of him would certainly include mention of the mustache and most importantly the tattoos. First thing a suspicious watchman would do is look to his arms. The disguise he'd be wearing, arms bared below the elbow, would rule him out with one glance.

"And now it's time to shave." Ratcher held up the razor.

Geth heaved a sigh, stroked his mustache. "I'm gonna miss this damn thing."

Ratcher motioned Geth to sit. "I don't know what you're complaining about." He started by sawing at the big warrior's shoulder length hair. "I'm the one who has to shave my eyebrows."

"Just carry the swords under your arm like you're making a delivery," Ratcher said when they finally prepared to leave. "Don't look anyone in the eye. Especially any watchmen."

"Not my first day on the job, Ratcher."

The assassin snickered. Closing the shutter of his lamp, they crawled out of his little lair and into a humid morning. Geth wiped sweat from the bumps on his shaved head, resisted the urge to scratch. An application of some sort of oil had helped, but not much. At least the assassin had a spare sword for him.

"I'm keeping one of these blades afterwards," Geth told him.

Ratcher motioned to the left and they set out, northward. A black-robed cleric of Vorda and a clean-shaven blacksmith soon joined the stream of laborers, housewives, beggars, shouting children, and stray dogs wending through Paellia's streets. At Geth's insistence, they would search for Phelan, Melagus and Gahalus—news of them at least—before anything else.

"We'll start at the garrison," Ratcher said.

"We're headed toward the palace." Geth frowned. "I hope you don't mean the garrison of the watch."

"That's exactly what I mean. We've got to rule out the possibility they didn't make it out."

Geth bit down a curse. They weren't dead. He wasn't even going to entertain the idea.

"What if some ball-scratch recognizes me? Or you for that matter?"

"Have faith in the Dark Lady." Ratcher smirked. "And her barber. You do look better without the mustache, by the way. That's a strong nose, but still."

"And you look like a freak. You do know it's only the zealots that shave *everything*?"

It did work though. Ratcher looked totally different. He hummed all the way to cistern plaza. They passed the still water and its basalt statues, the sun already beating down hard enough to put a shimmer of steamy air above the surface.

At plaza's end, the three arches of the Leonine Gate reared up before them, the series of stairs and the Lion's Den itself rising behind them. White-clad guardsmen eyed the pair sideways, but a pious bow from Ratcher got them halfway inside before one of the lilies caught Geth by the shirt sleeve.

"What about this one?" the young guardsman asked his sergeant. "He's no holy man."

Ratcher intervened, dipping that fresh-shaved head. "Apparently a few of your brothers departed for my mistress's realm last night."

"And?"

"Do you expect me to carry the bodies all by myself, child?"

The sergeant stepped over, looked Geth up and down. "I reckon you picked the right scratch for that job."

Geth shook his arm free. Beside him, Ratcher just set a hand across his heart and gave the lily that pious bow again. He looked like a real nut without his eyebrows. The young guardsman must have agreed. He spit to ward off evil and waved them through.

Ratcher aimed a wry smile at Geth. "Child's play."

They strutted past the stone lions to either side and entered Elius's stronghold.

Inside, they turned left, moving under the shadow of the ramparts. About halfway to the side gate Geth, Phelan, and Melagus had entered through the night before, they arrived at the garrison of the watch, a squarish edifice built into the curtainwall. It hummed with watchmen, gold-tasseled armbands everywhere. Beads of sweat ran unobstructed down Geth's head.

Ratcher made small talk with a few gold-bands, lamenting the death of the two guards he himself had killed. "Have the rites been performed then? What about the other bodies? Oh, it was only the two?" He made sure to address all the watchmen as "my child."

Geth breathed a sigh when a seasoned old watchman confirmed beyond a doubt that they only had two bodies awaiting rites.

"Anyone injured, my child?" Ratcher asked. "My prayers may yet be needed if someone else has been wounded. Or imprisoned."

The old boy shook his head and moved on. Ratcher snooped around the entrance to the dungeons for a time, but it soon became clear no new prisoners had been stowed away. He led them back out the Leonine Gate and past the wide cistern.

"Well, we can't be certain they haven't covered it all up, but there's a chance they're still alive."

"Escaped, gods willing."

"Then again, Lyanne might want to hide the bodies, cover her tracks."

Geth glowered at the assassin. "There's some things you oughta keep to yourself, you know that?"

"I'm only trying to eliminate possibilities. She's a devious woman, the queen."

Geth cursed her as they walked. "I could see her hanging on to Phelan and Melagus just to spite us, the nasty wench."

"Let's hope they escaped then."

But that begged a different question.

"What of Prince Gahalus then?" Geth asked. "He would know. She'd have to shut him up as well if she'd killed or captured my friends, wouldn't she?"

"Makes sense we ask him, doesn't it?"

"Damn right."

"Then follow me."

Geth marched after Ratcher in silence. They were alive, his friends. Period. He wiped more sweat off his head, cursed the assassin and his stupid disguise under his breath. He didn't ask where they were going though. He had no choice but to leave that to Ratcher.

They went in and out of several watering holes, but the prince couldn't be found in any of his usual haunts. By and by, Ratcher steered them back to the inn where Phelan had found Gahalus a few nights earlier. They took a seat in a corner. Geth kept his eyes down, just in case, as Ratcher moved piously toward the bar for a round of drinks.

"I threw out a couple hooks while I was up there," he said as he returned to take the seat across from Geth. "The prince hasn't been here today. But no one's whispering about anything suspicious either."

"So, what's next?"

"Next, we talk about assassins on our trail. You know, the people that will be trying to kill us?"

Geth set his tankard down harder than he intended. "Phelan and Melagus could be dead already."

"We're hoping they're not, aren't we? But if they *are* in Lyanne's clutches, you can't do anything for them—or King Hadean either—if some knifeman gets to you first."

"Fine. Let's talk with your...colleagues. What do we do?"

"Well, what we *don't* do is rush. We *think*." Ratcher tapped the side of his shaved skull. "For starters, we identify the marks."

"Well. I'd say it's you and me that are the marks, but I reckon in this case you mean the men who're coming for us."

"That's right."

"And who is that?"

"All of them."

Geth leaned back in his chair, muttered a curse. "So," he ticked off fingers. "The Claw, The Lordling, and Three. Cloak and Brickhouse. The Frog, Starling. And Snake Eyes. Weeping Willow too. Who am I missing?"

"That's a pretty good list. I'm impressed. But we can rule out a few of them."

Geth eyed Ratcher sideways.

"You know that I am the one that's called Blacksheep, right?"

"Sure."

"Well, to some clients I'm also known as the Lordling."

"What?"

Ratcher spared a glance to either side. No one was paying them any mind. "In this business, discretion is of utmost importance. Secrecy. Clients have been known to go after the assassin they themselves have hired, just to keep things hush."

"Tie off loose ends." Geth nodded. "Cold, but I reckon there's a logic to it."

"That's why I keep an ear to ground, operating as more than one contractor. See, if a client hires Blacksheep and then contacts the Lordling about eliminating me, that's valuable information. I have no choice but to terminate the relationship of course."

"And I thought being a sellsword was tough."

Ratcher blew out a sigh. "It's tiring, let me tell you. But at any rate, we can rule out the Lordling."

"How about the Frog?"

"Now there's a real worry. We'll have to deal with him most certainly. I'm not sure how just yet."

"Alright, well how about Snake Eyes? Or The Number Three. Should we start there?"

Ratcher shook his head. "Three's a legend."

"Is it true he kills a man three different ways?"

"He does. But some say the name comes from three special talents he has, like stealth, archery, and such. By my reckoning, truth be told, he's got more than three special skills at his call."

Geth frowned. "Well then how do we kill him?"

"We don't. As I said, his accomplishments are unmatched. Thankfully, he's been retired for years."

Geth mouthed a silent prayer.

"As for Snake Eyes," Ratcher went on, "they're back in Umbel."

"They?"

"You've met them. A pair of twins in the employ of Palladine."

Geth resisted the urge to spit. "I remember. We'll deal with them later, that's a promise."

"We could start with the Claw." Ratcher said. "Then again, maybe we should work up to that one."

"If you say so. How about Starling? What's his game?"

"She," Ratcher corrected. "Not that it's such a bad idea. You see, Starling is a markswoman, an archer without equal. She also works a sling at times, throwing knives, poisoned darts on rare occasion. What do they all have in common? She strikes from afar. You won't see her coming."

"We'll want to get to her before she gets to us, I reckon."

"You said it. But we've got time to deal with her. She'll take her time, you see. She'll need to set up, pick a nest, lay her trap. Better we start with something more pressing."

"Alright then, how about we start with Cloak?"

"Cloak." Ratcher rested his elbows on the table, steepled his finger to look over them at Geth with a grimace. "Well, you see, the thing about Cloak..."

It took Geth a moment to work it out. "Thram's balls, you're Cloak too, aren't you?"

Ratcher spread his hands, smiled ruefully. "Better safe than sorry."

Geth rubbed his temples. "What have I gotten myself into?"

He just wanted to go after Phelan and Melagus. But to what end? If King Elius was really behind the poisoning at Hadean's wedding, Geth had no doubt he would, indeed, try again before long. Helping Ratcher kill these assassins would at least buy Hadean time to deal with Towdric. They could circle back to Elius later.

"Alright," he said. "What about Weeping Willow? Should we start there?"

"I can't say I know much about that one. Except that she's some kind of enchantress. Or poisoner, perhaps. Some say she doesn't even exist. Let me think on that some more."

Geth waved at the barman for two more drinks. He sucked foam from the lip, waited for the man to leave. "Well, that leaves Brickhouse. Unless you're him as well."

Ratcher smiled. "Not a chance, not that bastard. A real slimy ball-scratch, Brickhouse. And as good a place to start as any."

Even with all his worry for his friends, his temples hurting and his scalp itching, Geth was hungry. Ratcher didn't let him eat though. They could take a meal at their next stop, he promised: Brickhouse's base of operation.

"It's a dumpy little drinking cellar," Ratcher said, "down near the wharves. I reckon he lives nearby. They call it the Rabbit Hole."

"Catchy." Geth walked beside him, adjusted those two sheathed swords held in his arms across his chest.

"He's not very clever, as contract killers go. It only took me a few weeks studying him to realize all correspondence led back through that place."

"Can we finish with him quick and get back to hunting for the others?"

"As soon as he shows his face."

By the time they arrived it was late afternoon. They weren't far from The Netmender's Daughter, the same ramshackle inn Geth had brought his friends to when they'd first arrived. He wondered if there would be time to sneak over for a plate of fried smelts before Brickhouse arrived. Ratcher squashed the idea.

"Get yourself something to eat at the Rabbit Hole," he said. "We need the time to draw him in. Make sure to ask about him."

"Should I make it like I want to hire him?"

"Here." Ratcher reached over to smear the makeup on the underside of Geth's forearms. The swirling tattoos immediately showed through.

"You sure that's a good idea?" Geth asked. They'd ducked into an alley but plenty of foot-traffic moved past just yards away.

"We're gonna make sure he knows exactly who's asking after him. He'll know Lyanne wants you dead."

"Then give me that rag. Let me clean it all."

Ratcher shook his head. "Just the bottoms, like it rubbed off and you didn't notice."

"This way he thinks I'm here on the sly, eh? Trying to get to him before he can get to me."

"Well, you are, aren't you?"

Geth had to smile. He passed one of the two swords he'd been carrying to Ratcher and checked the blade on the other. Razor sharp.

"Now that I think about it, if this scratch Brickhouse is so deadly, it doesn't seem like a wise thing to just sit there waiting for him, does it?"

"He won't just strike. There will be a distraction. Normally, you wouldn't see him until it was too late. The good news is, we know he's coming."

"And where will *you* be?"

"I'll be watching your back, making sure he doesn't slip your notice."

"Slip my notice? Sure."

Geth stalked out of the alley in the direction of the Rabbit Hole. A set of worn stone stairs led to a low door. It was a squalid little cellar. A man Geth's height had to enter bent-necked. A barman and a handful of winos looked up as he stepped inside. Geth made a show of surveying the rickety barrels that stood in for proper tables.

The barman grumbled something, but Geth's black-smith disguise seemed to be working. Instead of holding his sword, he'd thrust the sheath through his belt now. He chose a seat against a wall where he could see both the front door and the bar, in case there might be any arrivals from the rear.

With a wave, the flabby-jowled barman brought food and drink. Geth didn't have to fake a suspicious look as the man set down a thin soup and watery ale. Geth frowned as he dipped his spoon, thinking of those fried smelts a few doors down. He rested his elbows up on the barrel-top to display his half-covered tattoos as Jowls returned for the empty bowl.

"I hear this is the place to come if you need a house built," he told the man, voice low. "Is that right?"

"This is a tavern. No stonemasons here."

"What if I needed a *brick* house?"

The barman's eyes narrowed. They flicked to Geth's arms and quickly away, but it was clear he'd noticed. He pulled a towel from his waistband to wipe an imaginary puddle from the surface, buying time to think, Geth reckoned.

"I may be able to point you in the direction of one bricklayer," he said finally. He flashed a smile, revealing a mouthful of rotten teeth. "And I'll bring another ale, on the house."

Geth nodded. The slinking bastard disappeared behind the bar and didn't return with the drink for a good long while. When he did, he flashed that winning grin again, wiping the table with renewed vigor.

Geth waited. The soup had done nothing for his hunger and the ale only made him want to piss. He studied the hunched-over drunks best he could in the dim light, women and men, most of them sitting alone with short cups of harsh rye liquor or unwatered wine. Now and again, one of them staggered out or a new one staggered in. None of them looked dangerous.

Geth tried to imagine what sort of distraction Brickhouse might stir up. Ratcher ducked inside sometime later, his robes gone, dressed as a sailor in baggy breeches now, but he didn't acknowledge Geth as he sauntered up to the bar. The big warrior started to wonder how the man had dug up that outfit when a bedraggled couple tramped in, cursing each other roundly.

"Nutless bastard can't even buy a lady a drink," the woman said, a bony creature with the look of an aging, over-taxed whore. The scratch with her, a slack-jawed laborer judging by the dusty trousers, mouthed curses of his own.

This is it, Geth told himself. His hand closed on his hilt, and he scanned the room. A few of the regulars looked up, grinning as the insults flew back and forth. Movement flashed to the left and Geth caught sight of the barman himself rushing from behind the bar. Geth drew a few inches of steel, waited for him to close the space, but a thump and a cry behind the big warrior froze Jowls wide-eyed and mid-stride.

Geth spun, drawing his blade at last. A few stools away, Ratcher stood over a body sprawled in a growing pool of blood on the floor. A wicked looking dagger rested on the floor near the dying man's hand.

CHAPTER TWENTY-TWO

G eth blinked. "Son of a..."

He was smaller than Phelan, the dead man, with a weak jaw and long shock of womanly blond hair. Jowls still stood a few paces off, mouth agape, looking down at the dead assassin. Geth cuffed the old bastard across the face for good measure. He crumpled and the big warrior stepped over him to walk behind his bar and take the back exit out.

Ratcher met him in the alley. He fished around behind some crates and returned with his satchel. That black robe went over his head again and he tossed a loose-fitted tunic and a wide-brimmed hat to Geth.

"You're a farmhand now," he said.

Geth watched as Ratcher wiped blood off a knife with those sailor's breeches and left them on top of the crates. "I'm your gravedigger, let's say."

The assassin waved Geth to follow and they hustled away. Even at such a sordid hovel as the Rabbit Hole, the city watch would be along eventually. Geth flicked one glance over his shoulder before sheathing his sword.

"One down," he said. They slowed to an even pace. "Brickhouse, eh? More like 'Doll-house' I reckon."

Ratcher shook his head. "Who could have imagined? He pulled off some pretty big jobs, really made a name for himself."

"I have to admit, I was looking at the barman."

Geth motioned Ratcher down a side lane, toward the water. The sun had sunk below the rooftops, casting long shadows as night approached. It had been almost a day since Phelan and Melagus disappeared. Far too long.

"I have an idea," Geth said. "Melagus has contacts throughout the city. With any luck, he's already got in touch with one of them. You said yourself you've been tracking us for a while, did you happen to follow the old scratch, see anything?"

"You're asking if I know any of his contacts?"

Geth started to growl but he didn't get a chance before Ratcher winked.

"Well, I do."

"I never doubted you."

"After you dealt with Brega, both Phelan and the old snake slithered out, headed in different directions. I guessed that Phelan was headed for the prince, or perhaps simply to find some brothel for a roll. But Melagus, what was he after?"

"Thram's balls, Ratcher, just say it!"

"Well, I don't know. But he was definitely looking over both shoulders when he left. I followed him to an embroiderer's shop. They closed the doors and shutters, but he was inside for half an hour. And he didn't come out with new stitchwork, if you understand me."

"Let's go."

Ratcher led the way. It was across town, near the Oak and Hart, and it was fully night by the time they arrived. The chirp of crickets and the buzz of cicadas replaced the clamor of passersby, carts, shouting children, and barking dogs. Geth thought of Eora, decided her inn was the next stop if this embroiderer didn't turn anything up.

They stopped in front of the door. The shop was shut for the night, but the owner, no doubt, lived on the second floor. Geth could only hope the embroiderer was the contact himself, and not someone in his employ, a customer, or someone else.

He frowned, gave it a think. "Have you got anything green?" he asked Ratcher. "Anything at all?"

The assassin frowned, reached under his black cloak, digging around in his pockets. He pulled out a lot more odds and ends than Geth had suspected, unfolding a patch of cloth finally.

"How about this kerchief?"

Geth smiled. "Perfect."

Ratcher melted away, taking both of the swords with him. Geth didn't want to appear menacing at this late hour. The big warrior knocked on the door. He had to knock hard, for a long while too. A shutter swung open finally on the second story.

"Neyna's blessed light, what is it? The shop is closed!"

Geth stepped back from the front door to crane his neck up at the lean face of an elderly woman in the window. He mopped at his shaved head and face with the green kerchief. "I'm looking for a friend of mine. Little fellow, green cloak? He passed this way yesterday."

The woman rolled her eyes.

"Could we talk inside? This heat is turning me *green*."

"Enough!" She shook her head, still muttering. "By all the gods..."

The shutter closed. Footfalls sounded and the door to the shop cracked open. A slender hand waved Geth in.

A lantern glowed in the hands of the old woman, the embroiderer, unless Geth was mistaken. "And the Asp?" she asked, watching Geth's face.

"I didn't know anyone outside of Umbel knew his nickname."

"I take it you're his bodyguard, the local boy?"

Geth couldn't help but smile a little at that. "Sure. Have you seen him though? Has he passed any message through here since last night?"

The woman frowned. "He sent for the ship to meet him in Sorn. But that was yesterday afternoon. I assume he's already left."

Geth clenched his jaw but held in the curse.

"I see from your face that isn't the case." The embroiderer pursed her lips. "If he does come by, is there any message I should relay?"

"Just tell him I came looking for him," Geth said. He started to go but the woman caught him by the arm.

"King Hadean's people have gone silent as well. I should have had a pigeon from them by now. Maybe it's nothing."

But judging by her look, she didn't believe that herself. "Thank you," Geth told her.

She saluted, fist to heart, Umbel-style.

Geth caught up with Ratcher down the street. His pale, hairless brow and slick head seemed to float though the darkness, the rest of him invisible in his black robes. He fell in beside the big warrior.

"No luck I take it."

Geth grunted. "We may as well check in with Eora while we're out this way."

"Eora?"

"At the Oak and Hart. They may have circled back."

"It's possible."

They marched in silence. Two big men wearing swords weren't at great risk, even at night, but Geth watched the shadows anyway. Once or twice, someone ducked deeper into the shadows of a doorway or scurried off down an alley, but no sane criminal dared confront a man wearing a face like Geth wore.

"After the inn," Ratcher said, "whatever the news, we should consider our next play."

"Don't worry, I haven't forgotten about Lyanne, Elius, or any of their hired blades. But without Phelan—" he shook his head. "Melagus too, the little toad. I swear I was just starting to like him."

"We'll find them. While we headed up this way, talking about your friend, Eora, an idea came to me."

"What kind of an idea?"

"I think I know how to get to Weeping Willow."

Geth turned to face the assassin. "I thought you said she might not even exist?"

"Well, I've been thinking about that. If she *is* an enchantress, and not a poisoner, she may have been able to hide her existence. From regular folk that is."

"But not from other witches."

"You get it. We could use another witch to locate her, I reckon. Now as it happens, I've got my hands on a knife she used in a recent job. I'm told there are sorceries that rely on the possession of an artifact. With some luck, a woman I know—a witch herself—might be able to conjure something up."

"It's worth a try," Geth said, "But only after we check with Eora."

"She—"

Ratcher's eyes shot past Geth. Without warning, his sword flashed out of its sheath. Geth ducked, anticipating the threat behind him by the direction of Ratcher's look, and the assassin swung over his head. The sound of steel on steel rang deafening in his ear but a second attacker had already materialized out of the shadows ahead of Geth.

There was no time to draw his weapon. He got the blade up, still in its scabbard, just in time to parry an overhand blow from a man in a Lach-style vest. Somewhere behind

Geth, Ratcher cursed, trading strikes with more than just one enemy by the sound of things.

Geth skipped to one side, battered sheath still stuck to his weapon, but fought with the damn thing just like it was. A second swing came at him crossways. He parried and threw out a side kick, catching the bastard in the midsection and sending him stumbling into a stack of clay pots, shattering the lot.

Another swordsman attacked from Geth's left. A saber slashed straight through the sleeve of the big warrior's tunic, but he'd twisted just enough to dodge any real contact. He snatched at his mangled scabbard, scraped his blade free finally, and squared up his enemy.

But Saber-man's exaggerated retreat gave away the approach of yet another attacker behind Geth. Whirling to face this threat, Geth drove straight forward, smashing the man's guard to one side with a wide swing and following through with a shoulder barge that knocked him off his feet. Geth teetered as well, caught his balance, and turned just in time to deflect a thrust from Saber.

The strike opened up the man's defenses. Geth swung a low, left-handed punch at his exposed middle. Knuckles crunched into some kind of armor hidden beneath a plain tunic, but the force of it sent Saber-man off balance, careening into the Lach bastard, who'd just regained his feet among the shards of broken pottery. He went down again with a curse, his fellow right on top of him.

Geth left them there, turned again to find the enemy he'd shouldered over back up. *Thram's balls!* Steel sounded off steel to Geth's right somewhere, but he couldn't spare a glance for Ratcher.

With the two behind him certain to regroup in a moment, Geth had no choice but to attack. He skipped right and slashed with both hands. His enemy backpedaled, absorbing several blows, stalling, waiting for his friends to take their quarry in the back.

Geth couldn't let that happen. An arcing swing backed this foe up and he turned back toward the Lach and Saber. The latter rushed to meet him, slipped on a shard of pottery—by the gods' own luck— and impaled himself on Geth's blade.

"Ahhh!" he cried

"Ha ha!"

Geth wrenched his blade off Saber to charge the Lach before he could set himself, launching a series of cuts until the wall on the other side of the street closed the man in, allowing a hack straight down through the skull. His eyes rolled up into his head and he went down. Geth whirled, but the third attacker had turned toward on Ratcher.

They had him surrounded. And the flow of battle had taken Geth several yards away, too far to get to him in time. He started to shout a warning but roared as loud as he could instead.

"Arrrggghhh!"

It was enough. The fighter creeping up on Ratcher's back flinched, half turned. That bought the assassin enough time to hurl something from under his robes in the face of the man before him. That one coughed and spluttered. A straight lunge from Ratcher dropped him. A slash behind the knee hamstrung another. Geth had arrived within striking range by the time Ratcher turned, but the last of their attackers ran for it.

Geth started after.

"Let him go," Ratcher said, panting.

"Why?"

"He won't go straight back. The Claw won't hear of this for a while yet."

Geth scowled. "They know our disguises, that we're traveling together. And how do you know they were sent by the Claw, anyway?"

Ratcher waved that off. "They already knew our disguises. They must have. I reckon they've been tailing us for a while and just waited for us to amble through a dark place like this to catch us by surprise."

He was right. *We aren't the wolves anymore, we're the sheep.*

But another thought struck Geth as well. "Wait, they know your face, who you are. You told me you'd kill any man that knew who you were, just to keep it secret."

"I did." Ratcher said. "And I meant it."

CHAPTER TWENTY-THREE

Ratcher knelt down to study the bodies, took several knives and some coin, then straightened and waved Geth on. The big warrior wasn't keen on sticking around anyway. More than a few shutters had cracked as bystanders watched from their homes. The watch would be along sooner or later.

"Definitely the Claw," Ratcher said as they hurried away. "No one else would go for brute force like that. And those weren't standard army weapons either. Even if they'd left their whites behind, lilies and watchmen alike favor familiar blades, the sort they've been issued."

Geth worked that through his mind. "We can't go to Eora then. For the same reason we can't go back to Umbel. Not yet anyway."

Ratcher nodded. It didn't need any explanation.

"You were right from the start," Geth told him. "Better we kept our enemies in front of us than let them get behind. We've got to take it *to* these bastards, each in turn. And I reckon we better start with Claw."

"Then follow me."

There was nothing for it but to focus on the list of assassins they faced. Brickhouse was down. Weeping Willow, The Frog, Starling, and the Claw remained, legends, each of them, almost as much as The Number Three. Geth rehashed all they'd discussed as they crossed town again.

Starling, Ratcher claimed, would wait to strike. They had time there. As long as they didn't put anything in their mouths, they should be safe from the Frog as well, Geth reckoned. Weeping Willow could pose a problem, but they'd have to take that chance. If Geth was right, hitting the Claw before he learned they weren't dead just might give them the edge they needed to scratch him off the list.

Geth looked to Ratcher. "Seems like you know where you're going," he said, marching beside him in and out of grey moonlit patches and deeper shadow.

The assassin nodded. "The Claw doesn't bother to hide. Anyone can find him if they dare. He's done enough work for the watch that they don't trouble him either."

That could only mean one thing. "Thram's balls. How many fighters will be with him?"

"Hard to say." Ratcher scratched at one of those shaved eyebrows. "Dozens, I'm sure. Hard men too."

"And the place itself? The battleground?"

"You'll see. We're almost there."

They came to a halt in front of a narrow door jammed between a crumbling stone tenement and a shopkeepers' row, merchandise all stowed away for the night. A rusty lock sealed it shut.

"What is this, an outhouse?"

Ratcher snorted. "You aren't far off."

With one of the knives he'd taken off the dead, he worked the lock until it clicked open. A fetid smell hit Geth's nose, and he closed his mouth. Inside, a set of stairs led down. That was it, the space wasn't wide enough for anything else.

"The Tributaries," Ratcher explained. "More than a few rivers run under the city until they reach the Arm. I'm sure you've heard of them."

"The Tribs." Geth shook his head. "You're telling me he lives in a sewer?"

"It stinks down there, but he's made quite a fortress out of it. There're several ways in, all of them guarded, all of them leading down to the water. I found this one a few years back though. I'm not sure anyone else remembers it's here."

Ratcher started down the stairs. Geth closed the door behind them, and they moved gingerly through utter dark. A shudder ran down his spine, remembering the tortures of the Tower of the Moon. He was glad the darkness hid that from Ratcher.

The smell grew stronger and the sound of running water reached Geth's nose as the steps abruptly ended. "This way," Ratcher whispered. "Stay close to the wall on the right."

With one hand against stones, they crept forward for what felt like miles. A faint glow lit the place, the odd sewer grate, spaced at far intervals, admitting the moonlight. As Geth's eyes adjusted, he made out a barrel roof and the shimmer of water down the middle of a long passageway. Ledges a few feet wide provided a walkway to either side. They moved in silence for a long time, turning right twice, down side passages just as large as the first, the stink constant, and the tinkle of flowing water.

A faint orange light appeared some distance farther on, growing more obvious as they neared it.

"Shhh." Ratched breathed.

"What is it?"

"A barracks. Of sorts." The assassin pointed up ahead on the right. "Further down there's another. After that is his hall."

"His hall? You mean they eat and drink down here, with the rats?"

"Nasty sonsabitches." Ratcher's teeth glowed whiter than his head as he grinned. "But yeah. And the Claw will be there. So, what do you think? You're the great captain, the breaker of sieges, Wolf of the Hills. How do we get to him?"

"These ain't no hills." Geth muttered.

He looked at the water, down the tunnel at the faint yellow glow that marked the first barracks and the second further on. Farther still must have been the 'hall' as Ratcher called it. But Geth couldn't see it. No matter, he knew that's where the real shit awaited. He looked down at the water one more time. He was fairly certain he saw an actual turd float past.

It was flowing in the direction of the Claw's stronghold.

Hmmm. Geth reached for his mustache, rubbed his smooth chin instead.

"Anything?" Ratcher asked.

"I think I've got an idea."

It was a fool's gambit. But if anyone could make it work, Geth reckoned, it was a formidable swordsman and a deadly assassin. He relayed his plan—most of it anyway.

"It's late, these men will be sleeping. How hard can it be?"

Ratcher pursed his lips, repeated what he'd heard. "So, we sneak down to that barracks there, take out anyone who's awake before he can cry the alarm. If we do it real quiet, we can just prance in after that and murder the rest of the men there, one by one, as they sleep."

"Exactly. I had to do the same thing more or less to break Phelan out of prison a while back. Once the first man was down, the rest didn't stand a chance."

"Gods above and below. You're a bloodier bastard than me."

"After that, we move on to the second barracks and repeat the whole thing."

Ratcher looked at Geth like he was seeing him for the first time.

"I know it's a tall ask, to count on getting lucky twice," said the big warrior. "But even if we wake up the others in the hall, it's the perfect place to meet them when they come running, the perfect battlefield. Standing here on this ledge, they can't come at us more than one man at a time."

"Well and good, but even if we get past the two barracks, and cross swords with whoever's in the hall, we'll never batter our way through to the Claw. If we even get close, he'll turn the other way and run."

"Not if one of us is already behind him."

This was the part Geth hadn't revealed. Ratcher looked understandably confused. "How...?" He blinked. "Frozen bloody hell. The water?"

Geth wore an evil smile. "We throw the bodies in, watch them float past. Then one of us gets in with them and floats by like just another corpse. He crawls out after they've rushed past and sneaks up to flank them."

Ratcher's shaved eyebrows rose. He looked from Geth to the water and back. "If you say so, brother."

Geth nodded. "Let's go."

Ratcher started forward, completely silent, right down to his breathing. Geth had to admit he was impressed. He didn't do half as well, but it was quiet enough. At the edge of the barracks—a chamber that opened like a cross-cut cave to their right, they paused to study the enemy. A man sat cross-legged, back to them, whittling at a chunk of wood while another half dozen dark forms snored on their pallets. Orange lanternlight glinted off weapons leaned against walls or laid flat on the ground beside sleeping warriors.

Ratcher put a finger to his lips, motioned for quiet. He drew a knife from his belt and waited for Geth to do the same. They crept into the room together, but Geth left the assassin to do the honors on the whittler.

He didn't disappoint. The unlucky bastard never knew what hit him. Ratcher's knife was in his back, his left hand over the man's mouth before he could turn his head. The blade must have struck the big vein in a man's torso, or the heart itself. He didn't struggle for more than a few seconds. Ratcher eased him down to his side with the knife still in him. He used both hands to release the weapon, sliding one finger inside the wound as the blade slid out.

Not a man missed a snore on the pallets. Geth thanked Mighty Awer, dedicated the coming kills to the Red God. With a nod from Ratcher, they each moved toward another enemy, striking in deadly silence.

In a matter of minutes, seven men were dead. Only one had woken at the sound of his fellow's weak thrashing. But Geth had leapt on top of him to slash his whole throat out before he could scream. Blood pooled the floor and the smell didn't improve, but Ratcher's smile matched his own.

"I like your plan," the assassin whispered. He winked. There was a twinkle in his eye, the sick bastard.

Geth really was impressed though. "Wait. What's the deal with the finger in the wound?" He waggled a bloody digit.

"You saw that? Good. I'm glad you copied it too. Sometimes it makes a noise when you pull out your knife."

"What kind of noise?"

Ratcher looked thoughtful. "Kind of like a fart."

Geth just shook his head. As he had on the street, Ratcher took coins and the odd ring off the dead. And knives. He seemed to have a thing for knives. They wiped their bloody blades off and moved back out to the ledge beside the water, toward their next victims.

Once again, they paused to study the sleepers at the edge of the barracks. This time, by some miracle, not a man seemed to be awake. Ratcher nodded, motioned with his knife to one side. Geth started in the other direction, and they crept inside the room.

But the big warrior's boot brushed an empty bottle, tipped it and sent it rolling with a hollow, scraping sound. Geth winced. That noise seemed impossibly loud, to carry on impossibly long.

And yet not a man stirred. Geth exhaled. And then the bottle continued over the edge of the gutter to drop with a 'plop' into the tributary's fetid water.

"What the—"

Ratcher's knife was in the speaker's chest a moment later, but he cried out, the sound of his struggle with the assassin echoing off the round ceiling. Geth cursed, kicked the nearest man hard in the face, hurrying to kick or stomp on each of the others near him before he'd even drawn his sword.

Those kicks did enough. With a hiss, the big warrior's blade finally rasped out of its sheath. He spun it in his grip to bring it down execution style into the first man's spine. Wrenching it free, he swept it across the neck of a second, spraying the room with blood. The third had an axe in hand already and managed to parry Geth's swing and square him up.

The din of melee, shouts and cries, echoed weirdly off the barrel vault overhead. It was like a whole army made war in those confines. Especially after all the silence.

By the sound of things echoig over Geth's shoulder, Ratcher had drawn as well. He seemed to be fencing with two of the Claw's men at the same time, not that Geth could spare him more than a glance. He launched himself at Axe-man instead, blow after blow parried with head or haft of the weapon. The crusty-eyed scratch just didn't want to die.

With a toss, Geth shifted his sword from right hand to left, an old trick. Before he could circle toward the bastard, however, a hand clutched his ankle, tripping him down to his side among bedrolls, blankets, and half-dead enemies.

Geth rolled as he hit the ground, a habit learned in the Pits, and narrowly avoiding a chop that sent sparks up from the axe's blade. A miss from a heavy weapon like that took its bearer off balance, however, required an extra heartbeat to recover from. In that span, Geth grabbed the edge of the blankets under Axe-man's feet and yanked hard.

He went over with a curse, landing on the scratch that had tripped Geth in the first place. Geth gained all fours, dove on top of Axe-man, smashing the heavy counter-weight of his sword into his face. That blow bought Geth enough time to sit up and lean back, sawing at the bastard's neck to slit trachea and arteries in one go. A measured strike ended Ankle-grabber as well.

Geth looked up to find Ratcher choking one of the Claw's men from behind with a garrote of some sort. Where the hell had he gotten that? The floor around him was littered with mangled enemies. The last of them went limp in Ratcher's clutches and the assassin let him fall. He reached down to retrieve his sword, pierced the man's chest just to be sure, then slid the weapon in its sheath. He ran a hand over his brow to wipe away sweat, replacing it with a smear of blood by accident.

"C'mon," Geth said. He grabbed the first body, dragged it to the edge of the water and rolled it in. Shouts could already be heard from further down the tunnel, the Claw's hall.

With Ratcher's help, more dead men joined the first, drifting slowly downstream. "Well," said the assassin. "I guess it's time."

Geth nodded. "I wish you luck." He looked down at the filthy river and shuddered. "You're a brave man just for getting in there."

Ratcher's eyes widened. "Me?"

"You thought I was getting in?"

"This was your idea!"

"You're the assassin, Ratcher. Who better to sneak up behind these bastards and slit throats?"

"Ha! You slit throats as well as any man, Wolf."

"That's almost true, I reckon. But do you want to be the one facing the angry mob on this end? And do you really want me to be the man that takes down the Claw?"

Ratcher scowled.

"Plus, you've got all those knives."

"Thram's pimpled ass."

They just stood there looking at each of for a long moment, Ratcher's face red from more than just blood and lamplight. "You're a real sonofabitch, you know that, Wolf?"

"It's the only way," Geth told him. "We need Claw to think someone came alone, remember? They need to think it's *me*. Would an assassin like Blacksheep really launch a frontal attack like this, all alone? Never. But I'm just a dog of war, he won't expect anything clever from my sort."

Ratcher uttered another curse. The voices were drawing nearer. "Fine. We'll meet topside afterwards. I'll signal once the Claw is dead."

Geth nodded. "Here." He reached over to smear the blood on Ratcher's forehead down onto his cheeks. "In case they look at the bodies, so you look one of the dead."

"Did I say what a sonofabitch you are?"

Geth grinned. Then he pushed Ratcher over the edge.

CHAPTER TWENTY-FOUR

Ratcher spluttered filthy water and directed a crude gesture at Geth before rolling to his back to begin the float downriver. Several bodies were already in the subterranean river, but Geth dragged the rest in after his friend. A flotilla of corpses meandered slowly into the darkness toward the sounds of the yelling.

"Claw!" Geth screamed. "Your boys are dead, Claw! Come and join them! I challenge you! Kill me yourself if you can!"

For good measure, he loosed a wolf howl. The voices were almost upon him. He cast a glance around the chamber that served as the dead warriors' barracks until he found a shield. He wrenched the Axe-man's weapon from dead fingers and stepped out onto the ledge beside the dark water.

He slid his right arm through the shield's loops. The proximity of the wall on his right would limit the use of his sword, but for the time being he sheathed the weapon altogether. It was the axe he hefted in his left. When the first cursing, torch-bearing minion came within a dozen feet, he hurled that weapon as hard as he could.

Getting the rotation right wasn't easy, but the axe haft clattered into the bastard, made him stumble long enough for Geth to draw with his left hand and close on him with a straight thrust. The strike punctured his ribcage under the arm, sending him backward into the man behind him before he staggered and fell into the dark water with a splash. Geth's sword flashed again before the next man could really set himself and a second dying man joined the flotilla.

"Awoo!" This one was a howl of joy. Geth couldn't say how many men he faced, how far back the file of enemies went, or which one was the assassin himself. But another casualty joined the first two within seconds.

It was almost too easy. Most warriors just weren't used to fighting a lefty. And in the bottleneck the Tribs present-ed, on that narrow ledge of stone beside the water, there was no margin for error. Geth's shield offered cover while his left hand did the business. After watching three of their

fellows fall dead into the filth, the Claw's men—the first
bunch at least—turned and ran.

Geth started to curse himself for not dragging things
out longer, but noises of triumph echoed up the tunnel to
his ears a moment later. By torchlight he saw why. Shields
much like his own were being passed forward, along with
long pikes. Armored up, with pikes to keep Geth at a
distance, the tide of battle could only go in one direction.

"I'm coming, Claw!" Geth shouted.

But even as he said it, he fell back. With any luck, Ratcher was already behind the bastard, sneaking up and leaving
a silent trail of death. He'd said there would be a signal
once he'd killed his rival assassin. So far, Geth had heard
nothing.

He had to buy more time.

"You'll pay, foreign mutt!" a shield man said, coming
within yards of Geth, pike flashing forward. Geth parried,
backpedaled.

"Where's your, master?" the big warrior goaded, still
backing up. "I didn't come here to drown a few water rats.
Where's that craven weasel that calls himself Claw?"

The shield-man cursed Geth, still driving forward, darting thrusts from his pike.

But these were streetfighters, knifemen and bodyguards,
not real soldiers. The enemy in front of Geth, at least,

didn't really know his business with a pike. The big warrior deflected each blow with his sword or shield, edging backward all the while.

Whatever their skill, he had no choice but to retreat. If he didn't, the second man in the file would get his pike over the top and Geth'd have two foes to deal with. He didn't have Neary or Hack to protect him from overhead strikes either.

"Who's the craven now?" they cursed him, growing in confidence.

But that gave Geth another idea.

With a glance over one shoulder, he located the barracks chamber behind him. He backpedaled even more, led his enemies on until he stood at the edge of those quarters, the wall no longer protecting him on his right. The Claw's cutthroats hooted and jeered. But it no longer protected them either. As the first of them stepped into the open space after Geth, the big warrior skipped to his right, gave another howl, and barged him, shield against shield, right over the lip and into the water.

A second man lunged with another pike at Geth's head, but the big warrior had been expecting it. He brought his shield up to catch the blow, sliding a thrust under to pierce his enemy's gut. A high-pitched shriek left the man's throat before he stumbled and fell into the water. The

Claw's next fighter hesitated, blocking his fellows from joining the fray. They might have done Geth in, three or four men at once in that open space, but the big warrior rushed to halt them outside on the ledge again, their pike and shield men now floating down the river with the rest of the dead.

"Claw!" Geth cried between swings. "Where are you, Claw?"

It was Ratcher's voice that answered from somewhere down the tunnel. "The Claw is dead! Slain at the hands of Blacksheep! The legend dies here, and a new legend is born! Weep, sewer rats! Weep and wail! Your master is no more! Scramble for some hiding hole..."

Geth didn't hang around to listen to the rest of Ratcher's speech. He bolted back the way they'd come in, past the two barracks, making two lefts this time, all the way to the stairway and up into the open night. Outside, he breathed deep of the clean air. His stomach lurched and he vomited, once, twice. Then he ran.

———†———

Best Geth could tell, no one followed. He ducked inside a dark doorway, watched and waited. A form came around a corner a few minutes later. Judging by the smell, it could only be Ratcher.

Geth stepped out, raised a hand.

"That you, Wolfie?" Ratcher's boots squelched with each step. His cloak dripped but he wore a grin. "Well, the Claw's had his nails trimmed, eh?"

"We did it." With no pursuit apparent, Geth allowed himself a smile.

"Better keep moving though." The assassin looked down at his soiled clothes. "If I don't get changed, I think I'll puke."

Geth turned to hide a sheepish smile. He looked to the moon. It was hard to say, but he put it past midnight at least. Grim thoughts of Phelan and Melagus flashed through his head. He squashed them. He'd find them yet.

Ratcher must have read his mind. "No time to waste. We need to see the witch I mentioned about Weeping Willow. Maybe she can help with your friends while we're there. If the gods are merciful, she might even give me a change of clothes."

Geth fell in beside him and they started off. "If she can use her magicks to find Weeping Willow using that knife, you reckon she could do the same to find Phelan? I've got a pair of his dice."

"It's worth a try."

That was enough to buoy the big warrior. They crossed the dark streets of the Golden City for what seemed the tenth time that night. They almost bumped right into a pair of watchmen near the Great Shrine of Thram, but the Hunter's own luck was with them. The watchmen were good and drunk, too drunk recognize them, or to give chase when they ran for it.

Ratcher pulled Geth to a halt just a few blocks later. "This is the place. Her name is Feru-Lea. And she's beautiful."

"A beautiful witch?" Geth gave the assassin a meaningful look. "Bad combination."

Ratcher nodded. "Goes without saying you'll need to be wary. But we've worked together in the past, her and I. She's an ambitious thing, even if she means well. And we have something she doesn't, something she can use."

"What's that?"

"Muscle."

Geth snorted.

He'd been used for that for about as long as he could remember. Beside him, Ratcher stooped for a stone, tossed it up to rattle a shutter on the second floor of what appeared to be a chandler's shop. The window cracked then shut again. Footsteps sounded inside and the door to the shop opened.

"Well look who it is."

If this was, Feru-Lea, she was indeed a beauty. But Geth felt those dark, sultry eyes weigh him in a manner only the highborn could manage. He was plenty wary of that sort already, with or without the warning from Ratcher.

"I need a favor," the assassin told her.

"Do you now?"

She waved them inside despite Ratcher's foul stench and the blood that must have stained them both. They stood in a room packed with shelves of candles, the scent almost enough to quell the stink of the sewers. Almost. A pair of lit wicks cast their yellow light on Feru-Lea's perfect features.

"We need to find one of your sisters," Geth said. "A witch."

Feru-Lea frowned. "Give up a sister of my coven? To a pair of assassins? Why would I do that?"

"Forgive my friend," Ratcher hurried to explain. He forced a smile. "But she's no sister of yours, we've discussed her before. Unless I'm wrong, she's not of any coven at all. But she uses your arts. I thought that might aid in the finding."

"Still..."

"If you help us eliminate her, you move up amongst your kind," Geth said. "Isn't that what you want?"

"And what is it that *you* want, *friend*?" She emphasized the word. "The queen? You can't get to Lyanne. That would be suicide. And Lord Black here isn't in that sort of business."

Geth didn't ask how she knew about all that. *Bloody magicks.* But there was clearly plenty of familiarity between the witch and Ratcher.

"I'd strangle the queen if I could," Geth said, "You've got me there. We're not after Lyanne though. Not yet."

"We're after Weeping Willow," Ratcher said.

Feru-Lea didn't blink, not once. But she didn't reply and the moment stretched on. Geth could tell she was working up a price. Folk like her always were.

"What do you offer in trade?" she said finally.

Geth opened his mouth, but Ratcher beat him to it. "A job. Anyone. And my friend will help as well."

"I—"

A look from Ratcher cut Geth short.

"Fine." The big warrior took a breath, smoothed the front of his tunic. "But only if you can find my friends as well."

The witch shrugged. "I can try."

Geth reached into his belt pouch and drew out Phelan's dice. "I took these off my friend when we first arrived, to keep him out of trouble."

"And Weeping Willow?" Feru-Lea asked.

Ratcher handed over a slender, wicked looking knife.

"Wait here."

Feru-Lea took the possessions upstairs. Geth watched her with a frown. He looked to Ratcher.

"Didn't you say there was a chance Weeping Willow never really existed? Something like that? What if this witch sends us in the wrong direction?"

"Well, *someone* killed a man with that knife. And Weeping Willow got credit for it. But it's true, in all my years of hunting her, I'm still not sure if I was chasing shadows all the while."

Maybe they were wasting time on that front. But Geth was more worried about what Feru-Lea made of Phelan's dice anyway. When the witch came back down the stairs, it was the knife she held in her hands. She handed it hilt-first back to Ratcher.

"She is in the city."

"And my friend?" said Geth.

"I could not find him."

Geth's stomach dropped. "What does that mean?"

"It could mean one of several things." The witch looked at him evenly. "Perhaps they've left, traveled far enough that my arts cannot track him. He could yet remain in the city, but if Lyanne holds him, she would likely set the man behind wards. Or it could mean that your friend is no longer among the living."

"But," Ratcher lifted a finger, "he could just as easily still be alive."

Geth started pacing. He reached for the end of his mustache, cursed. He clenched the hilt of his sword instead. "Well, is there some way to find out if Lyanne's got them?"

"We could ask her."

Ratcher's eyes went wide but he held his tongue. Geth stood there blinking, anger rising. Did this mean the two of them were in league? He breathed in and out.

The witch spoke before he could say anything rash. "I am going to do you a favor. Three actually. But when I call in the favor you owe me, it will not be a small one."

"Murdering someone never is." Ratcher muttered.

Feru-Lea flicked a smile in his direction. "First, I'm going to burn your clothes, Lord Black. And replace them."

"You knew I was going to ask for that, didn't you?"

"Second, I will attempt to speak with Lyanne, to learn if she has your friends."

Geth's eyes narrowed. "You would do that?"

"You will give me one of your possessions in return."

"So you can magick me?"

"So I can *summon* you. When it is time for you to fulfil your debt to me. Think of it as a kind of...insurance."

Geth watched her, eyes narrowed. He wished he knew more about witchcraft, but then again, he knew he'd do anything to find Phelan. And that little worm Melagus too.

"Done." He reached into his boot and pulled out a knife, handed it over.

Ratcher cleared his throat. "I don't mean to sound ungrateful, but you said you'd do us *three* favors."

Feru-Lea dipped her head. "For the last, I'll give you a piece of information you may not know: Prince Gahalus has left the city. Unexpectedly. I'm told he was ushered out under cover of dark, perhaps on the orders of the queen."

Geth looked to Ratcher. "What the hell can that mean?"

Ratcher didn't answer, but a few things came to Geth's mind.

First, it could mean the prince had tried but failed to protect Phelan and Melagus, that Lyanne feared retribution toward her son from the likes of Geth and had forced him to leave. Or it could mean the lad angered her so much that she'd banished him, a penance for going against her wishes.

Then there was the chance the prince had double-crossed them all and had decided to flee the scene of his crimes.

"How do you know about Gahalus?" Geth asked finally.

"In the Golden City, one must keep a close eye on the Lion at all times. And the Lioness."

Geth snorted. It didn't matter. It changed nothing. He had to believe his friends were alive and he had to keep looking for them. All while dealing with Pellon's deadliest assassins.

"What of Weeping Willow?" he asked. "You say you've found her?"

Feru-Lea nodded. "I saw the statue of Neyna, a side street, and a spice shop. These workings are not exact, but a better solution would have taken hours."

"That's enough to find her I reckon," Ratcher said. "What about Lyanne? You'll ask about our friends?"

Feru-lea disappeared upstairs a second time. She returned after only a few minutes.

"The queen would not receive my greeting."

"She couldn't, er, hear you?" Geth asked.

"She refused to."

Geth exchanged a look with Ratcher.

"It could be she's angry, or suspicious," the witch went on. "Or simply busy."

"Either way," said Geth, "what you're saying is that she's not talking. About our people or anything else."

"You should get moving," Feru-Lea replied. "She may wonder what I could have wanted, and she just might come by to investigate."

Ratcher frowned. "And what happens if she somehow learns we were here? You won't be in danger, will you?"

Feru-Lea laughed, those pretty eyes sparkling. "Well, maybe when I contacted her, that's what I was trying to tell her?"

CHAPTER TWENTY-FIVE

The statue of Neyna that Feru-Lea mentioned must have signified the plaza dedicated to that goddess, a meeting of four streets adorned at the center with her stone likeness. Geth led the way, feet aching by now, until they were almost to the square. But Ratcher pulled him toward his little hideout in the dilapidated building first.

"I wouldn't have asked for the change of clothes if I'd have known we'd be back this way so soon," he said. Ducking inside, he shrugged out of the borrowed clothes and into his own. Geth found the remainder of their cheese, shared it out, and washed it down with plain water. He felt a new man, almost, after that.

"So, what's it between you and that witch?" he asked. "I reckon you wouldn't have agreed to her bargain if you didn't trust her. She know your secret?"

Ratcher nodded. "She knows my secrets and I know hers. We go back a long way. She can be wicked, make no mistake. That's why I warned you. But you could say she's a friend."

"So it was worth it, what you promised her?"

"We'll find Weeping Willow, of that I'm certain. And the fact that Gahalus has left the city, that has to mean something. Shame though, that Fera's craft brought us no closer to your friends."

Geth frowned. "Can she really summon me? Using that knife?"

"She can."

"Will she?"

"Not if you're dead. But let's see about Weeping Willow and make sure that's not how it happens."

They found the spice shop after a half hour searching the small streets around the square. The back of the two-story building butted directly against the homes behind it, there was no back entrance. But a narrow cellar hatch was set in the ground beside the shop next door, a rugmaker's business according to the signage.

Geth examined the buildings to either side before turning to Ratcher. "I think we can get on the roof down there—" he pointed to a nearby tenement—"and come all the way across to the spice shop and get in one of the upper story windows."

"If she's really an enchantress," said Ratcher, "it won't be easy to sneak up on her. She may have some kind of sorcery to warn her. On top of everything else."

"So, let's come at her from two sides." Geth flicked his chin at the trap door to the cellar. "That might lead into the rugmaker's shop, but it's the same building. There's gotta be a way to break through to the spicer's basement from there."

Ratcher nodded slowly. "Alright, you take the roof. I'll take the cellar. She's probably on the second floor so we'll catch her between hammer and anvil there."

Geth started off but Ratcher caught his elbow.

"Feru-Lea gave me this." He reached under his tunic to display a little pouch on a leather thong around his neck. "It's supposed to help me slip through. So wait for me to strike first."

"I reckon she didn't have a second one."

Ratcher grimaced. "Be careful." He reached toward his belt and handed Geth a pair of knives. "If you have no choice, stall for time. I'll be at her back quick as I can."

This time he let Geth go. The big warrior had already picked a good spot to climb, it wasn't hard. He moved as quiet as he could across several roofs until he was looking down at Ratcher in front of the spice shop.

The assassin gave him a wave and knelt down to work at the lock on the cellar. He had it open in less than a minute and disappeared inside. Geth counted to one hundred, allowing time for Ratcher to work through any locked doors in the basement itself. Then he lay flat on the roof, reached down, knife in hand, to slip a shutter latch. He pulled the window open, swung his legs in, and climbed down and inside.

A cat hissed at him from the shadows.

"Gods all be damned!" Geth breathed. The hairs on the back of Geth's neck were up straight. He growled low but deep in his chest until the animal bolted past him, out onto the window ledge and across to the next building.

Geth moved quietly toward the nearest door, studied the place. Moonlight slicing through the open shutter gleamed on what looked like a collection of knives and weapons of various kinds, laid out on tables, hung on the walls, stacked in the corners. The room was still mostly dark, and he didn't stop to take inventory, but at least he knew they had the right house.

But the hairs on the back of his neck still tingled. Out the door and down a hall to a second room, he found more weapons but no Weeping Willow. That's when the fear washed over him, clenched his chest tight, drew out a startled gasp.

Gods above and below!

Could it be? Ceter, alive after all this time?

No, it was a similar feeling, but more animal somehow, less icy, inhuman.

And it wasn't directed at him. Rather, it washed past. Geth thought of Ratcher and the amulet Feru-Lea had given him. His gut told him that wasn't going to be enough to save him.

Careful to step at the edge of each stair, Geth hurried down toward the first floor, then on to the basement. He left his sword in its sheath at his side but drew a second knife to match the first, moving as fast as he could without making a ruckus. The fearspell seemed to thicken the further down he went. He pushed through. By the time he reached the cellar, his heart was beating in his throat.

"...the infamous Blacksheep," a woman's voice was saying. "More like a donkey than anything if you want my opinion. I reckon your pet wolf should be along any minute now as well."

Geth froze. The room was almost pitch black, but from where he stood, he could just make out a slender form standing over a second, kneeling figure. Weeping Willow hadn't heard him, hadn't yet turned, best he could tell.

The only detail he could make out with certainty was the faint gleam of a blade in her right hand.

He didn't trust his aim throwing a knife in the dark, and that was if he even got the spin right. Any killer worth her salt would slash the throat in front of her before turning to deal with the threat from behind. Geth swallowed a curse, tried not to stare too hard at her back lest she get that sixth sense of him.

Her head turned, ever so slightly, but Geth knew it was already too late.

"And here he is."

By the Thram's own luck, the enchantress left Ratcher where he was to face Geth. With no time to think up anything, the big warrior made do with what he had, which was nothing. He stiffened up, pretended to be stuck, frozen with fear himself. He felt her eyes on him more than he saw them, such was the darkness. Behind her, Ratcher hadn't moved. He couldn't.

"Welcome, Wolf of the Hills. Yes, yes, you are indeed welcome. The wolf and the sheep together."

Weeping willow's voice dripped out of her like acid, words mouthed in some accent he couldn't place. She took a step toward him, just one. He could throw those knives now, but if he missed...? What else did she have up her sleeve? He needed her to get closer, to be certain. He lifted one of his knives slowly, like it was almost more than he could manage. He didn't have to fake the tremble in his arm.

Across the room, Weeping Willow purred. "So strong. Oh, the life to be had from your blood! You're no dithering old heiress, no inconvenient child-bastard. No tiresome, whining, mistress. No, you're *alive!* The both of you. The power..."

Bile rose up Geth's throat, even if he understood only the half of what she was saying. This was a creature of pure evil, of that he had no doubt. Her fearspell grew as she took another step toward him and Geth shook where he stood, uncertain whether he was still pretending or if he was actually held fast.

She took another slow step toward him, close enough for Geth to see white teeth in a dark face. He couldn't let her get closer, let her magicks get a hold. Grunting with the effort, he lunged for her with both knives.

The resistance he'd gained battling Ceter cut through her spell like a cleaver through a joint of beef. He staggered as he broke through but caught himself in time to sidestep a slash of Willow's knife. His own weapons found flesh. The enchantress gasped as they struck home.

Her knife lashed out again, backhand. Geth let loose his two handles and twisted to dodge. The slash grazed his collarbone, just short of slicing his throat. He felt the burn of his cut at the same time Ratcher sucked in a rasping breath and collapsed forward onto the floor.

But Weeping Willow still stood there, blood gurgling up through her lips, quivering with fear or rage or both. She raised that knife again, impossibly, and surged at Geth with a screech, slashing as she came. He sidestepped to let the strike pass, slapping the back of her hand away and drawing his sword in one motion. She turned to come at him yet again, stumbling like a damn marionette, until he swung his blade in one final arc, taking her head clean off her shoulders.

Like a tree being felled, Weeping Willow's decapitated body teetered and went down stiffly to one side. Her head rolled in the opposite direct to land beside Ratcher.

"Agh!" The assassin scrambled away from the thing.

"You alright?"

Geth reached down with his free hand to help his friend up, wincing at the burn of the cut at his collar. Ratcher shuddered, stuck out a foot to kick the dead assassin's head further away.

"What the hell was that?" he said. "Fera's amulet went all cold and then...I don't know."

"Some sort of magick. In Ilia, they call it a fearspell. Don't feel bad she got to you. I've had a run in with that sort of thing before. It seems to have less power once you've faced it down a few times."

Ratcher stepped gingerly toward Weeping Willow's dismembered body, peered down wide eyed. "Dear gods! And she just wouldn't die either, would she?"

"I guess she really was an enchantress."

Ratcher patted himself down, checking for injuries. Geth led him up the stairs, wiped his hands on his pants as if that could wash away the evil. He had half a mind to rummage the cupboards for something to eat but thought better of it. He hadn't forgotten the hoard of weapons on the second floor though.

"C'mon," he told Ratcher. "If you like knives as much as I think you do, wait 'til you see this gal's collection."

He found a lantern and unshuttered it to throw some light. They went up the stairs, pushed open the door. Geth whistled as he got a full view of the arsenal.

But Ratcher had gone stiff at his side again.

"You alright?"

"Look."

Geth followed the assassin's eyes to a row of bows mounted on one wall. A variety of arrows completed the set. More knives rested on a table beside a pile of little lead balls. "Are those slingstones?"

"Starling," Ratcher whispered. He sucked in a breath. Without warning he started laughing. One hand came to rest on Geth's shoulder for balance as he doubled over.

"Oh, dear gods! ha!"

"What the—"

"She's Starling!" Ratcher looked up, took Geth by both arms. "Don't you get it? Like I'm both Cloak *and* Blacksheep!"

"And the Lordling," Geth mumbled. "And Lord Black. And the gods only know who else."

Ratcher's hands went on his cheeks, his mouth open, eyes wide. "Dear merciful, sweet, and glorious gods! Thram and Awer, I swear I'll never malign your underparts again!"

"So, you're saying," Geth frowned, "that we just took down Weeping Willow and Starling in one go?"

Ratcher belted out another laugh, nodded between breaths. Geth found himself giggling too, just a little at first, then more, until he was holding his side and shaking with laughter. "Gods all be damned."

"This night deserves a song," said Ratcher. "A proper tale. The Number Three himself would be proud. What operator ever took down *four* competitors? And all in the same night? Not even Three."

"If he had, they'd call him Four."

That earned another round of laughter.

"I wish he could see me now." Ratcher wiped his eyes. "He'd be green with envy!"

Geth supposed he would. Brickhouse, the Claw, Starling and Weeping Willow...He wasn't sure you could really count the last pair as two separate 'competitors,' given the facts. But he wasn't about to take the wind out of Ratcher's sails.

No, the assassin was right. The sun had begun rising by then and they scooped up a half dozen daggers and knives between them. It *had* been one hell of a night.

—————†—————

Ratcher led the way back to his lair, the pair of them jubilant if exhausted. But Geth hadn't forgotten about Phelan and Melagus. Assuming his friends had managed to slip through Lyanne's net, where might they have gone? He didn't believe the witch had them—he couldn't allow himself to believe it.

But he was just too tired to come up with anything. And that slice across his collarbone, however small, burned like hell. Sleep took him almost as soon as his back was against one of the crumbling walls of Ratcher's cave-like hideout. He woke to the sound of the assassin returning with breakfast, just as he had the previous morning.

"Bread," Ratcher said. "Fresh this time. Apples, some cherries. And goat cheese."

"The mushy kind? Hand it over."

Geth split his half of the bread down the center and smeared cheese inside the crack. Apple and cherries served as dessert, washed down with a good deal of plain, luke-warm water. He would have dozed off again after that, but an idea had come to him.

"Melagus's embroiderer said Rondah's ship had been made ready, right?"

Ratcher nodded from across the little chamber.

"But she said they depart from Sorn," Geth went on. "What if they're there, waiting for me, as we speak?"

"Then we should go. Feru-Lea said Gahalus had left town. And that both of your friends were out of the range of her senses. Maybe they left together?"

"I suppose they could be gone already, at sea, thinking I didn't make it out. Someone at the marina would have seen something if they passed through, don't you reckon?"

"It's as good a plan as any."

Ratcher climbed to his feet, tucking away various knives and loading his satchel. Geth had his sword and little else. He poured water on the itching cut at his collar and, with a reapplication of makeup to his forearms, he was ready. They stepped outside, melted in among the midday foot-traffic.

"We'll get there faster by boat," Ratcher said, leading the way toward the river. "Lyanne will be expecting us to escape by sea. But let's be ready just in case she has eyes on the river. Put this on." From inside his satchel, he produced a red robe, the kind worn by the servants of Awer, God of War.

Geth laughed.

"What?" Ratcher had already pulled a fresh black one over his own head. "Two holy men, out for a stroll. War and Death. What could be more natural?"

They passed plenty of watchmen supervising trade at the river, but either Geth's bare forearms or the gods' own luck deflected any suspicion. And Ratcher had taken enough coin off the men they'd killed to buy passage to Far Adus and back if needed.

"I've been thinking," the assassin said when they were finally aboard a ship, oarsmen working them upriver. "I think we're done."

"With what?"

Ratcher looked down at the muddy water, squinting in the bright morning. He leaned back, eyes closed, to let the sunlight hit his face for a moment before turning back to

Geth. "We've taken down almost all of my enemies, the assassins Elius and Lyanne sent. What I'm saying is, if we do find your friends in Sorn, you should leave with them."

Geth frowned. "What about the Frog? You said yourself he's about the worst of them."

"He is." Ratcher muttered a curse. "Hiding behind his poisons, always lurking in the shadows. Should be called the Spider, cowardly bastard. Or just the Bug. I swear I'll squish the sonofabitch."

"He tried to poison Hadean at his wedding," Geth agreed. "That's a special kind of nasty. You sure you can manage without me?"

"That's the thing. I've been thinking it backward and forward. I don't know how to get to him. Except to lure him out."

"Sounds dangerous."

"But more to the point, it'll take time." Ratcher met Geth's eye. "He'll come, don't worry about that. Especially after I ruined the job on Hadean. But when?"

"You don't think he'll take a second stab at Hadean before coming after you?"

"No chance. And don't worry, once he does slink out of his hiding hole, I'll make sure he never slinks back."

Geth could appreciate the determination in those words. The river glided by, brown and lazy, dappled by the sun. Heat rose off the surface in waves. He watched Ratcher, lounging across from him, more relaxed than he'd ever seen him, even as they spoke of his deadliest adversary.

"You're gonna quit, aren't you," Geth said. "The business, I mean."

Ratcher eyed him sideways. "What gave it away?"

"I don't know. But what are you gonna do with all those knives now?"

"Good question. My cover's been blown, I'll never sneak up on anyone again." They shared a smile. "Then again, I could always fake my own death..." Ratcher tapped a finger on his chin. Geth snorted a laugh.

They made Old Sorn an hour short of nightfall. A bored looking watchman fidgeted with the tassels of his armband, muttering to himself as he walked the quays. He paid the pair no mind. Geth scanned the marina until his eyes found the Windskimmer.

He left Ratcher settling up with the boatmaster to hop the gunwale and hurry down the planks in search of Rondah. She grinned when she saw him, hand on hips, standing on the deck.

"Master Geth!" But when she looked past him to find only Ratcher in tow, her smile faded.

"They haven't been here, have they?" Geth said.

"No."

The captain waved them aboard. Geth moved like a man in a dream. Somehow, he'd really believed he'd find his friends in Sorn. So much had begun in that town, perhaps there might be a happy ending there as well. Or so he'd thought.

Rondah fed them but skipped the small talk and got straight to business. "There's something you need to hear." She sighed.

Geth felt himself tense. He shared a look with Ratcher.

"Thing's have gone awry in the king's camp. I don't know what, but I should have heard from them."

Geth swore. "Melagus's people in the Golden City said the same thing."

"The message from Melagus was urgent. He wanted to leave straightaway. Apparently, he'd learned there were spies in King Hadean's camp."

"Spies? Could it have something to do with that? The reason we haven't heard anything?"

"I don't know. But that's how Towdric's men got in and out clean when they burned his supplies."

Geth wanted to spit. It made sense, he should have probably considered the possibility already. Perhaps that was the long and short of it.

But what if there was something more? Like the assassin Snake Eyes. Was Hadean in danger?

Of course he was.

"We need to get back to Umbel."

Rondah nodded slowly. "It's too late to set out now, but in the morning perhaps."

Geth didn't argue with that. He needed more time to think, to be certain.

And maybe, just maybe, Phelan and Melagus would arrive to join them by then.

Chapter Twenty-Six

Geth led Ratcher across town to the Acorn and Branch. They had to spend the night somewhere. And could an assassin really judge anyone, even the son of a whore? Geth decided he didn't care either way.

He found the Lady Largess at a table in the sparsely occupied common room, braiding the hair of a young colleague. "Hello, Mother."

The lass batted her eyes up at Geth and Ratcher, arched her back just so to accentuate her curves. Mother dropped the girl's tresses. Her eyes lit up.

"There's my boy!" She stood and hugged Geth.

He still wasn't used to that. "Uh." He patted her on the back awkwardly. "Just thought I'd stop in. We were in town and in need of a roof."

"Of course, of course!"

"We can pay," Geth added. "One of the nicer rooms. My friend is...um, a cleric as you can see."

Mother watched Ratcher with narrowed eyes but the girl with the half-braided hair reached out to take the satchel from him, still working those lashes. If Geth wasn't mistaken, the fool had winked back.

They started upstairs for a room. Eyelashes passed the satchel over to Geth when they reached the landing, tried to pull Ratcher in the other direction.

"He doesn't have time," Geth said. "Not tonight."

"Maybe tomorrow?" Lashes purred. "What girl could resist a man in robes?"

Geth rolled his eyes. Ratcher watched her float off then ducked into their chamber with a sigh. Geth followed Mother in the opposite direction to her quarters.

"Well, I won't say you look better than the last time I saw you," she said, "but I reckon you've got an explanation. You haven't really taken in with the Reds, have you?"

Geth had almost forgotten about his own cleric's robes. "Me? Not a chance. Much as I've cursed him, I doubt Awer would have me."

"You've done plenty of his work, enough for a temple of your own I daresay."

Geth snorted.

"Why the hair though?" Mother asked. "I know it's not the fashion in Pellon, but I liked the length. And even that mustache."

"Finally, someone agrees." Geth rubbed at his bare lip. "But that's the thing, I've made some enemies it seems. Again. You'll want to be careful, keep an ear to the ground."

He reached for his belt pouch, pulled the whole thing off and handed it over.

"What's this?"

"Just in case you need it."

She looked down at the pouch in her hands. She didn't judge the heft of it this once, or count out the coins. "I can't take this."

"I can't take it back either. And anyway, I have rich friends now, remember?" He forced a smile.

Mother smiled back. Taking Geth's hands in her own, however, she squinted down. It became a frown.

"What happened to your tattoos? Oh, I see."

"Part of the disguise," Geth said.

She sniffed. "Stage makeup. If you want this to last, let me fix it. The mix I use really holds on, if you know what I mean. Whether you're in the bath, if you rub it, if you sweat—"

Geth winced. "I get it, please."

She sat him down on the bed and turned to sort through some bottles on the sideboard. She had to mix a few colors to get the right shade, but a liberal application covered his tattoos so well he really didn't need the leather bracers. He put them back on anyway, just in case.

"What happened to your friends anyway?" Mother helped lace the bracers up, standing over him as he sat on the edge of the mattress "That thin fellow had a tough look, but that always hides a tender heart."

"Tender heart? Melagus?" Geth would have laughed under better circumstances. "We got... separated. I don't suppose you've seen them? I thought they might come this way to meet with our ship, but it looks like I'll be going back alone."

"Back to Umbel?"

"I have to."

She nodded. "I reckon that's your home now."

Geth reckoned it was.

"Listen," he said. "I'm real pleased to see how you've changed your life. And truth be told, I wouldn't mind passing through more regular. But this time, I can't stay except tonight. If things get hairy, I want you to think about leaving as well."

"Leaving?" Mother's eyes widened. A hand went on that huge bosom. "You're serious, aren't you. I guess that coin purse makes sense now. But I can't leave, son. Where would I go?"

"Anyplace, I don't know. I just don't want you to suffer for the things I've done. I've made plenty of enemies here in Pellon, even more than usual this time."

Somehow that made Mother smile. "Show me an important man without any enemies."

———†———

As usual, Ratcher was awake before Geth the next morning before him. "About time you got up," he told the big warrior.

"Did you already eat? I swear I'll starve to death if I don't get something in me." Geth said.

"What I need is a bath." Ratcher waved the big warrior up. "They're pouring one for you as well. The pantries are full downstairs if you feel like cuffing a snack while you wait."

Geth rubbed the sleep out of his eyes and headed to the kitchens. He talked the cook out of a loaf that was half-stale anyway and slunk behind the bar to pour himself a pint when no one was looking. He found Ratcher in the bath chamber, already submerged to the neck. His face was red, but he looked damn comfortable in the steamy water.

"I still can't believe we've done it," the assassin said, not bothering to open his eyes. "Brickhouse, Starling. And the Claw..." He turned his head, cracked one eyelid to look at Geth. "Right into the belly of the beast and ate its liver while we were there."

"I suppose we did."

Ratcher nodded. "There should be a couple of girls...around," he said, wiping sweat from his brow. "Nothing like a good...scrub...by a... pair...expert hands."

Geth frowned at the effort in his friend's voice. And where were those girls? It wasn't like the ladies of the Acorn and Branch not to at least make the attempt. Geth looked to the assassin's bathwater. His heart skipped a beat.

"Ratcher, I think—"

The assassin's eyes opened wide in the middle of Geth trying to say it. He sat upright in the tub, looked down. Before he could utter what they both must have been thinking, the door cracked and a bent old woman with a scarf over her head hobbled in.

"Geth!"

Instinct told the big warrior all he needed to know. He was already backpedaling away from the old woman as she closed in, a slick-looking knife slashing at him. Her head came up to reveal a pair of bulbous eyes, a flat, pasty nose, and a toothless snarl.

That knife kept coming, flashing too fast for Geth to do more than dodge. He backed off until he was out of space, up against the edge of his own waiting tub. Teetering on the edge, over steamy, poisoned water, he threw out a desperate kick.

Thank the gods he still had his boots on. Thick leather soles deflected that knife, bought enough time for him to lean back up and away from the lip of the tub. Geth's drew his own knife, and he squared up his attacker.

"Frog!"

The poisoner hissed a wordless challenge through that hideous smile, producing a second knife at the same time. Ratcher breathed weakly from the other tub.

"Geth..."

The Frog didn't so much as spare him a glance. "Yes, we meet finally." He licked his pale lips. Gods but someone had really nailed it with that nickname.

"I'm gonna kill you, Frog." Geth said, eyes never leaving those two blades. "Squish you like the bug you are."

"You would do that?" That toothless smile broadened. "Finish the job for your friend? Don't you see you've been used, Wolf? Just like always. Once you've killed me, you'll have cleared out all his competitors, left him the last man standing."

"Geth..."

The Frog flicked his chin toward Ratcher, up to his bottom lip in the water, struggling, one arm dangling out. "He's dead already, Wolf. Be your own man for once. *Think.* Come for me if you want, but a nick from one of these knives will mean your end as well."

"I'd gladly kill you, Bug. Hadean's wedding—"

The Frog's stance shifted, but whatever he planned, Ratcher cut it short, popping half out of the water to hurl something. A knife—and he got the rotation just right. The blade sunk hilt deep into the Frog's pasty neck with a wet thud.

Geth wished he had a sword just then, or any weapon with reach, to finish the bastard. But the Frog collapsed to one knee, no help needed, his eyes panicked. He dropped both of his own knives to clutch at the weapon protruding from his neck. He pulled the blade free with a whimper, only to let loose his life's blood in a spurting red fountain.

Blood pooled on the floor. Those bulging eyes rolled up in the Frog's head and the poisoner toppled straight forward, smashing his head against the lip of one tub. His body slid unceremoniously down the side of the wooden vessel to rest in a heap on the floor.

Geth hurried toward his friend. "Ratcher!"

But the assassin held both hands out in warning, standing now, dripping suds and water.

"Don't touch...the water!" He climbed out himself.

"I thought you were done for?"

"Faked it. Mostly. Get me some...fresh water...and ash from the hearth."

Geth hollered out the door. He wrapped a towel around Ratcher. The assassin sat on the edge of his tub, looked down at his dead adversary.

"We got...the bastard."

A girl arrived with two buckets, but Geth shooed away the rest of the ladies that tried to gather outside the door. Ratcher pushed the big warrior away and began wiping himself down. The ash came a moment later. He mixed it with water, washed again. Then a third time with plain water.

"Is that it? Are you gonna be alright?" Geth asked.

Ratcher shook his head. "The only reason...I'm not dead already... is the 'antivenom.' I knew...the Frog would come...so I took... precautions."

"Antivenom?" Geth frowned. "Sounds terrible."

Ratcher gave a weak smile. "You took it too. I put it...in the berry wine."

Geth felt dizzy again at mere mention. He helped his friend back into his clothes. There was only one place they could go.

"We've got to get you back to Paellia. To Eora."

Ratcher just looked at him blankly.

"She's a healer," Geth said. "The best of them."

He didn't wait for an answer. Mother had heard the commotion by then, but Geth sent her right back out the room and upstairs to gather their things. When she returned, he hugged her and turned to go.

"Wait!" She fished in a pocket, retrieved the belt pouch Geth had given her and pressed it in his hand. "And if you need anything else—anything—just ask it."

Geth pushed the coin back at her. "If anyone comes asking for me, just run."

"What about your friends? What if they come?"

"Tell the I'm headed home."

Chapter Twenty-Seven

Before Geth could go after Towdric, he had to get Ratcher to Eora.

He half-dragged, half-carried the hefty assassin to the Windskimmer. Captain Rondah's eyes widened at the sight of them. She snapped her fingers and two of her men helped haul the assassin aboard.

"He's been poisoned," Geth told her.

Rondah spit a curse.

"We need to get him to the Golden City. I know a healer. It's his only chance."

Ratcher lifted his head. "Whatever happens...we did it. The Number Three? Ha! Blacksheep...will live...in legend."

"And retire to hear the tales retold." Geth helped lay the assassin out in Rondah's cabin. "Number Three got to retire, didn't he? Why not the infamous Blacksheep?"

Ratcher nodded, sweat trickling down the stubble on his head and eyebrows. His chest heaved with each breath, but he squeezed Geth's hand tight then settled himself and closed his eyes.

Sailing downriver, they covered the distance quicker than they had rowing up. The glimmering walls and rooftops of the Golden City came into view a few hours short of sundown. Rondah and her crew helped get Ratcher from the marina on the river to the Oak and Hart, arriving just as the sky began to purple.

They burst through the front door and into a common room, turning heads, drawing a gasp from some, curses from others.

"What's happened?" Eora said.

"He's hurt."

She motioned them into the kitchen, scattering bowls and sprigs of dried herbs off the cook's counter. They laid Ratcher down. The assassin's head lolled, his body gone limp.

"Poison." Geth wiped sweat from his friend's brow. Ratcher's chest rose and fell, if weakly. He wasn't dead yet.

"Out." Eora pointed the way they'd come. "Get a drink and meal. This will take time, if I can save him at all."

Rondah waved her men through the door, back to the common room. Lifting her captain's hat to smooth down the silver wisps standing out of her red hair, she set it back on her head, blew out a sigh, and motioned Geth to a table near the bar.

"Can she do it?" she asked as they sat.

"Eora can raise the dead just about. She brought me back, a long time ago, and I had one foot in the grave, the other kicking dirt on it."

He forced a smile. Rondah and her men tried to return the gesture. Geth hailed Eora's barman for wine and food.

"What now?" the captain asked. "Even with the healer's touch, your friend will be laid up for a while. I wonder if I shouldn't circle back to Old Sorn, wait for Melagus, just in case?"

Four cups of wine arrived. Geth rubbed at the wound on his collarbone, thinking. "Can you take me back to Umbel?"

Rondah blinked. She gave a nod.

"Thank you. I'm not giving up on them, but I don't know how much longer we can wait."

"I'll send my men to prepare the ship. We'll leave in the morning."

At a flick of the head from Rondah, the two sailors rose and headed out. Geth downed his wine, jaw clenched, neck itching. The wound had scabbed over, but it still burned. The heat of summer seemed to have reached a crescendo as well. Sweat beaded his forehead, even then, in the middle of night. A storm would be coming soon, he reckoned. That was about the only thing that could break such heat.

A tray of grapes, olives, cheese, and bread arrived, borne by none other than the Lady Brega, eyes half-glazed like a simpleton. Geth prayed Eora's magicks could do more for Ratcher. With Rondah's men gone, there was far too much food for two people, but the big warrior ate nervously, hour after hour, leaving only a modest share for the captain.

The night stretched. Rondah departed for the Windskimmer as well. Geth recalled how Eora had healed his own wounds so many years before, told himself that all would be well. A small, jealous part wondered if she pressed her body against Ratcher as she had against him, willing her magicks into his flesh. He shook his head. If the man survived, he had to be happy, however it came about.

The common room emptied by ones and twos until Geth was the last patron. Eora finally emerged from the back sometime before midnight, circles under her eyes. Geth watched her expectantly but couldn't bring himself to ask.

She slumped into the chair across from him. "He'll live."

Geth exhaled. "I never doubted you."

"Tell me what happened."

"The Frog, one of the Queen's assassins. He did something to Ratcher's bath water."

"But your friend must have ingested some kind of protectant beforehand," Eora said. "Otherwise, he wouldn't have made it. That was a potent concoction he was poisoned with."

"He drank something called 'antivenom.' Supposed to help against such things."

"Whatever it was, it slowed the process, nothing more. Another hour and his liver would have been beyond repair." Eora reached across the table, tore a crust of leftover bread and chewed.

"What now?" Geth asked. "He'll need to stay here I reckon."

"That's fine."

Geth reached toward the purse at his waist, but Eora held up a hand.

"It's alright. I'll take it out of Phelan's share."

She grinned, a rare twinkle in her eye. Geth hadn't seen that since before she'd bid him begone, years past. Rather than smile in return though, he felt his shoulders sag.

"I'm sorry, Eora. For everything I've laid at your feet. Again, and again."

"It's alright."

"Well—"

"You really have changed, you know? I see that now."

Sitting there at that moment, his two friends missing and another half-dead, Geth wasn't sure she was right. But he didn't havre the strength to argue.

"Master Melagus told me about your trial," she went on, "that he sentenced you to die. And yet there you were, slapping backs with the man like he was your uncle. You forgave him. The old Geth didn't know how to forgive. And he didn't want to learn."

Geth looked down at his hands then back up. "I have a child on the way. Maybe that changed me."

Did she look disappointed? Or did he imagine that? Maybe she really *had* changed her stance. She fumbled in her pockets, retrieved the green-jeweled ring he'd given and held it out.

"What?" Geth said. "That was a gift."

"For me? A man's ring?"

"Well—"

"It was payment. But I don't want it. Your coin is no good here." There was that twinkle again. "Phelan wouldn't take it, would he?"

Geth started to disagree, but as she pressed the ring into his hand, she gasped, recoiled.

"What?"

"Stand up."

He did, feeling a little lightheaded from the food and wine.

"Are you sure you weren't poisoned as well?"

Geth frowned. "I don't think..."

He trailed off, one hand rubbing at the cut just above his hidden mail shirt. Eora rounded the table to unlace the collar of his red robes, hissing softly as she laid eyes on it.

"I got nicked. A scratch, nothing more."

"Shush." She laid a hand on the wound, closed her eyes. Several heartbeats passed. She took a step back, gazed up at him, eyes round as saucers.

"This is bad, Geth. Very bad."

"It's just a scratch."

"There are at least two evils at play here. There's a poison, something not unlike what ails your friend. But there's an underlying curse as well. Blood-magick. Deep and overpowering."

Geth's eyes narrowed. "Overpowering? Overpowering what?"

"Your will to live." She ushered him down into his chair.

He looked back at her, resisting a sudden urge to scratch furiously at the cut. Ratcher's words about Weeping Willow, that she was an enchantress or maybe a poisoner, came back to him. Perhaps she was both. Eora moved to stand behind the big warrior to rest cool, soft hands against the sides of his bare neck.

"I'm going to try to strip it away. Don't move. This shouldn't hurt, but it could take some time."

Geth couldn't see her face, standing behind him, but he knew her eyes had closed. She didn't sing or hum, just breathed slow, even. His mind drifted, like he'd laid down his head for an afternoon doze. When his thoughts refocused, Eora was on the ground at his feet, sweating and shaking.

"Eora!" He scooped her up, carried her upstairs to her chamber. He laid her on the bed, wiped her brow with the edge of the sheets.

"I'm alright...just tired."

Geth blinked, touched his shoulder. "Well, whatever you did, it worked. I feel a lot better."

But Eora shook her head. "It didn't work. The curse is still there. And it will grow with time until it consumes you. Unless I draw it out."

Geth frowned. "You won't be doing anything tonight."

"No. And it will take weeks anyway."

"Weeks?" Geth thought of Hadean, of that bastard, Towdric. "I don't have weeks."

"No, you don't. The blood-magick in your veins will kill you inside a fortnight."

Geth paced the room, cursing. He cursed Weeping Willow, Starling, Elius and Lyanne. He cursed Towdric and Palladine. He cursed every god and the Shaper as well. King Hadean needed him, damn it! That bellowing bastard Towdric would become more entrenched behind Umbel City's walls with every passing day. And if he really did have spies in the king's camp, Geth reckoned he'd be looking to kill off the true king sooner than later.

Geth could do nothing to help Hadean from Paellia, but Eora had already fallen asleep. He checked on Ratcher, tucked in bed in a spare guestroom. Brega sat beside him, unblinking, eerie and silent. But he had to trust Eora's ministrations would work. On the assassin and on himself.

He laid himself down on the floor at the foot of Ratcher's bed and only awoke when Eora came back in some hours later. Dawn had broken judging by the faint light around the edges of the window. She beckoned him wordlessly back to her chamber.

"Sit," she said.

Geth took a seat on the edge of the bed. "Are you going to try to heal me?"

"I don't think I can. Not by myself. But I can postpone the effects until others can be found to help. With another pair of hands—or better yet two more pairs—I'm sure we can clean this evil stain, once and for all."

"I have to get back to Umbel, Eora. How long will it take to find another healer?"

She frowned. "If I chip away at it, I might be able to heal you over time by myself."

"You don't know any other healers, do you?"

"Not in The Golden City."

Geth swore. "Well, I know one. She's in Umbel."

"Geth—"

"You said you could postpone the magicks. Do it, Eora. I have to get back to King Hadean. The witch Amalia can heal me after that."

"I can't say how much good it will do if I try to heal you again right now. It could take almost two weeks just to get to Umbel. And what if you can't find this woman Amalia soon enough? Even with my touch, you won't last a month without a healer."

"Then three weeks will have to do." Geth closed his eyes, sat up straight. "Do what you can."

Eora muttered something like a curse. He felt those cool hands again, the drifting of his mind. This time it was only a matter of minutes though. It was still morning when

Geth opened his eyes, and Rondah would be waiting for him. Eora helped him sling a satchel containing his meager belongings over one shoulder. He buckled the sword Ratcher had given him to his waist and slid Melagus's ring on one finger.

"I'll take good care of your friend, don't worry."

"Tell him..." Geth paused to think. "Tell Ratcher I said thank you."

"Good luck."

"And thank you too."

Eora embraced him. He breathed her scent, closed his eyes, wished things had been different. There was no magick in that hug, except the old-fashioned kind, the kind that never failed.

———†———

Geth found Rondah waiting at the marina, as promised. They pushed off, downriver, past the last glimmer of the Golden City, and out to sea. It was nearly as hot on the ship as it was on the streets of the city, but Geth thought only of Hadean and Towdric. He had no plan except to get back.

He thought of all that had passed behind him, all that awaited ahead: Hadean and everything righteous that he stood for, the dozen, and Agrem and Iyngaer up in Ilia.

And Vriana, of course, with his child in her womb. Seeing Eora had reminded him what the love of a woman could do, something he'd forgotten and had only begun to remember in the company of the chieftess. If the gods were kind, they'd give him a chance to do what needed doing for them all.

They could be, if they wanted to. The wind was with them for several days and they were on course to reach Umbel City ahead of schedule. But on the sixth day Rondah steered them into the harbor of Sirona, a small port city at Umbel's southernmost reaches.

"Towdric knows my allegiances," she told Geth. "We can't put in at Umbel City. He'll have the mouth of the North River blockaded as well, no sailing up to meet Hadean that way."

"So, what's the plan? Leave the ship here and continue on horse?"

She nodded. "It's the only way to be sure we don't get snared by the Paellian fleet. Over land, it will be another seven or eight days to the king's camp."

The Windskimmer banked into port, sailors hustling with oars, ropes, and fenders. It didn't take a scholar to deduce that they'd lose at least two days traveling on horse-back, but there was no point complaining. He hadn't told Rondah about the poison lingering in his veins and he didn't intend to.

He looked down at his fingers, counting digits. "Thram's balls." Those two days could be the difference between life and death. Eight more would put him at a fortnight, leaving perhaps a week to find Amalia, assuming she could do what Eora could not. She could be far to the north, in her woods.

And what of Hadean himself? What could have silenced his messengers? Would they find the camp in shambles? Abandoned, or worse?

The king is just fine, he told himself. Pigeons sent ahead would have alerted Hadean to the depths of Elius's betrayal by now, but Geth would relay the loss of Melagus in person. A hand went to his hilt of its own accord. Gods willing, Phelan and the counselor yet lived. Either way, he'd take it out on Towdric. Geth squeezed that hilt til his knuckles went white.

And one day, he'd go back for the king and queen of Pellon.

CHAPTER TWENTY-EIGHT

They left the ships and port of Sirona after little more than a meal and a stretch of the legs. Geth had stowed his red robe and now openly wore the chain he'd taken from Towerrock's armory, long before the journey to Pellon. A wide brimmed hat protected his stubbly head from the sun, but it could do nothing for summer's flies or road dust in his eyes.

Within a few days ride, dizzy spells began to strike him as well. His head went light each morning as he first stood up, and getting on and off his horse. Sweat ran down his sides from more, he feared, than the summer heat.

Eora's healing touch had begun to wear off. Or Weeping Willow's curse had grown. Geth couldn't imagine he had another week—not on his feet anyway. He was running out of time.

But Rondah seemed as eager to return to the king as the big warrior himself. Riding hard, they shaved a full day on the road. The walls and towers of Umbel City and Erehan Keep appeared atop Umbel Hill on the afternoon of the sixth day. Hadean's camp spread to the north and east of the walls. As the rows of tents and banners came into view, something in the eyes of the green-cloaks they passed raised the hairs on the back of Geth's neck.

His heartbeat quickened. The pickets had already announced his arrival, and ahead, Brant emerged from Hadean's tent, face grave. He saw Geth but his smile was fleeting. The big warrior braced himself.

"Master Geth."

Geth knuckled his brow, slid out of the saddle. "Lord Brant." He leaned against the animal and pretended to check the cinch until the dizziness passed.

"We've heard the unfortunate news of King Elius, Lyanne, and Pellon," said Brant. "But come, I have unfortunate news from Umbel as well."

Geth swore under his breath. *He isn't wearing Hadean's crown*, he told himself. *How bad can it be?* He followed Brant back inside the tent.

"We're doing everything we can," the lord said and looked down at his hands.

"Thram and bloody Awer."

The king was laid out on a cot. He wasn't dead, no, but laying there with his arms folded over him, he looked like it. His wife, Eynid, sat beside him, dabbing at his forehead with a cloth. The witch, Amalia, stood to one side, as did Brant's Captain, Worran.

"Poison," Amalia explained.

Geth swallowed. "Will he live?"

"He will. I was able to get to him in time."

Before Geth could breathe a sigh of relief, however, Brant cleared his throat. "We face another problem though, perhaps as a result of this."

"What could be worse?"

"The king can be healed, the Lady Amalia assures it. But word of Towdric's brazen strike has shaken the troops. Our allies are grumbling. Men have deserted. I'll not mimic like the traitor of Turey Hill and hang a man for such a crime and they know it."

"Awer's purple cock."

A shuffling sounded from the cot and Hadean's eyes opened. He smiled. "I know that voice."

"My king!" Geth knelt beside the bed, took his hand. "I'm back. All will be well, Towdric will pay in blood. If I have to strip the flesh from his bones with my teeth."

Hadean managed a weak smile. He patted Geth's hand, but that was all he had. Settling back, he closed his eyes again.

Geth sat there holding his hand, the hand of the man that had stayed his execution, placed his trust in him, raised him from dungeons and gutters to the lofty ramparts of his citadel. He would have stayed longer if that could have helped, but Amalia waved them all outside where Brant led them to his own tent and called for food and drink. Geth found all eyes on him as the meal finished.

"Melagus is dead," he blurted out. "Or lost, anyway. Same for my friend Phelan. They couldn't be found. When I heard things had gone awry back here, I had to quit the search."

"Melagus dead?" Brant shook his head. "I won't believe it until I see the body. He's too clever, that man."

Amalia nodded. "Tell us what happened."

They sat around a small table, the witch leaning in as close as Brant. Geth recounted the meeting Gahalus arranged for them with Lyanne. He told them of Ratcher, how the king's assassins had come after them, how they hunted those bastards in turn, and how they'd searched in vain for the counselor.

"Lyanne has him," Brant concluded. "She knows his value; she'd never let harm come to him."

Geth wasn't sure the lord knew Pellon's queen as well as he did. But he prayed the man was right.

"I'll sue for his release," Brant went on. "Master Phelan too. She may demand a hefty sum, but when the dust settles, she's the one who will pay."

"Well and good," Geth said, "but we can't do anything for them until that blowing bastard in the keep's been dealt with."

Brant opened his mouth. "The king—"

Amalia cut him off. "The king shall not leave his bed for at least a week." She looked exhausted herself, that grey beehive of hers tilted to one side, loose hairs spraying out in places. "I will continue to work on the poison daily, but I assure you, I cannot do more than I already am."

Geth felt a twist of guilt. He'd almost asked for help with his own condition. But here, under the shade of a tent, and with a fresh meal in his belly, he felt better anyway. He could make it another few days.

"How do we dislodge the usurper?" Brant asked. "If it was so simple, we would have done it long since."

Captain Rondah stepped through the tent flap just in time, saluting with fist to heart. "Just the topic I'd hoped to discuss." She swept a grim glance from one face to the other. "Perhaps it's time to bring up the fleet."

"A bold move," said Brant.

"We have the ships. Those lilies can't man the walls and the oars at the same time. If we attack both—now, before our entire army melts away—we just might take the city."

"Storm the walls?" Brant's eyes widened. "A bloody proposition."

Geth grimaced. "As bloody as they come."

"And one Hadean would have avoided at all costs," the lord added. "Is it time? I'm not sure. And I'm not keen to give the order in his absence."

"But can it wait another week?" Rondah asked. "How many more will desert us by then? I've never seen a more defeated lot than this one."

"She isn't lying," Geth said.

"It would cost countless lives," Rondah went on. "I know it. And ships. And cause bad blood for generations between Umbel and Pellon, not to mention within our own kingdom. But something must be done." She punched her own hand, shook her head. "I'd sooner drown to the depths than let the kingdom fall into the hands of that traitor, Towdric."

Brant's eyes went to Amalia, like the witch might have the answer.

"Why can't we just assassinate the bastard?" Geth asked.

"We tried. It was Melagus's idea, but I didn't gainsay him. And we didn't tell the king."

"It failed?"

"Towdric surrounds himself with his most loyal troops. And he's naturally distrustful. It's hard to get close to him."

"So, let's try again." Geth rose from his seat. Not for the first time, he wished he had Ratcher beside him. "Melagus said he had a way into the city. I'll do it myself."

Amalia smiled. "Even without your mustache, Towdric would still recognize a wolf in sheep's clothing."

"Besides," said Brant, "only Hadean knows the way to the postern entrance. It is a secret the kings have always held close, for fear of it being used against them in just this sort of a way. Melagus is the only other person who knows where that entrance lies."

"Should we at least send for the ships?" Geth asked. "Rouse the troops now, give them hope, while we still have men to hold the banners?"

They looked from one to another, each slowly nodding in turn. "Let's do it," Brant said finally. "At least they would be in position to strike, should it come to that."

Geth clasped his shoulder, nodded. But he knew it wasn't enough. Not nearly.

He stepped outside the tent. He didn't know where he was going though, and Amalia caught him up from behind. The fading light cast deep shadows across her face, accentuating the lines on her cheeks and forehead, the frown she wore.

"You look tired. I will have them raise you a tent."

Geth shook his head. "We need help, Amalia." He thought of Neary and the dozen, still at Towerrock, but didn't mention them. He liked them in the north, out of harm's way. "It's like you told me once, a while back. We need allies."

"What are you thinking?"

"Iyngaer. If we're going to war, we may as well bring the tribes with us."

"It could take them weeks to get here."

"Perhaps just a few dozen, to remind the men that Hadean has friends. Fierce ones at that."

Amalia pursed her lips. "More than that would play into Towdric's hands, allow him to tap into fear of the Ilars. It could do more harm than good."

"Perhaps just a few of the chieftain's best men then."

"Are you not thinking of a woman, in truth? Of Vriana?"

Geth exhaled. "Maybe."

Amalia's smile was grandmotherly. She reached out to rest a hand on his elbow. Just as Eora had though, she hissed and recoiled at the touch.

"I've been poisoned," Geth told her. "But I have a friend back in Pellon, a healer. She did what she could."

"There's more than poison there." Amalia shuddered. "And your friend must have done more than I could do already. You should be dead."

Geth blinked. Seeing the worry in her eyes, he did his best to recover. "It's nothing." There was still time he told himself. "I'm not dead yet. And I swear I'm not going anywhere Towdric doesn't go first."

It was Amalia's turn to blink. "You had hoped I could heal you." She opened her mouth but Geth spoke first.

"No matter. Heal the king. Afterwards..."

She nodded, that grandmotherly face replaced by a grim one. "I will think on how it can be done, there must be a way. Until then, let me ease the burden best I can."

She took his hands. Her eyes didn't close, only went distant. She hummed, just as Eora had done with Brega's tea. Geth found his mind drifting in that way. When he blinked himself back into the present, Amalia's breathing came in deep draughts.

"I did what I could," she panted. She let go her grip, adjusted her great beehive, and closed her eyes for a moment. "It is an evil thing upon you, Wolf of the Hills. Not easily turned loose, and not carelessly either."

Geth didn't know what that meant. But as with Eora in Paellia, her ministrations had noticeable effect. He patted himself, shook his head. The dizziness had passed at the very least.

"Thank you." He started to go, then stopped. "Wait. Can you speak to your sisters and, uh, such, from afar?"

"What is it you need?"

"Lyanne."

That grim look showed itself again. "I will search for your friends. She can try to hide them, but if I can raise the queen, she cannot lie to me."

This once, Geth got the answer he wanted to hear. "I thank you, Lady." He dipped his head and started off.

"Get some rest!" she called at his departing back.

Geth marched on, uncertain where exactly he was headed. Green-cloaks lazed about in front of tents but snapped straight at his approach. He took some consolation in that. He saluted with fist to heart. They whispered, wide-eyed, as he passed.

"It's the Wolf. He's back!"

CHAPTER TWENTY-NINE

Geth followed Amalia's advice, found a tent with some familiar faces and invited himself inside to plop down on his bedroll. He felt better, sure, but he was still tired. And he knew he hadn't truly been healed. He would die of that scratch to his neck, by and by, unless the Lady of Witchwood conjured up some strong magick indeed.

But Geth reckoned there was another witch that might be more practiced in the sort of magick that ailed him, someone with a dark streak as wide as a barn door. Someone not so far off either. *Pythelle.* She was inside the city, unless he was wrong, just the place he was headed.

For all his thoughts of the witch Pythelle, it was Agrem Geth dreamed of when he finally fell asleep. And Eko. The wolf found him, ran a joyful circle around his legs, then led him through hill and dell, over streams and under the eaves of Ilia's forest, all the way to his master. The Seer looked up at Geth's arrival, shook his head so those spikes of hair swayed. He rose from his campfire, rested a hand on the big warrior's shoulder and hummed in that familiar way, long and low. "Mmmm."

Eko howled.

That was it. Geth woke with the sound still in his ears. His hand moved, half-hoping to find soft fur against his leg. But the dream was gone. *Maybe I really am dying*, he mused. Seeing spirits of the dead, even the spirit of an animal, was never a good sign.

It was still an hour or so before dawn, but Geth rose, gathered his things, and left in search of his horse. The night's rest had hardened his resolve. No one could end Towdric's reign but him. No one else was as desperate to either.

He found a soldier to help with a fresh shave of his head and beard, then checked to make sure Mother's makeup still covered his tattoos. He stashed about a half-dozen of Ratcher's knives on his body then pulled that red robe on over his head. The men in this camp knew him, but the disguise might work in Umbel City. He'd left there months ago. And to the lilies Palladine had brought, he was a complete stranger.

"Where are you going, Captain?" the Umbel-man-turned-barber asked as Geth climbed in the saddle. "Or should I call you 'Brother?'"

The big warrior snorted a laugh.

"All you need is a basket to beg for alms, Captain. That will send anyone running."

"Wish me luck." Geth adjusted his sword, smoothed the front of his red robes. "Time to make an offering to the Red God."

He climbed into the saddle and flicked the reins. A wide circuit took him south of the city, then back up the coast. He left the beast a few miles from the city, slapped its flank, hoping it might return to Hadean's camp. He found a fisherman to ferry him around the breakwater and into port. Remembering what the soldier had said, he paid extra to take an empty basket with him.

"Go with Awer's blessings," Geth told the man as he climbed up on to the pier

The Umbelman eyed him sideways, counted the coppers he'd been paid, and pushed off.

Geth strode down the length of the port, shaking that basket at everyone he passed. Green-cloaks and lilies questioned all who entered through the Harbor Gate, except Geth when he thrust that basket at them. Him, they waved him through, a grumble their only offering.

"Awer's broad shield protect you, brothers."

The Oathstone gleamed darkly ahead, at the center of Holrain's Court, a great jagged hunk of obsidian, best Geth could tell. This was where it had all began; an innocent fight, a trial, conscription, and a whole war to follow. A whole new life, truth be told. Geth frowned, muttered a curse. He had to kill Towdric. Otherwise, it would all have been for nothing.

But what did he know about being an assassin? Sweat beaded his forehead, whether from the heat of day, the curse in his veins, or just nerves, Geth couldn't say. It was one thing to kill a few, another to master the trade. What *was* certain was that he was no expert bowman, no poisoner, no witch, no master of disguise, and no leader of a troop of murderous sewer-rats. He muttered another curse and turned from the great monolith to peer back out the Harbor Gates.

And there stood Towdric's man, Bushy-brows, a file of lilies behind him, his gaze fixed on Geth like a hungry cat on a mouse.

Geth ran. He bowled over passersby, dodged a tall chunk of wood oddly placed in the middle of the plaza, and ducked down a lane leading uphill. Bushy-brows and those Paellian sonsabitches came right behind.

"Get the bastard!"

Pedestrians cried out, plastered themselves against the walls of shops and homes to either side. Lilies grunted and cursed in pursuit. With a glance over his shoulder Geth realized the same pedestrians moved coyly to hinder the white-clad foreigners. Head shaved, robed in Awer's red, there was no way anyone recognized him. They just hated the lilies that much.

But sweat streamed down Geth's face, his breath ragged, panting as he ran. He'd hoped to lose Bushy-brows and his gang, using his strength to outrun them going uphill like a bear outrunning a doe. The curse in his blood was too much though. He had to turn and fight eventually.

Scaffolding built up against the side of a building further ahead caught his eye. Buckets, timber, and tools sat in piles along the platform stretching just over a man's height across the frontage. With a lowered shoulder, Geth ran full into the nearest support, dumping those supplies behind him to tumble into the street and downhill.

The impact spun the big warrior halfway, but he drew his sword in the same motion, bit down the pain, and reversed course to charge after the little avalanche. The first lily looked up, eyes wide, and dove to one side. Geth hacked through the parry of a second man to batter him down and send him cursing into the knees of a third.

The fourth man was Bushy-brows. He skirted around his downed comrades to feign a slash at Geth from the left. The move steered Geth toward the three fallen men, but the big warrior hopped over one then another and surprised everyone, including himself, by continuing at a dead sprint downhill, back the way he'd come.

Sword raised, he screamed at the stragglers of the pack, kicking a bucket as he went, parting them like startled cattle. "Argh!" He passed the first pair, barged over another that didn't move quick enough. He was almost free.

"Someone stick the filthy mutt!" Bushy-brows swore behind him.

A narrow alley on Geth's right offered a way around the last of the lilies and Geth made for it, thighs burning, breath coming in gasps. Bushy-brows appeared around the corner behind him, leading the pursuit. But he was blowing almost as hard as the big warrior. Up ahead, a man stepped out of a back door, presumably to take a piss, but seeing Geth and his pursuers, jumped halfway back inside.

His head peeked out once more. "This way, man!" he hissed and flung his door wide. "Shit-stinking foreigners!"

Geth pounded through what looked to be a small tavern, upsetting a tray of drinks by accident before bursting through into the street again.

"Sorry!"

Outside, he doubled half over, hands on his knees to suck in a few breaths, then took off again at a run. He made a left at the first turn. The harbor and the sea beckoned down below.

Bushy-brows yelled somewhere behind him, but a vague notion of escaping back out through the Harbor Gates sent Geth downhill at a stumbling run. Sweat rolled down his face, stung his eyes. The sword in his hands, that chain shirt, seemed to weigh a thousand pounds. He slowed to a walk and sheathed his blade as he reached the wide plaza of Holrain's Court, trying to blend in, to walk right out the gates.

He didn't make it three strides.

"Leaving already?"

That voice, from over Geth's shoulder, froze him where he stood. *Palladine.*

Up ahead, those twins—Snake Eyes—materialized, knives at their sides. By the time Geth turned around, pedestrians were already scrambling away. Palladine waited with sword ready, cuirass gleaming. His shaved head flushed pink from too much sun or the usual amount of ire. Geth didn't waste any breath on words. He drew his blade and charged.

Palladine parried Geth's arcing swing with a smooth sidestep, deflecting the brunt of it as the big warrior slid past. The clang of steel on steel echoed across the plaza and a woman screamed as Geth whirled and slashed again. The Paellian skipped and moved, dodging, weaving expertly out of the way.

He was good. But Geth knew he could take him.

"Argh!" He battered at the Paellian, from the left, from the right, thrusting straight. Palladine gritted his teeth but managed to stay clear. *Buying time.* With a wide sweep, Geth backed the lily captain away then turned in time to hack at one of the twins, throwing a kick at the other. Both fell far short. These two weren't keen to cross blades with the big warrior and they knew they didn't have to. Sweat was coming down Geth's face in rivulets. His mouth hung open as he sucked in air.

He whirled back toward Palladine, switched his grip from right hand to left. He almost had the bastard.

But his arm failed him. The thrust he aimed at the opening at the Paellian's armpit came in low, clanked off that cuirass instead. Palladine grunted, recovered with a slash of his own, and Geth was forced to leave him to swipe at a twin before that one could slip up close with his knife. As Geth turned again to face the captain, the world spun.

It was over. He found his footing, but the three bastards surrounding Geth just wore at him, one thrust at a time, driving him one way then the other. "Bastard...sonsa..."

It was all Geth could manage. As one twin slid close to threaten with his knife, Palladine darted up from behind to sweep his back leg with a kick. Geth collapsed to one knee, swung a backhanded slash at the other twin. Pain exploded across the back of Geth's head, and he caught sight of Palladine's boot in the fraction of a second before he hit the cobbles.

"Been wanting to do that for a long while," said a voice.

And then everything went dark.

CHAPTER THIRTY

It was the same cell they'd stowed Geth in almost a year before, beneath the stones of Erehan Keep. But it was hotter than he remembered. So very hot. Maybe it was just the time of year, or maybe it was his sickness. If not for the curse in his veins, he was sure he wouldn't have been caught in the first place.

At least they hadn't beaten him much—they didn't have to in his weakened state—and Geth had the dungeon all to himself this time around. He found that odd. Then again, he was no mere tavern-brawler, no foreign nuisance, but a known and reviled enemy of the regime.

As such, Towdric came to *him*.

The usurper's booming voice announced his approach, echoing off the stones. "The gods love me! What a day! Ha!"

"Bloody bastard," Geth muttered from his seat on the floor.

The sound of several pairs of boots stopped in front of his cell. Keys rattled, the bolt ground across its slot, and the door opened.

Towdric squinted in at him. "What's wrong, Wolf? Got the mange? You look terrible."

"Come to gloat?" Geth rasped. "Why bother? There's no one to hear it but me."

"There will come a time for something more. For now, your mangy ears are enough." Towdric grinned.

Geth said nothing, just glared back until the usurper rested hands on hips, leaned forward, giddy almost by the looks of it.

"Don't you get it? You've handed me the kingdom. And I didn't even have to draw a blade. Hadean's half dead already, you know that. And his army's melting away like...well, a prisoner in the dungeons in midsummer. But what better way to make it clear that the boy's day is ended than by putting down his infamous pet wolf?"

Geth lifted his chin, croaked a laugh. "You really believe that will work?"

"I know it will. Hadean's allies will be lining up to make amends with me once they see your head on a spike."

Towdric looked like a he wanted to say more, but the sound of footfalls coming down the stairs turned him. A familiar voice, a voice that Geth hated as much as the usurper's, sounded.

"A fine capture, is it not?" Palladine said. "But don't make any plans to mount those antlers on your wall. The fugitive returns to Pellon with me, as agreed. *Alive.*"

Geth couldn't see more than Towdric and a pair of jailors through the frame of the doorway, but the lord shot a hard look to his right. "Not now, Captain. We can discuss the details later."

"We agreed—"

"Things have changed."

"Nothing has changed. Except that I have once again furthered your bid for the throne."

"I *have* the throne."

"But little more than that. And if you think killing—"

"He needs to die!" Towdric slapped the pommel of his sword. "Here in Umbel, where everyone can see it!"

Silence from the other end of the hall.

The tension in that dungeon was like a pot too long on the boil, trembling, foaming, threatening to spill over. Geth could still only see Towdric, but the usurper leaned into that stare now, rightwards, toward the place Palladine must have stood.

For the first time since he'd been caught, Geth felt a glimmer of hope. If he could drive a wedge between Towdric and the Sworn Realm of Pellon, his strongest ally, it didn't matter the cost. An idea sprang to mind, but a female voice chimed in before he could think more on it.

"If I may, the both of you speak truth. Each in part."

The witch, Pythelle. Geth licked his lips. She must have been there all along. Not that there was anything for it. Towdric's eyes narrowed as he turned toward the sound of her voice, hands back on his hips, chin raised. "Speak your thoughts and be plain."

"I know your mind, my king. You mean to execute the wolf atop the walls, where your enemies can all see it, break their spirit."

"That's exactly what I mean to do."

"But tread warily." Pythelle came into view, moving closer to Towdric. "What if you only anger them, spur them to vengeance? Do not underestimate what a lead wolf means to the pack. If you want a bloodless revolution, this isn't the way."

Towdric snorted. "So you say."

"Neither is it the way to appease the captain." She flicked a glance in Palladine's direction. "Who profits if the false king attacks the walls? Or if the Paellian fleet returns to the Golden City—" her eyes turned back up the hall,

"—returns with no fugitive in hand and an angry young king on the throne of a sworn ally? Neither of you."

Towdric spat. He opened his mouth, but Palladine spoke first.

"What do you propose?"

"First, and above all, you don't want Hadean to storm the walls. Even in victory, it would cost many lives. And it's no secret that your men, Captain Palladine, are already unhappy with their visit to Umbel."

"Not entirely true."

Pythelle ignored that. "Now that the false king has sent for his fleet, what do you think will happen? Things won't get easier, that's certain. Your soldiers may have to cede their ships and endure a siege behind these walls. Or fight a battle at sea they may well lose."

Towdric snorted. "Let the boy come. If he finds his courage at last and attacks, we'll thrash him."

"Perhaps. But why take the risk? Why not draw things out, let his forces slip away until victory is all but assured?"

Palladine cleared his throat. "Perhaps we don't kill him at all. As promised. Without his guard dog to protect him, it's only a matter of time before one of the queen's contractors gets to Hadean. We've almost got him now. Worse case, I can send the brothers."

Towdric's eyes narrowed. But he didn't immediately squash the idea. He could be shrewd, Geth reckoned. That's what made him dangerous.

But when those eyes swung back around to Geth, the hatred in them told the big warrior all he needed to know. "You speak truth," Towdric said. "I won't kill him straightaway. I'll make sure that Hadean and all his allies know we have him first, let them stew. When word of it spreads, those allies and all their men will be running out of Hadean's camp like sweat down a plowman's back. I'll kill him after that."

"You agreed he would be *mine!*" Palladine hissed. "Breaking promises before your reign has even begun? What will the king and queen think of that?"

"Watch your tongue, Captain! You are speaking to a king now."

Pythelle pursed her lips. "And yet, does he not make a valid point? What would they think, indeed?"

Towdric put on that big, fake, smile. "Of course. It is not my intent to cheat anyone, least of all you, Captain. You deserve better. But I still want his head. I *must* have it. So then, how about a compromise?"

The question hung for a moment. Geth could feel Palladine's anger rising. Towdric continued before he could speak though, raising both hands.

"Don't judge the offer before you've heard it. I think it's a good one. I must have his head, and you want it. But what if you, sir, were the one to swing the axe?"

CHAPTER THIRTY-ONE

By the sound of things, Palladine was first to leave. Towdric aimed that broad smile of his at Geth one last time, then turned, rubbing his hands together as he went. Pythelle, however, stayed behind with two grim-faced jailors.

"You probably wish you'd accepted my offer of employment last year," she said.

Geth tried to laugh, but no sound came out. He didn't have the energy for it.

"You really are in bad shape, you know." She motioned to the jailors. They stepped into the room. At her instruction, they drew steel, resting a cool tip on either side of Geth's neck. He didn't bristle, didn't have the strength. The witch followed them inside, crouched beside the big warrior with a frown. A hand touched his leg.

As with Eora and Amalia before, she recoiled. "You're dying."

Geth smiled. This time he made sure his laughter was heard. "I guess that'll put a damper on Towdric's plans, won't it?"

Pythelle shivered, reached out again, rested a hand directly on his chest. "Blood magic. The killing sort." She pursed her lips. "No, that won't do."

Her eyes were closed, expression unreadable, but the two jailors looked uncertainly from one to the other. She wouldn't harm him, Geth knew that, but he felt something. His heart skipped and his head went light. It was over in a few moments. He knew she'd healed, not harmed.

Some measure of strength was back. He shot out a manacled hand, took Pythelle by the throat, even as two sword points dug into his trachea from opposite sides.

"Watch it, Wolf!"

Geth ignored them. "Why shouldn't I kill you?" he told the witch. "You've given me the strength to do it. And Towdric's going to execute me anyway. Why shouldn't I take you down with me?"

Pythelle just made a choking sound, both hands clutching at his grip until he loosened it a hair. She gasped.

"Because," she croaked, "you know I don't deserve to die. I'm just like you after all."

"You and me alike? Ha!" Geth spit. "What are we then?"

"Survivors."

Geth cursed her roundly. They were nothing alike. But something wouldn't let him kill her, not like that, unarmed, and right after she'd healed him. He shoved her away.

Pythelle stumbled backward onto her rump, but only snorted a laugh, rose to her feet and stepped out into the hall. The two guards backed out after, swords up. Geth pushed up to his feet, doing his best to stare down at them from his considerable height. They took no chances, slammed the door shut.

"At least you feel better," Pythelle called through the little barred window. "Don't forget it was I that gave you that."

"And why did you?"

"So you live to see your execution day of course."

Geth's curses trailed her up the stairs and out the dungeon. When she was gone, he sank back to his seat against the wall. He had some measure of strength again, true, but it really was as hot as an oven beneath those stones.

These were what they called the 'dog days' he reckoned, when all you wanted to do was lay down in the shade and wait for it to end.

But Geth wasn't ready for it to end. And he certainly wasn't going to lay down and wait for it.

"Thram's twisted, hairy balls. How do I get out of this dungeon though?"

Days passed. Neary never showed up to break Geth out and Ceter the warlock didn't arrive to upset the balance of the fortress either. No singing of Amalia could turn Geth's waking nightmare to a dream escape and Ratcher with his blinding dust and disguises was far off in Paellia. What strength Pythelle had given the big warrior began to wane. Sweat beaded his forehead, dizzy spells washed over him even while he remained seated. Hope faded until shuffling footfalls sounded outside his door and a bony hand thrust itself between the bars of the little window.

"Who's there?" Geth growled.

The hand shook, a cloth of some kind wrapped inside its grip. "Hurry, m'lord! Take it!"

Geth rose to his feet, peered through the bars. Outside in the hall, an old woman stood trembling, looking back the way she'd come. Geth took the parcel, opened it to reveal a piece of soft bread, some ham, a slice of cheese. After days of stale crusts, the smell of it set his mouth watering. He shoved a bite in—why worry, he was already poisoned anyway?—and swallowed it down like an animal.

"You have friends in this city, my lord!" breathed the woman.

And just like that, she hurried off the way she'd come. Geth didn't dare call after for fear of setting the guards on her. He started to wipe his chin with the cloth, until he noticed crude markings on the inside. He held it up to catch the light. It was a rough sketch of a dog. He tore into another bite and muttered to himself between swallows. "Dog days indeed."

It couldn't be much longer, Geth reckoned. He was going to die. But the old woman's small act of kindness, of defiance, gave him new determination. She said he had friends. He doubted he had the sort of friends that could break him out of that place, and yet it was something. He wouldn't die without a fight.

Strangling men with his manacles though, or kicking and punching bastards to their death wasn't an option, not in his weakened state. Neither was running. He had to have a plan. The only prospect that came to mind was to the tension between Towdric and Palladine. If he could get close to the captain, there was still a chance.

Towdric himself arrived to haul him out the very same day. His jailors entered the cell with bared steel, but it took Geth some effort just to clamber to his feet.

"Ready, Wolf?" Towdric wore that wide smile. "It's your big day. I know you spent some time with the Mog. If you believe how they tell it, you'll soon have an army of slain enemies to look after you in Vorda's Hall."

"Eat shit, Towdric."

The usurper chuckled. "It almost makes me hesitate to kill you, Wolf. Except that it would mean that you, and all your slain enemies, will be serving *me* one day as well." His smile went even wider. "Not for a long while yet though."

"You think they won't avenge me?" Geth asked. "My friends? You think King Hadean and all the rest will just forget?"

Towdric laughed. For all the scorn, there was real mirth in it too. "They've already forgotten about you, Wolf. Where are they now? And where are you? After all you've done for them."

"They—"

"They know where you are. Don't make excuses. I made sure of it, made sure they *stewed* on it. And tomorrow, when it's all done, I'll send you back to them." Towdric motioned with a finger across his neck. "Well, the upper bit anyway."

"You'll get what you've got coming," Geth said. "By all the gods."

"You should have sworn to me, Wolf. I offered, remember? You refused. You risked everything for that fool boy and the rest of them." He put all the scorn he had into his words. "Where arc they now, Wolf. Not here. No, they left you to die. Alone."

He turned on his heels and marched out, head high. More guardsmen waited in the dim hallway, Bushy-brows among them. They hauled Geth by the manacles, up and into a grim, overcast day. Wind whipped the green and white banners on the ramparts, the promise of a storm on the air.

Green-cloaks jeered as they marched Geth out of the keep. Up ahead, he saw Towdric and a column of riders along with several dozen footmen, descending the switch-back from the great fortress toward the thatched rooftops of the city below. Sweaty laborers and plain-clothed womenfolk watched the column pass with dull eyes as they reached the shops and homes of the city. A thin crowd lined the avenue. Geth tried to hold his chin up, but that walk was exhausting, even if it was all downhill.

Sweat rolled off the stubble on his head. He clenched his jaw and concentrated on each step forward. He wasn't about to give these bastards the satisfaction of watching him stumble.

But where was Palladine? *I'll be standing in front of the bastard soon enough,* Geth told himself. *Or kneeling, more like.* He thought of Hadean, of Vriana and Agrem, of Eora, of Phelan and of the dozen. Still, it was Palladine he wished for.

That wish was granted.

"I'll take him from here."

Geth looked up, almost in a daze already and still only halfway down Umbel Hill. The captain stood there in his polished cuirass, flanked by the twins known as Snake Eyes and a handful of his own white-clad soldiers. Bushy-brows passed Geth over without argument.

The big warrior waited until that one was out of earshot. "Just the man I wanted to see," he told Palladine.

"I could say the same." The captain waved and two big lilies took Geth at the elbows. Palladine came behind him, almost near enough to whisper in Geth's ear.

"I just wanted you to know that even when this is over for you, it won't be over for me."

Geth held his own words back, let the man spill whatever information he might.

"I'm coming for your mother next, back in Sorn. Do you hear me, Stray? I'm coming for all your little friends, especially that thief. And once I have them, I'm coming for your child."

"I don't have a child."

Palladine laughed. "You will in a few months."

Geth felt a lump of ice form in his stomach.

But he shook his head, willed himself to stay focused. *Empty threats.* He had to choose his words, not waste his breath on curses. If he didn't speak soon, he might be too sick to speak at all.

"He's using you, Palladine. Don't you see it? He's cheating you."

"He's trying to."

Geth craned his neck but failed to turn far enough to catch a glimpse of the captain. "He'll double cross you first chance. And he'll laugh when he's done. He's probably laughing already. But you can have it all, all that you deserve."

Palladine snorted. "You think you know what I deserve?"

"Take me back to Pellon. I won't fight it. That's what you want, isn't it? Don't let Towdric have his way. He needs you. You have the power here. Don't give in to that blowing bastard just for the asking."

Palladine didn't answer.

Had he done it? Geth prayed. He would still probably die, but at least there was a chance. And for Hadean, a rift between Towdric and Palladine would be enough to turn the tide. If Geth did die, he reckoned he'd still have won.

He felt like he might die right then and there. A wave of dizziness swept over him and he felt himself teeter into the lily to his right. The man cursed him, hauled him up. But Geth moved like he was in a dream. A bad one at that. He smelled blood and his vision was a little bright, like he'd taken a crack on the head. He heard the voice of Lord Wels cackling. And he saw faces in the crowd lining the way, some jeering, some mournful, some strangers, others familiar but impossible, like Ratcher, Agrem, and even his mother.

"Don't die on me yet, Stray," Palladine said.

They pulled him to a halt at the edge of Holrain's wide court. Geth was thankful for the rest. A veritable crowd had assembled, packing the cobbles to watch, solemn-faced. Green-cloaks looked on from balconies and windows. They lined the edges of a wide, cleared space. Towdric and his mounted column waited there, the Oathstone shadowing over them, a headsman's block at the center of it, beneath the shadow of the great monolith.

Lilies pushed a pathway through for them and the crowd parted. Geth recognized the block of wood ahead as the same piece he'd dodged a few days earlier. The wind whipped and a little patter of rain struck him. Even the weather was against him. He started to mutter a curse, but Towdric cantered up on his horse, hands raised to gather attention.

"Loyal subjects!" he bellowed. "You've been called forth to witness the execution of a heinous criminal! A foreigner, a consort of northern enemies! A murderer and a traitor to the peaceful realm of Umbel!"

He paused, tugged his reins to turn his mount in a half circle to make sure those behind him were listening.

As if they could miss all the blowing, Geth thought. *Shit-stinking whale.*

"Order, my people, is what holds a kingdom together! Law is what guides us to ensure peace and order! And when a man *betrays*," he paused to let the word hang, "*lies,*" another pause, "*steals,*" pause, "And *kills*...justice must be meted out!"

Towdric let the words sink in a moment then gave a dramatic sigh, shook his head, chin down as if saddened. He pointed to one side of the court. "It pains me to know that this same criminal killed a man just there." He wagged his finger. "It pains to know he stood trial for it, under a weaker man, and walked away with no punishment. Indeed, he was rewarded!"

Geth opened his mouth to holler back, but a jab in the side took his breath, doubled him over. He would have collapsed all the way to the ground if not for the sturdy grip on each side of him.

Towdric bellowed on. "My subjects! It takes *strength* to serve justice! *Sacrifice*! *Courage*! The same virtues that see us through times of war, through pestilence, through famine! I thank the gods, one and all, to have such strength, now and until my death, for the service of this great kingdom, and you, my flock, within it!"

A shove from behind started Geth into open space and toward the headsman's block. The corners of Towdric's mouth were turned solemnly down, but there was no mistaking the twinkle in his eye. At least the Umbelfolk around the court seemed to disapprove. Not a one of them hooted or spit.

"And here he is!" Towdric backed his horse up a few paces to make room as Palladine and his lilies pushed Geth toward the block.

Standing on death's door, the big warrior's head cleared though, his heart pumping with one last measure of strength.

"Well?" Geth craned his neck back toward Palladine. "You really gonna hand that gloating bastard all he wants? And let him laugh at you forever after?"

The captain's eyes were as icy as ever. "As long as I kill you—*and* those you love—that will be enough."

CHAPTER THIRTY-TWO

Palladine hefted a wicked-looking axe as his lilies shoved Geth toward the headsman's block. Geth struggled against them, skidding forward on the heels of his boots. They tried to double him over as they went, but he arched his back. Head up, his eyes landed on an unlikely patch of hope, sandwiched in among the onlookers.

Agrem?

He *had* seen him. The Seer's lips moved. Impossibly, from across the cobbles, Geth heard his voice like he spoke directly in his ear.

"You are not alone, mmmm?"

He followed the Seer's eyes as they moved and a few paces down, there stood Iyngaer's man, Fork-beard, decked out in Sunlander dress. Further still, he saw Captain Rondah, and, against all odds, Ratcher, aproned like a blacksmith, carrying a sheathed sword. Last of all, his eyes found Phelan. The little man winked.

Everything happened at once. A commotion sounded under the Harbor Gate and a cluster in Paellian white marched into the plaza and through the crowd, right toward himself and Palladine. From somewhere up the hill, the sound of hoofbeats could be heard—reinforcements, Geth reckoned—but the Paellians arrived first.

"Stand down!"

Geth blinked. It was Prince Gahalus, cuirass shining, flanked by a gaggle of lily officers. Geth heard an intake of breath from one of the soldiers holding him.

But Palladine only kicked Geth savagely behind the knee, dropped him expertly onto the headsman's block so that his chin landed right in the cup.

"Stand down, I say!" Gahalus snarled. Geth's head was too low to see, but the sound of swords scraping out of sheaths rang in his ear. "Think, Captain, before you make a misstep from which you can never recover!"

Palladine hesitated and Geth sat halfway back up.

But Towdric's voice echoed loud. "What is this?" He kicked his mount to block Gahalus's path, straightened the gold band on his head pointedly. "You must be the prince. Leave the business of Umbel to us, sir. This is no place for outside intrusion."

Gahalus dipped his head. "Leave, you say? I intend to. And I leave you to it." He looked past the usurper, stabbed a finger at the lily soldiers holding Geth. "You heard the king, leave him."

They didn't need to hear anything else. The hands on Geth loosened and they backed away. Palladine, however, moved in to take Geth's arm, that big axe wedged up under his chin.

"This man is wanted in Paellia. As a Hand of Justice—"

"I know your station, Palladine," Gahalus's voice dripped with the kind of scorn only a prince could manage. "And I've come with instructions that supersede your orders."

"Supersede?" Palladine's blue eyes narrowed.

"That's right." Gahalus turned to address the lilies all throughout the court and up above them on the walls. "Brothers! I am here to rescue you." He flashed a smile. "That's right, pack your things. We're going home!"

A hoot went up from more than a few Paellian soldiers, a veritable cheer from the Umbelmen and women all around. Lilies started off in the direction of the harbor in twos and threes, clapping each other on the back and hailing the prince as they went. Gods but they loved the young scratch.

Towdric moved his horse in close to Gahalus. "You'll regret this," he hissed. His hand went to his hilt. Palladine's axe still scratched the underside of Geth's chin as well.

Gahalus ignored the usurper. "Leave him, Palladine." The prince lifted the bare blade in his hand, only a few steps away now himself.

"I know what you're at," Palladine said, voice cool and even. "Taking quite a risk, but then, you always were a rogue. What will your mother say when she learns what you've done?"

"*You're* the rogue. You've steered the entire realm down a path of folly, just to save face, to get revenge! Taking sides with a usurper? Where's your honor?"

Palladine lowered the axe a hair, but Towdric snorted from his saddle. "Take your ships if you wish. Strip the captain's cuirass. But it's him that's right. When word reaches your mother, those same ships will be headed straight back."

Gahalus said nothing, sword still bared, but Palladine hissed at Towdric over Geth's shoulder. "See to it this one dies."

Bushy-brows and several other green-cloaks moved in to take Geth roughly in hand. Snakes Eyes appeared from out of nowhere to flank the captain as he stalked away.

"Give him here," Gahalus said, gesturing with his hand.

Towdric just shook his head, baring that evil smile. "I don't think I will."

CHAPTER THIRTY-THREE

"Get me that axe!" Towdric said, climbing down from his saddle.

Bushy-brows laughed like that was the funniest thing he'd ever heard. Gahalus shouted a protest and Agrem, Fork-beard, Rondah, and Phelan rushed to join him.

"This man is wanted by the Justicar in Paellia," said the prince. "He comes with me."

"He's already been sentenced to death," Towdric growled. "Here, in Umbel. And by my order, the king. It's time for him to die."

Green-cloaks with drawn steel fell in around the king, surrounding Geth and Bushy-brows as well.

"Towdric—"

"Your turn to stand down, Princeling!" Towdric said. "Do you think you can supersede me too? In my own realm?" He pointed and a pair of his men dragged the chopping block over.

"Bastard!" Geth bucked, swung an elbow into the man on his right. But his hands were chained, and they were all over him. Fists pummeled him from every direction. They dragged him in front of the block, bent him double over it with a punch in the ribs.

One fat boot appeared at the edge of Geth's vision and sweat dripped off his head to wet the cobbles beside it. The shadow of that axe fell over him as Towdric took position. "This traitor is sentenced to die! By order of me, the king!"

"You're no king!" someone shouted. A collective gasp sounded from hundreds of onlookers.

Geth twisted the best he could, but there was no need to see—the hoofbeats he'd heard, the green-cloaks, it all made sense. Hadean himself had come.

No, Geth wasn't alone at all.

"You!" Towdric pointed that axe in the direction of Hadean's voice. "Take him!"

Green-cloaks started toward the king. But in all the commotion, Geth sat up enough to see that Hadean hadn't come alone. They weren't a fearsome lot, the ten-odd men mounted at his side, but Geth had never been happier to see them.

Kerrel moved to Hadean's right, Hack to his left. Towdric's men formed up as well, cursing as they neared. Melagus kicked his steed out in front of them all, however, arms raised.

"Stop! Men of Umbel, pride of the realm! Do we spill our own blood here beneath the Oathstone? Will sworn brothers forsake the green they both wear, the people of Umbel City—King Hadean's people—against the kinfolk of their own beloved Queen Eynid, and the other way around?"

Even half-bent over a headsman's block, Geth laughed. Bold, the little bastard, and clever, reminding Towdric's men that their lady would still be queen even if their lord lost. What were they fighting for, some of them must have been asking themselves. They hesitated.

At the same time, the counselor's words called on the people of the city. *Hadean's* people They did not fail him. The gathered crowd responded by surging through the thin line of green-cloaks holding them at bay around the court. They weren't armed, but a mob of angry citizens piled in behind Hadean to stare down Towdric's warriors.

"It's over," Hadean said. "Surrender, Towdric. The Paellians are leaving. You can't hold the city."

"This city is mine!" Towdric bellowed. "Who are you? The boy who nearly lost us the north? The boy who rubs elbows with savages, releases killers and criminals to pray on decent folk? You are no king. And no Turian sword can say otherwise. I am the king!"

Agrem appeared, Fork-beard beside him. The Seer's hands raised in imitation of Melagus and Towdric earlier. "The tribes do not recognize you as king. Sunlanders must not kill each other, must not war, mmmm? So, there must be a trial."

"A trial?" Towdric barked a laugh. "I have the soldiers. I have the city. I am the king!"

Agrem lifted a crooked finger. "But he has the white army. He has the ships. Mmmm?"

Towdric's eyes narrowed. Geth, too, wondered what the hell Agrem was angling for. *Not another bloody trial?*

The usurper figured it out first. "A trial, you say." Geth didn't like the gleam in his eye. "A trial of *arms* is what you mean, isn't it? A duel for the throne."

CHAPTER THIRTY-FOUR

Mutterings of approval swept through both sides. None of these green-cloaks really wanted to kill their countrymen. Hadean had clearly never wanted to attack his own city either. But even from Geth's position over the block, he could see that the lad was still pale, only half-healed from his poisoning. He was an able fighter, a hero even, but he'd never beat a seasoned warrior like Towdric in this condition.

Melagus stepped between the two parties again.

"Thram and bloody Awer..." Geth cursed. He knew where this was going.

"Yes!" Melagus lifted both arms. "Trial by combat! Call forth the champions!"

Melagus, Hadean, Phelan and all the rest swung triumphant looks in Geth's direction. The big warrior cursed again. They didn't know he'd been poisoned.

But Towdric knew.

"The gods stand beside me. I need no champion." The bastard could barely contain a smile as he flicked a sideways glance in Geth's direction. With a wave, the two jailors arrived to unshackle the big warrior.

What choice did he have? Geth forced his shoulders back, stood as tall as he could. The gathering stepped back to clear a space. Towdric rolled out his shoulders, swung his sword through the air. Geth wiped sweat from his brow, fought down a wave of dizziness, blinked to clear his eyes, and set his jaw.

"I need a sword." He turned back toward his friends. Phelan moved within touching distance, squeezed his arm. Agrem nodded up at him. Fork-beard offered his weapon. Hadean dismounted, however, to pass over the sword of Umbel's kings.

"Vingil." Sweat dampened the lad's hair beneath his crown. His face was pasty, gaunt, but there wasn't a hint of doubt in his eyes.

Geth wiped his hands on his pants, took the sheathed blade, drew it slowly. He examined the flawless length. His arm tried to shake. He took the weapon in a double handed grip to steady it.

"Turian steel, the finest."

Hadean frowned. He hadn't missed the tremble. "You don't look well, Captain."

"Me?" Geth mustered a laugh. "I've been dreaming of the day I get to swing a sword at that bastard. Nothing could keep me from it."

He turned before the king could say more. He knew he was weak, but he was still the best, he told himself. And what was Towdric, but a grunting old pig, long past his prime?

"Long past." Geth mouthed aloud. He swung Vingil a few times, did a high step to limber his legs and get his blood pumping. That seemed to help. "Now let's kill this bastard."

From the center of the space, Geth caught Melagus watching him. The counselor blinked, doubt flashing across his face for the first time. But he composed himself quickly. His mouth went tight, and he nodded. He cleared his throat, raised both arms.

"By the oldest law," he said, loud enough for all in the court to hear, "a dispute for the kingship may be decided by combat. So has it been agreed between Hadean and Towdric. Either may yield, but both and all must abide by the outcome. No blood shall be spilled this day, unless it be in this trial. So we all swear before the Great Shaper and all the gods!"

Oaths were sworn, hands on the Oathstone itself, but Geth hardly listened. *How do I win?* His mind was fuzzy, he could hardly remember how Towdric liked to fight. There was little to be gained from studying the battleground either. The cobbles were mostly even, with no obstacles of course, except the headsman's block, hauled to one edge of the fighting circle. Towdric saved his bellowing for once and just glowered at Geth over the tip of his sword.

"Let it begin!" Melagus said.

Towdric met Geth near the center of the space, crown replaced with a helmet, shield on his left arm. Their blades touched. The bastard charged.

Geth parried one blow, then another, skipped back a pace, flicked a thrust in return. The usurper knocked it aside, teeth gritted, but he didn't press further.

It had been a test, and Geth passed. Towdric must have wondered just how weakened the big warrior was. He knew now that Geth wouldn't simply collapse onto his sword. Not yet anyway. Towdric watched him, circling warily.

Geth tried to think, searching for some weakness, something to give him the advantage. Towdric had that helmet, mail, and fought with a round shield in addition to his sword, where Geth carried only Vingil, wore nothing but a sweated-though tunic. No matter. The weight of extra

trappings would have only slowed him down in his com-
promised state. Would they slow down Towdric? He could
only pray.

A wind gusted as if in answer, a few patters of rain
fell, then ceased. It would take a well-placed strike to kill
the scratch, Geth mused, armored as he was. And Geth
didn't reckon Towdric would be the first to tire either. He
snorted a grim laugh. No, there was nothing for it but to
attack.

He surged forward, feigning a high swing, only to bring
the cut in lower, with the intent to follow it up with another swing from the left then right. But Towdric took it on
his shield and skipped back. Chasing the bastard forward
made Geth's head swim. He had no choice but to pull up,
let him retreat.

Towdric frowned. He hadn't missed it.

He came to some sort of decision, Geth could see it
in those malevolent eyes. Towdric circled toward his left.
Geth switched his sword to that hand, dipped at the knees
and sent a thrust below the shield at Towdric's leading leg.
It slipped under, but there wasn't enough in it to pierce
the skirt of the usurper's mail.

The crowd hollered, some jeering Geth, others calling
encouragement or cursing. Towdric kept moving, circling,
feigning lunges, stepping back, stepping to either side. A

few onlookers at the very edge of the fighting space heckled the usurper as they were forced to move further back, opening the space wider. But Geth could see what he was about.

He was trying to wear Geth out. Not by getting too close where a lucky strike could find him, but by keeping the big warrior always on the move. It was working too.

"Come to the skewer, piglet!" Geth cursed him. He sucked in a deep breath and struck a series of cuts, right, left, right again. He thought he'd put his weight behind it, but Towdric parried them evenly.

From over the rim of his shield, the bastard smiled. That gleam was back in his eye. He was winning and he knew it. Gods, how Geth hated him.

Towdric circled toward his left again, flicking darting thrusts. Geth concentrated on deflecting each, unable to try the same under-shield strike that had almost worked before. Without warning, Towdric shifted his attack to circle right, swinging heavy, arcing blows. Geth was nearly caught by the first of these, stumbling as he switched directions, head gone light.

But as Towdric pressed, still swinging those arm-shuddering arcs, Geth thought of poor Eko, gathered his rage, parried with all his remaining might. He grunted, knocked one last slash aside, lifted Vingil in both hands to hammer down at the usurper from above. Towdric took the blow on his shield, knees expertly bent to absorb it, throwing out a kick to catch Geth in the thigh right after.

Geth stumbled again. The crowd gasped. His head spun. Somewhere in there, Towdric's blade licked out like a hot tongue to cut a burning line across one tattooed forearm. Geth cursed, looked down. The bracers he wore had saved his tendons from being sliced, but blood welled and ran down to his elbow.

Towdric bellowed a laugh. "A worthy foe," he said, loud enough for all to hear. "A hero, they say! And yet the will of the gods cannot be denied!"

He swung at Geth again. But even the big warrior could tell he was pulling his punches now. Geth parried, sent a blow back. Towdric made a show of blocking it with a hard, clattering cut of his own.

Damn you, Towdric!

He didn't have the breath to mouth it aloud. The bastard was managing appearances, making a show of his things, as always. He'd come out of this as king, and the man that had beaten Hadean's best swordsman to boot.

Geth retreated a step, ran the back of his hand over his brow to clear the sweat. The world tried to spin but he squinted, blew out a hard breath, steadied himself. He couldn't keep this up. He'd lost. Maybe it would be smarter to just let the bastard stick him, he mused—refuse to play the game, be made a fool. But he had to hope, for Hadean and for his friends.

He roared a futile challenge and swung with everything he had left, stumbling into the blow. Towdric grunted, parried hard, and knocked Vingil clear out of Geth's grip, the big warrior's momentum carrying him right past the usurper to land in a heap on the cobbles.

Instinct made him roll. His hand found Vingil and he came up to all fours with the blade in one hand. But Towdric hadn't taken advantage, hadn't advanced. No, he was sure of the victory now. He was just savoring it.

"Up, dog!" he said. "Get up!"

Towdric was breathing hard too, sweating down his slick head, but nothing like Geth. Still, he knew the usurper would grow tired of the charade before long. Then it would come, the death blow. A few yards behind Towdric, to his right, the headman block rested on its side, inside the widened fighting space now, a reminder of what awaited.

And yet it was the one thing that gave Geth hope. The block sat too far back to trip Towdric up, but if he himself was the dog they named him—loyal and determined by nature—then his adversary was a swine—greedy, petty, always wanting more.

Geth howled. For dead Eko, for Baby, for all the rest. For Phelan and Vriana, Agrem and Melagus. For the dead-man dozen. For Hadean and his vision of Umbel. He threw everything he had into a charge and a swing as hard as the time before and harder.

Once again, Towdric sidestepped and parried. This time, however, Geth released Vingil on purpose. It clattered to the ground ahead of him, just beyond the headsman's block. Geth watched it skid to a halt as he fell himself, landing as he had before on the cobbles with a grunt.

But this time he didn't roll. And once again, Towdric didn't rush in to finish him. Geth rose to all fours, dragged himself toward his sword.

"That's right, crawl, foreign dog!"

Geth collapsed right in front of the block, panting and sweating like a man that was already dead, one hand stretched toward his blade but well short of it. His head swam. A little voice reminded him that he was dead already—or soon to be—if this didn't work.

But there was enough life in him for one last gambit. He dragged himself forward, stretched his head just over the wood, then went slack, the back of his neck presented to Towdric. He heard the usurper sidle up, unable to resist, saw that boot move into position again. The crowd fell silent. Geth *felt* the sword go up over his head even if he didn't see.

"So let it end," Towdric said. "And—"

With the last of his strength, Geth flung out a hand and yanked at that boot. Towdric gave a yell, went over. He hit the cobbles with a crash of armor on stones, his helmet rolling off across the cobbles.

It took all Geth's strength to scramble on top of him, pinning Towdric's sword arm underneath him. But the bastard managed to roll to his belly underneath the big warrior, bucking up to gain all fours. Geth rode his back like the hog he was, then sat up, lifted both hands together, bringing them down against the back of Towdric's head. The usurper cried out. Geth struck again. And again. Towdric finally groaned and collapsed. Geth teetered off him, eyes rolled up into the back of his head.

CHAPTER THIRTY-FIVE

A ruckus woke Geth. He wasn't sure if he'd been laying there for a minute or an hour, but Holrain's Court was full of shouting, cursing green-cloaks and civilians, and lilies, and even a few Ilars. The sun had peeked through the clouds to blaze hot on the pavers underneath him. The Oathstone shimmered in the heat.

He pushed up halfway, off the hard stones, gained one knee. That was as far as he could go, but it was enough.

"Hadean is king!" a familiar voice shouted. *Melagus*, Geth thought.

"Hadean is king," the cry went up. "Hadean is king!"

Geth felt arms pull him up. He shook his head to clear it and saw Towdric laying still on the ground. Bushy-brows rushed to roll him over, uttered a prayer when the usurper's eyes fluttered. But the same jailors that had held Geth earlier slapped their manacles on Towdric and hauled him off.

Towdric's green-cloaks looked nervously around. Hadean raised his hands though, already assuring them that all differences would be put behind them, all transgressions forgiven. Geth tried to look after Towdric—the danger wasn't over if he survived—but he didn't get a chance to think on it.

"I'll not be robbed of my justice!" a voice roared.

Geth didn't have time to turn. He heard the clash of steel on steel, curses, and a sharp cry. From either side of him, Phelan and Agrem whirled, taking the big warrior with them. Palladine stood quivering at the center of a sea of swords, frozen in place, arm still upraised. Two green-cloaks lay moaning on the ground at his feet, but Ratcher had a blade pressed against the nape of his neck, Fork-beard had one just under his arm, and Kerrel had one at his throat. The rest of the dozen closed ranks around Geth as he watched. Even Melagus wagged a letter-opener, or something like it, at the Paellian captain.

Hadean pushed through toward Palladine. "Take his sword. And escort him to the Paellian ships. Inform Prince Gahalus that Captain Palladine is exiled from Umbel. Should he return, his life is forfeit."

"You can't hide behind your betters forever, Stray!" Palladine spit.

Fork-beard uttered a juicy curse in the Ilar tongue and snatched the sword from Palladine's raised hand. Hack took him roughly by the arm, Ratcher took the other. The Captain's eyes stabbed Geth like daggers until he was dragged finally out of sight.

Men crowded around, tried to clap the big warrior's shoulders, but Agrem shooed them away. "Amalia," he said "Where is the Mother of the Woods? This man is very sick, mmmm?"

"I'm fine," Geth lied.

"Make way!" Hadean waved men aside. "Make way!" He didn't look well himself, but at least he could stand on his own.

They carried Geth to the Journey's End, the inn where it had all started. A table was cleared and they laid him on it. He didn't know how much time had passed before Amalia arrived, and with her, Pythelle.

"You," Geth breathed.

The witch nodded. "The past is behind us, Paellian. I'm here to see to it everyone survives."

Geth closed his eyes. "Poisoned," he heard them saying.

"Cursed," someone muttered. "Blood-magic," and "Dying."

The Seer squeezed Geth hand, looked down at him, eyes wide. "This, I did not see," he said. "But we have strong healers here, mmmm? A witch, a warlock, another witch. The strongest of circles."

"The what are you waiting for?" Geth managed. "Work your magicks."

———†———

Geth was still in the inn when he woke up. At least, he thought he was. A wood-beamed ceiling hung overhead, rain pattering against the shutters to one side. It was hot, but he wasn't burning up, and a savory aroma wafted to his nose from a tray at his bedside.

"You're awake."

Geth's eyes went wide. He turned his head to find Mother sitting in a chair beside him.

"I'm dead, aren't I?"

Her big bosom shook with laughter.

"Well, if I'm not, how did you get to Umbel? I'm still in Umbel, right?"

"You're still in Umbel. And it's only been a few days since that terrible business down by the harbor. My, my! I can't believe you live your life like that!"

"That was a little worse than usual."

Mother shook her head. "But you asked how I got here? I sailed here with your friends, Master Melagus and that rogue, Phelan. The blacksmith as well."

"Blacksmith?"

"I dunno, he was wearing one of those leather aprons."

Ratcher. Geth smiled. And Phelan and Melagus. They were alive! And they'd done it too, fetched Gahalus, saved Umbel from Towdric, and saved a certain sellsword from the chopping block as well. Geth croaked a heartfelt laugh just thinking about it.

Mother watched him with a frown.

"What? I haven't gone crazy." He reached out, rested a hand on hers. "I was just thinking how lucky I am though, to be alive and to have you here."

"Well..." She looked down at his hand, smiled. Her usual makeup was gone, and she looked older, but to Geth she looked better than ever, sober and earnest.

If she wanted to say anything though, she didn't get the chance. Melagus, King Hadean, and Queen Eynid came in, faces flushed.

"He's awake?" Melagus said, breathing hard like he'd just run up the stairs. "Thank the gods!"

Hadean and Eynid beamed behind him. Geth realized he wore no shirt, pulled the blankets up over himself. He noticed his mother sitting straighter, smoothing her hair over as well. But her eyes were on the counselor, not the king and queen.

Hadean just stood there smiling. The queen spoke for him. "At last, we can thank you."

"Er...my queen?"

"For everything." She looked to Hadean. "For all that you've done. You put a stop to my father's madness."

"He lives?" Geth asked.

The queen nodded. "The gods have been better to him than he deserves."

By the tone of her voice, it was clear there was no love lost between father and daughter. Then again, he'd tried to kill her husband on her wedding day. And chanced poisoning her as well in the process.

"At any rate," she went on, "we're thrilled to see you recovering. And hope you'll accept such gifts from us as your loyalty and courage merit."

Hadean stood straighter suddenly, started nodding. Eynid must have pinched his hand or stepped on his foot. "Yes, yes of course!"

Geth founding himself chuckling again. The lad who used to blush at the drop of a hat was a married man now.

And they looked good together. The fight beneath the Oathstone was all a blur, but Geth did seem to recall

Hadean looking about as sturdy as a damp rag at that point. But he seemed much better now. Happy. Alive.

"We brought you a soup," Eynid put in, motioning to the tray at his bedside. She smiled broadly. "They say it's the best thing to heal a man."

Geth forced a smile of his own. "Thank you, my queen. But how did you get here so fast? I only just woke up."

"We've been sleeping at the Journey's End," Hadean explained. "We were afraid to move you, so I rented the whole inn."

Geth's mouth opened and shut.

The king bent to give his hand a squeeze, smiled down at him, and led his wife toward the door. "Get some rest," he said, turning one last time. "We're just glad to see you're doing well, and happy to be able to commend you for all you've done."

Geth saluted with fist to heart. Hadean and Eynid took their leave. Melagus stayed behind though. Mother rose, insisting that Melagus take her chair, then backed across the little chamber.

"Well?" the counselor said. "Aren't you going to thank me?"

He seemed a bit worse for wear, Geth mused, gaunt in the cheeks, greyer than he remembered. But that hadn't changed him, except on the outside.

"Thank you for what?"

Melagus just raised his chin, looking smug.

"You set me up for that duel and almost got me killed!"

"Well, how was I supposed to know you'd been poisoned?"

"Amalia knew."

"Now, now, my boy—" Mother started.

"She had to have told you."

Melagus's lip made a guilty twitch. "She did mention something..."

"Ha!"

"You won, didn't you? Really now, Towdric against the Dog of War? He never stood a chance."

"Thram and bloody Awer..."

"But back to the point. I was referring to our timely arrival, with Gahalus."

Melagus raised an eyebrow. Boy did he look smug.

But Geth had to give it to him. "Well..."

"Admit it, you were impressed."

"Lyanne against the Asp?" Geth said. "She never had a chance."

Melagus puffed. Geth didn't miss the glance he flicked across the room either. Mother smiled back at him.

"How'd you do it though?" the big warrior asked.

"That's a tale. I didn't think we'd make it, truth be told. But we did."

"I looked for you. We thought you were dead or thrown down some hole by Lyanne. I went as far as Sorn looking for you."

At this, Melagus breathed out a sigh. "And *we* thought *you* were dead. It was only when we arrived in Sorn ourselves that we learned you were still alive. We had intended to sail back with Rondah, but the prince was able to secure passage for us within a few days."

"Well, you arrived just in time," Geth said. "I assume you snuck in through the secret postern entrance?"

Melagus rolled his eyes. "Secret no longer. It was supposed to be just myself and the king, but your friend Phelan wouldn't take 'no' for an answer. He insisted on coming along. Likewise the tribesmen. And those fool soldiers from your file. And Rondah. And that fool blacksmith." Melagus frowned. "Turns out you've got more friends than I expected."

Geth didn't know what to say.

"Gahalus came straight through the Harbor Gates," Melagus went on. "But we were stuck hiding in the cellars of the keep until Towdric brought you down to the court. It took some coordination with the prince and his lilies, otherwise we would never have let things run so close."

"You may be the only man in the realm that could have pulled it all off," Geth said.

"In the *world*."

Melagus rose from his seat. He smoothed his tunic, nodded to Mother. His eyes landed on the tray at Geth's bedside.

"How I love a good soup. Nothing like it. Make sure and eat, Master Geth."

The big warrior flicked a glance at the tray, tried to smile.

Melagus cleared his throat, thrust out a hand. "I'm sure we'll be seeing plenty of one another. But in the meantime, I must offer a commendation of my own. It is not often I'm impressed. And what you did for the Kingdom of Umbel, for Hadean, and for me...that was impressive."

Geth reached for his hand, but Melagus drew it back, hacked up a ball of phlem, and spit it into his palm. His smile turned smug again as he thrust that slimy grip out. "Brothers?" he said.

"Gods all be damned."

But Geth took that nasty hand and squeezed.

Chapter Thirty-Six

Geth slept the entire day after that, exhausted by the visit. His strength wasn't back, not by half, but it felt good to see his friends. When he woke again it was dark outside his window.

Mother was still at his side, chin on her chest, dozing. She started awake. "Geth—"

"Go on, get some rest yourself," he told her.

"Not until you eat your soup."

"I have to use the bedpan," Geth lied.

Mother snorted but rose just the same.

"Uh, mother?" he said before she could go. "Just wanted to ask; what's your plan?"

She paused by the door. "Plan?"

"I mean, are you going to stay? I reckon I could take care of you."

She rested a hand across her bosom. "Well, that's sweet of you, child. But I can take care of myself, don't you worry."

Geth didn't want to think how she intended to do that. He clamped his mouth shut and said nothing. Halfway out though, she turned.

"I'll be just next door if you need anything. Let me know if Master Melagus comes calling. He'd make a fine catch, that one."

"Oh, dear gods."

The door was already closed behind her, but Geth wasn't alone for long. Ratcher's blocky head thrust itself inside the room, mouth stretched in a grin when he saw Geth was awake.

"I suppose I'll have to tell the rest of the boys that you're up," he said. "But for now, I've got you to myself."

Geth snorted. "Where's my blacksmith's apron? I want that back when you're done with it."

They shared a laugh. Ratcher settled into the chair beside the bed. He flicked a glance at the door, lowered his voice.

"I wanted to be the first to tell you the good news."

Geth frowned. "If it's good news, why are we whispering?"

"Because it has to do with my former...*trade*."

"We're not talking about smithing, are we."

"No."

"They don't know? None of them?"

Ratcher scratched his ear. "What can I say, I'm good. Melagus suspects, I think. And Phelan knows of course, but he promised to keep it hush."

"I don't want to know how much that cost you."

"It was worth it. You see, I've retired."

"That's great news!" Geth paused, frowning. "I think. How'd you pull it off? Can a man in 'the trade' simply walk away?"

"I've got plenty of shine, that's no concern. But with your help, and Eora's, I was able to fake my own death," Ratcher grinned. "Don't want anyone to come looking for me, after all."

"Well, you're welcome to keep that green cloak and ride alongside me. This really is good news, from where I'm standing anyway."

"Thanks, Wolf. I mean it. But's that's not the good news I was talking about."

Geth frowned. Again.

"Towdric is dead."

"You didn't—"

Ratcher raised both hands "Didn't touch a hair. But he was in pretty bad shape when they found him. His throat had been cut, his heart stabbed through, and his eye pierced."

"Does that mean—"

"What else could it mean?" Ratcher edged forward in his seat, eyes alight. "Three, Geth! The Number Three! He was here!"

"Is he's after you? Does he know you're still alive?"

Ratcher chuckled. "Oh, he knows." The assassin rubbed his hands together. "But he's not after me. That was a *salute!* His way of saying 'I saw what you did, and it was something'."

Geth wasn't sure he followed. But he'd never seen Ratcher so happy. He hoped he was right. "So, he killed Towdric in...honor of what you did?"

"What *we* did Geth. And yes. I suppose he wanted to one-up me as well—you could say he's a bit of a show-off. But he *is* the best."

"Well, did he ever take down five competitors in the same night?"

Ratcher waved that off, pushed up from the chair. "I'd tell you to get some rest but what's the point? Now let me go tell those knock-kneed bastards you're awake so they can come and mob you."

The sound of a file of soldiers hurrying up the stairs and down the hall announced the arrival of the dead-man dozen. They hugged Geth, clasped his hands, hooted and laughed. Somehow in the ruckus, Geth's soup got spilled. He loved them even more for it.

But when the pleasantries were done, an uncomfortable silence fell. Geth looked from one face to the other, counting. All of them were there, even Neary, Amalia on his arm.

"What is it? No one has died, have they?"

More silence. Finally Hack spoked up. "Don't worry, Captain. Kerrel and I aren't leaving."

It took Geth a moment. Then he laughed. "Well Thram's purple cock, men, the war is over! There's no shame in wanting to go home."

A few nervous chuckles sounded, then more as they realized he wasn't kidding.

Dodger, Red-eye, Sweaty, and Bird-man would all soon return to their families. Ever the thinker, Blink, had decided to devote himself to the Omnibus and learning, to becoming a cleric. Hack and Kerrel had their sights on a soldier's life.

"And what about you?" Geth asked, turning his eyes toward Neary, still arm and arm with Amalia at the back of the room. "Will there be a wedding?"

The lanky fighter colored. "Uh, well, we've already gotten married."

A fresh round of hoots burst out. Geth reminded himself the noise didn't matter. Hadean had rented the entire inn.

But it was decided they should drink and celebrate the occasion further in a week's time, when Geth would be more up to it. As the dozen filed out, Agrem and Fork-beard came the other way.

Agrem looked Geth over and nodded. He seemed content with what he saw.

"I guess your magicks worked," Geth told him.

"Mmmm."

Fork-beard just watched, stoic as ever.

"You are well," the Seer said. "We will stay for the feast, but after that, I return to Dues. Iyngaer still has much need of me."

"Of course," Geth told him. "You've already saved my life. What more could I ask?"

Agrem nodded once more. "Barid has a gift for you,"

Geth couldn't have said who Barid was until Fork-beard actually smiled, producing a small cask with a cork in one end. "Eyfra," the tribesman said.

Geth wedged the cork loose, took in a whiff. "Forest fire!" The strong, dark liquor of Ilia. He grinned. "You haven't told Phelan about this, have you?"

The two tribesmen hummed in unison. Geth couldn't say what it meant. Agrem squeezed Geth's shoulder and turned toward the door.

"Don't worry, mmmm? We will visit much in the days ahead."

"After Neary's feast you mean?"

The Ilar smiled. "I have *seen* it."

Barid muttered something in the Ilar tongue and Agrem laughed. The Ilar warrior gave Geth a nod. "Be well, Geth et Trulsa. And strong, as always."

Geth watched them go with a touch of sadness, even if they promised to stick around for the feast. He sighed, looked to the empty soup bowl on his nightstand, stomach growling now that all his guests were gone. He didn't get a chance to curse before his door pushed open yet again. "My king? That you?"

There was no mistaking Hadean's form, but he moved gingerly, hunched over something. One finger went to his lips. "Shh." Closing the door quietly behind him, he turned and straightened to display a cloth-wrapped bundle with a flourish. "You're going to appreciate this. Phelan is coming with the drinks. And Melagus agreed to distract your mother for a while."

Geth cringed, thinking where that might go, but all was forgotten as the cloth came off and the scent of warm meat and fresh bread hit Geth's nose. He could have cried.

"Just point me at your enemies. I swear I'd storm the walls of High Turia if you asked."

Hadean used his belt knife to cut up the meat, pink, seasoned beef by the looks. Geth tore into it. They each took a share and chewed down several mouthfuls in silence before Hadean raised one finger.

"Amalia insisted on nothing but soup, but she doesn't know you like I do."

"Or she just doesn't love me as much."

Hadean chuckled. Phelan slunk in with three foamy tankards, a wheel of cheese, and another loaf. It was a feast. Geth ate until he was full and then some. He slurped down the last of the ale, burped loudly, and sighed.

"You guys..." He didn't have the words.

Hadean slouched in the chair, patted his stomach appreciatively. Phelan sat at the foot of the bed and licked his fingers.

"I heard about Towdric," Geth said. He hesitated. "Is the queen alright?"

"She will be." Hadean shook his head. "Eventually. He wasn't much of a father, but still."

They fell silent for a while. Phelan spoke. "I guess that means the war is won. It's really over."

An air of uncertainty hung on his words, rather than triumph or pride. Geth cut straight through it. "What are you gonna do?" he asked his friend.

"I reckon I'm heading home." Phelan flicked a glance at the king. "If I've been released from service, that is."

"Of course." Hadean blinked. "With honors."

But Geth shook his head. "Pellon? You're a wanted man still, Phelan. Do you think Palladine will just forget about you?"

"He will." The little man straightened up. "At first, he'll think I'm here in Umbel. And then little by little, he'll forget. That's what people do."

"I'm not sure he's the kind to let sleeping dogs lie. If he finds out—"

"There're thousands upon thousands of souls crowded inside the walls back in the Golden City, Geth. We won't cross paths. And that's assuming Lyanne doesn't banish him to the Lows as soon as he gets back."

Geth reached for the last corner of bread and forced down his pessimism. He stuffed his mouth and chewed.

Hadean looked down into his tankard. Phelan cleared his throat.

"I guess this means you're not interested in coming with me, back to the inn?"

"The Oak and Hart?"

"It's mine now. Well, a part of it anyway."

"What about the inn up at Greenfell?"

Phelan grimaced, smoothed back his hair. "I was never more than a squatter there, you know that."

"I guess I just thought..." Geth frowned. "I thought maybe you were happy."

"With a stolen inn?" His friend looked truly hurt. "I'm trying to do better, Geth. Just like you."

The big warrior couldn't argue with that. But he didn't like it. Eora would have to look out for Phelan now.

"I suppose I should say I'm happy for you," Geth said, "and that I wish you luck. Because I do. But I can't join you. Palladine won't forget about *me*. And I don't reckon I'll be able to avoid notice either."

"Not if you grow that hideous mustache again."

They shared a smile.

"Well," said Hadean, "if you're staying, Captain, I have a post I would like you to accept. After your return from Ilia."

"Ilia?"

"I expect you'll want some time to visit the chieftess and your child."

"Right, of course. But not too long a visit. I don't think she'd allow it."

Phelan snorted a laugh. Hadean just shook his head. "Women are mysterious, aren't they?"

"You said it," the little man agreed.

Hadean turned back to Geth. "But whatever happens, you'll want to visit the child from time to time."

Geth nodded.

"Good. Because Towerrock is badly in need of some leadership these days. It's only a day's ride to Ilia from there."

"The Tooth?"

"Lord Brant would oversee you, as the fortresses is customarily held by the king's close kin. But we never did replace the Yardmaster."

Geth's mouth opened and closed.

"Brant has already told me he intends to stay in Waterset. Towerrock would be yours in all but name."

Phelan whistled.

"Will you stay?" Hadean asked.

Geth looked from the king to his friend as back. "Can you throw in a new sword?"

A MESSAGE FROM THE AUTHOR

Thank you for reading DOG DAYS, I hope you enjoyed it! If you're hungry for more, join my newsletter at www.deankastle.com/newsletter.html and get a free short story from Palladine's point of view about Phelan's infamous dice game and subsequent capture. Subscribers will be first to know when new projects launch and will also receive exclusive content, bonus material, special offers, and more.

All the best!

-DK

An Excerpt from LET SLEEPING DOGS LIE

Agrem's voice woke Geth in the middle of the night, sat him up straight in his bedroll.

"Go back!"

There was no Eko this time, no image at all, but the urgency—the *command*—in the Seer's voice had Geth looking around the low-burning fire in vain for his friend.

Trees swayed in the wind, smoke drifted up and away. The night sky spread purple, star-smeared above him. "Go back where?" Geth cursed out loud. But he knew.

Hack, sat up, scrambling for his sword until he saw Geth sitting there. The big warrior rubbed his face with both hands, pulled at his beard. "Gods all be damned."

"Alright, captain? Bad dream?"

"The worst. A message from Agrem."

Hack frowned. "Magicks?"

Geth nodded. "We have to go back to Ilia."

They broke camp immediately, started back the way they'd come. Geth's green-cloaks rode with hand on hilts, bows strung. They followed without question, but Geth couldn't have told them much anyway.

If the news of his mother had been bad, at least it had told him *something*. Not knowing was as bad as anything.

"Why, 'Grem?" He tried thinking of the Seer, to *will* him into some kind of waking dream-speak. That made his head hurt, nothing more. What had happened, what could warrant that command? He had no way of knowing.

That night, Geth tried again to summon his friend again. His dreams were of war and fire instead. And a cold, insidious fear.

He rode for Ehken Laer, he didn't know where else he should go. As they drew near, it seemed like fear was on the wind itself. Geth wasn't the only person who felt it, he saw it on the face of Hack and the others.

Things only got worse.

"Is that..." Hack breathed deeply, nose lifted. He turned a worried eye toward Geth.

The big warrior smelled it too: the thin but acrid scent of smoke. "Ride!"

Geth kicked his mount to a full gallop. Rounding one final bend, plunging out of the trees, the valley and hill of Ehken Laer came into view. Recognizing Geth, fighters on the walls opened the gates. Their faces look shocked, panicked.

Horse-face met Geth on a horse of his own. He waved him up the hill. "Come, Truslata. Fast. Vriana." He turned, spurred his mount, not waiting to see if the big warrior followed.

A great black pile of ash smoldered beside Vriana's hall, the source of that smell, Geth reckoned. It was the remains of a pyre, and a big one. Blackened bones rested among the cinders. Geth slid from the saddle without a care for where his horse went.

"Dear gods." His heart leapt up into his throat. "Where is Vriana? Where's the baby?"

"Inside."

Geth crashed through the high doors, sprinted down the hall, around the screens. The chieftess lay still on her furs, an old woman wiping her brow with a rag. Gods but Vriana looked pale. Their son's little crib was empty.

Want to read more? Visit www.deankastle.com/newslett er.html. By subscribing, you'll be among the first to know when LET SLEEPING DOGS LIE launches. You also receive a free short story and other exclusive content. In the meantime, thank you and happy reading!

-DK

ABOUT THE AUTHOR

Dean Kastle is the author the DOG of WAR Epic, the LEGACY Series, and many short works. In addition to a love of 'story' in every medium, he's a rabid foodie, and soccer fanatic. As far as he's concerned, Pluto is still a planet, and the oxford comma is a matter of taste. He doesn't wear a beret or write with a fountain pen, but he does own a life-size replica of the Iron Throne. From that perch, he plots his next tale. Readers can connect with Dean by joining his newsletter, on X, on Facebook, or at deankastle.com. He lives in fly-over country with his wife, three kids, and—yes—a dog.

Printed in Dunstable, United Kingdom